Shak...

Robert Low was a Scottish journalist and historical novelist. He made his name with the Oathsworn Viking series, still heralded as a leading light of the genre. In later years, his series focused on Scotland through the ages, with books set during the Wars of Scottish Independence, in ancient Rome and most recently in the Scottish Borders during the reign of Henry VIII.

He was also a war correspondent, reporting from Sarajevo, Romania, Kosovo, and Vietnam over the course of his career. An avid Viking historical reenactor, he was a full time fiction author until his death in 2021.

Also by Robert Low

Brothers Of The Sands

Beasts Beyond The Wall
The Red Serpent
Beasts From The Dark

Border Reivers

A Dish of Spurs
Burning the Water
Shake Loose the Border

ROBERT LOW

SHAKE LOOSE THE BORDER

1ᴒCANELO

First published in the United Kingdom in 2021 by Canelo

This edition published in the United Kingdom in 2021 by

Canelo
Unit 9, 5th Floor
Cargo Works, 1-2 Hatfields
London, SE1 9PG
United Kingdom

A CIP catalogue record for this book is available from the British Library.

Print ISBN 978 1 80032 258 5
Ebook ISBN 978 1 80032 213 4

Look for more great books at www.canelo.co

Printed and bound in Great Britain by Clays Ltd, Elcograf S.p.A.

Chapter One

June 1548 – St Monans, East Neuk of Fife

The smoke was thick, grey black, coiling and twisting like a snake out of the trench where they had lit the fires. It was so dense Batty could not see the flames from Newark Castle, but Sandy Wood, one of the Largo Lairds, told Batty of it as he wiped his streaming, blackened face.

'They sacked and burned it,' he complained bitterly. 'Took prisoners away in their boats. Bastards.'

'Prisoners? From the castle?'

'Servants and tenants hiding there. You knew some?' Sandy Woods asked.

'Will Elliot. I heard he was Steward.'

'He is – if he lives. They huckled them all down to the beach and their wee boats. Bastards.'

He turned away to roar at skeins of men moving up with pikes and hackbutts, but cut it short as a stocky figure appeared stumping along in boots and a jack hung about with bits of gilded latten chain. Hans Cochrane, face streaked with powder-smeared sweat, gave Batty as much of a salute as he always did, a half-flap of one hand; he did not even acknowledge the Laird of Largo.

'Where do you want these wee poppers then Batty?'

'Front of the line if you please Master Coalhouse,' a voice interrupted and they turned to see a spade-bearded face on top of a carapace of half-armour and tall boots. The voice was rough with smoke and yelling and he fought the restive horse as he spoke, some of his words lost as it circled and shifted.

'My Lord Wemyss...' Sandy Wood began and the commander nodded brusquely, but talked only to Batty, looking at him and thankful he had seen him before and knew what to expect.

Master Coalhouse, the expert gunner, was a brute club of a man, his face hawk-nosed and up-chinned, so that his knife of beard seemed to curve like a scythe. He had wary eyes set in a blasted landscape of old lines and new wrinkles, a big-bellied body encased in a jack with no sleeve on the left, for he had no arm to fill it. All in all, he was a man birthed out of fire and sword, Wemyss had heard tales of a bloody feud with the Armstrongs along the Border and a history of slow match and petards and gunnery. Just what the moment needed.

Batty knew what Wemyss was seeing and stared back at pouched eyes in a face terse with age and new strains. No Holyrood painting yourself, he thought.

'Load scattershot,' Wemyss said, heaving himself off the horse. 'When yon moudiewarts sort themselves out they will come up through the smoke and ower yon trench we dug last night because everywhere else is too steep. They will wheel on their fixed left flank, which is what I want ye to tear to shreds. Your guns and my hackbutts will rend them so we will.'

He laid it out with twigs and scores from his backs-word.

'They landed in the bay. Thought themselves braw and clever for coming ower the firth and landing in this wee backwater. Thought they would attack St Andrews when they cannot move out of Haddington to take Edinburgh.'

A score of the sword and some pebbles. 'We are on their left. Sir John Sandilands is ower on their right, though he has only a few men, mostly his own tenants including women and brave bairns. They scarce make a hundred, but they are watching his castle burn and are fired for revenge, making a deal of noise to seem more of a threat.'

A final lump of round stone. 'Sir James the Bastard Stewart is coming from the north. Those on the beach cannot come at us up the cliffs so must move forward, wheel on their left flank and rush us ower that trench. Sir James'll be here within the hour, bringing Frenchmen with him and then we can show these English how bulls run and chuckies row.'

'Bastards,' echoed Wood and the men nearest picked it up and yelled it back at him, laughing.

Not be laughing long, Batty thought bitterly. There are more than a few hundred skilled men on that beach, struggling to unload horses and ordinance; it was no small force and arriving like a thunderbolt, as Sandy Wood had said. Through the drift of smoke he could see the forest of masts from their fleet – and that meant stronger guns if they could be brought to bear.

But Sandy Wood and his brother and Sir John Wemyss had seen it long before, had set to preparing for it as best they could with what was to hand, which was not much but all good. So had the Privy Councillors back in Edinburgh, Batty added to himself. They sent me and three guns here, showing more resolve and cunning than they had in a year; one more day of gabbing round a table about it would have been too late.

'Hans – bring up the wee casks.'

Cochrane, a skilled gunner, knew the import of Batty's order and scowled. It meant close work and a frantic scrabbling to load and fire otherwise the enemy would rush them. The gunners sweated the small casks up and cracked them open, ladling spikes and nails and odd lumps of metal down the barrels.

Batty thought the guns too light – they were rabinets, small enough on a wheeled carriage to be trundled fast by a single horse and a brace of sweating men. They launched no more than a fist-sized shot if that, but the spray from a load of sharp metal would scythe men down to bloody pats. The trick with it, Batty knew, was to let them get close – but not close enough for survivors of the scythe to rush in.

Men formed on either side of them, spiking their Y-shaped rests into the ground and blowing on the matches to keep them glowing like red rat eyes. They will run soon as the enemy charges, Batty knew and if we don't run with them we'll be sliced like pie.

The Scots were armed and armoured decently enough, all the same – Wemyss had a few score of his retainers and the Lairds of Largo had even more from their estates, former seaman and shipmen of their old da, Sir Andrew Wood, once the Lord High Admiral of Scotland.

Batty eyed up his own men, the gun captains Cochrane, Tibault Roquenau and Piers Schoufrenne the Fleming. They and a handful of Frasers freshly fled from some feud in the north formed the battery and only one was armoured – Ewan Fraser in his ankle-length saffron serk and long mail coat, leaning easily on a massive two-handed sword. He peered out from under an ancient bascinet and grinned.

'Dinna fash, Master Coalhouse.'

He was still young enough to be dark of hair and beard, but the frets round his eyes told a different tale. He had washed-out blue eyes and a strong frame – slender too, Batty noted ruefully – but the look in those eyes was a pool of old misery. Batty knew why; Ewan and the handful with him were the last of his clan, the Lovats of Beauly. With 300 other Frasers he had gone into a battle with the Ranalds and McDonalds and other enemies across some norther marsh. The Lovat Laird was dead, his son and heir with him.

'I am the last Lovat of Beauly,' Ewan had told Batty when he had presented himself, sent from Lord Arran to act as an escort for the guns. He was bitter-proud of it and it did not astound Batty to realise that he would return one day and slaughter as many Ranalds and McDonalds as he could before dying.

The enemy sorted themselves out and swung into action; Batty heard the trumpets and did not have to do more than nod to Hans Cochrane to get ready.

The enemy came swinging up over the trench, round the rocky foreshore like a closing door, right through the fading smoke of the old fires. Nearest to them, the hinge of their swinging door, hackbutts appeared, cautious and creeping, to be met by a scatter of fire from either side of Batty.

'Hold,' Batty said, watching the banners and the ghost shapes through the smoke. Green horizontal stripes, white sheets, red crosses, they fluttered boldly. There was even a great white banner with a gold St George killing the dragon – and a fatter, whiter one banded at the top in blue and studded with little black crosses.

'Yon's Lord Clinton's badge,' Sandy Wood yelled out. 'He's commander here. Fire on that, Master Coalhouse. Blow his heid aff.'

The pikes nearest to him roared approval but Batty ignored him. He would fire when he was ready…

The shapes coalesced. Hackbutts spun and fell; something whirred between Batty and Ewan like an angry wasp, but neither paid it any mind – to Ewan's left, one of his men was shifting from foot to foot and roaring in his own tongue, frothing. Huw, Batty remembered, a hard-eyed youth who was never done smiling and boasting about what he had done in battle and would do again.

Ewan lifted his sword and whacked him hard with the flat, a blow on the blue bonnet that Batty was sure would lay the man out with a cracked pate until he realised there was a steel cap under it; the man stumbled a little and shook his head. Batty leaned closer to Ewan.

'Is he right in the head? What was he shouting?'

'He will be fine as sunny water,' Ewan shouted back over the increasing din. 'It's only Huw, asking for claymore – to be let loose to charge them rather than stand here and be shot at. Huw was on the brim of it but now is not until I say so.'

'Dinna let him,' Batty replied grimly, 'for if he runs in front of my guns there will be nothing for his ma to weep over.'

Arrows flew, but they were shot blind and came in spurts like rain. The English bowmen were using their bows as spades to try and shift out the smouldering bracken in the trench they ploughed through, but a great mass of men was pushing through – billmen, Batty saw. A length of wood shorter by several feet than a pike, with a thin axe-head on one side and a piked point on the other, capable of being used with a small, round strapped-on shield.

That's the English way – bills and bows, Batty thought, when everyone else uses pikes and hackbutts – but the killing power was all in their archers, who would launch shaft after shaft at the tight ranks of pike before the billmen closed. They will have mercenaries with them, all the same, Italians and Germans who fight and dress like Landsknechts, who in turn fight and dress like the Swiss, favoured sons of war. Those piked-armed lads would be the ones to take on Scots pike, not the English with their bills...

He felt Cochrane's eyes on him and nodded. Cochrane bawled out orders, touched fire to pan; there was a series of deep little popping sounds, a great gush of smoke and the front rank of the distant figures misted with blood and shrieks. Cochrane was roaring for spongers and charges and prickers.

They did it twice more and then Batty saw the moment the enemy found their courage – they had been surging back and forth and now, under a sword-waving captain, started forward in earnest. Batty stopped his men from reloading, waved his good hand round his head once or twice and then clapped Ewan Fraser on one shoulder.

'Away,' he said. 'Leave the fight to those suited best for it.'

He led the way, pushing into the massed pike ranks behind him until stopped by a burly figure who grinned yellow and gap at him. He shifted to go around and was blocked, knew it was thought a good joke on those scampering to the rear by the way the others around the man sniggered.

He had no time for pike jests. He hauled out his dagg and stuck it under the pikeman's bushy chin, watching the eyes grow large and round. It was fearsome, that pistol, a great long barrel and a butt ending in an axe head and the joker's grin had altered to a wet-mouthed grimace.

'Blood of Christ,' said his neighbour; there was a buzzing sound and the man next to him went backwards in a pink mist. The joker shifted to one side and Batty moved through, though he turned on the way for he would not put his back to them now.

In the rear, he went to where they had parked the train, which was too grand a word for two carts, some Border hobbies, casks and boxes of powder and shot. There was bread and hard cheese and thin wine, too, so Batty took his ease with the gunners, hoping none of the enemy who washed over his guns had spikes or the thought to use them. He and the Frasers ate and drank while the smoke and shouts and screams drifted over them.

Men stumbled out of the ranks, gasping or shrieking over their bloody wounds. Others were left like a snail's trail when the mass of men surged forward. Eventually, like a tide, they would surge back again.

Then there was a flurry of men, a series of knots stumbling and shouting; Batty watched them, arms pumping and empty of pike.

'Stand to,' he roared. 'They have broke.'

The air went like a spoon in gruel, thick and slow. Men broke to the right and left, running blindly, anywhere, away from the vengeful edge of the enemy; Batty heard a voice bawling for them to stand, to rally, but he did not think they would.

New figures loomed, stumbling and wet-mouthed, but slashing bloody edges. A bill flashed and Batty ducked it, stuck out the dagg and fired – the long lance of flame seemed to engulf the man, who vanished in it, screaming.

Someone else hurled forward, spattered with gore and yowling like a cat, his fingers like claws which was all he seemed to have; he fell on the edge of John Dubh's targe and the weight dragged them both down, snarling and cursing.

Another bill-edge flashed and Batty reared away from it, stuck the dagg back in his belt and scrabbled out his backsword, stabbing at the helmeted head until the man fell away, trailing blood.

Batty gave him no chance and leaped on him like the wrath of an avalanche, kicking him repeatedly until his bascinet helmet flew off and then keeping up the flurry in his black-bearded face, pale and blood-slathered and panicked. He beat him like a red-haired step-wean with the backsword and watched him jerk and writhe and scream. Then he drew back his arm and pegged the man to the ground as if he was a curing hide.

Men roared, the sound like surf on shingle as Batty struggled to pull the sword out again, then cursed and went for a new pistol instead. Men moved alongside him and he realised it was the Scots pikemen, returning warily and half-ashamed, waving their wee backswords and looking to find the long pikes they had thrown away in fear.

They enemy surged away, backed away until Batty was facing a wall of them a pike-length away; the fringes to either side heaved and struggled with other fights – but they were distant matters to Batty, who only saw the fear in faces at the way Ewan Fraser slid and ducked, his two-hander sword making a high, thin ping of sound as it snicked pieces from men.

9

A man came up alongside Batty, stuck his Y-fork in the blood-sodden turf, rested the long weapon and shot; the ball struck one of that enemy wall of men and shafts and the victim shrieked and half-turned, throwing up his arms; the bill in it spun like a lance of light and Batty saw it come down on him, could not move…

Light blew into him and skidded him to the edge of an abyss. Batty lay in a cave of ice, his head resting in a cold so hard it seemed to burn on that side; the rest of him pulsed and throbbed with a pattern he could see on the inside of his eyelids. His neck ached; he opened his eyes because someone demanded it and shook him relentlessly until he gave in. It took him a long, blurry time before he found himself staring into the red-speckled face of John Dubh, heavy with concern.

'You're up then,' John Dubh said and blew out his cheeks. 'There's a mercy. Will you try for standing or lie there a' day?'

Lie here a' day, Batty decided, listening to the wind mourn out of the sea over the dead and dying. It spoke of rain and tears; he struggled to rise.

Then, like a distant bird, Batty heard a trumpet, another and yet one more. Heads turned to look – cheers rang out and Wemyss came riding up, all Alamain rivet and plumes.

'The Bastard Stewart,' he announced triumphantly, as if he had personally summoned the man up. He looked down at Batty, who was finally spurred to levering himself upright; he saw the bill a little way off and John Dubh followed his glance and grinned.

'Aye, God smiles on ye, Master Coalhouse – you were clipped by the flat and if it had turned a quim hair either way it would have sliced you like a bridal cake.'

'Well done,' Wemyss beamed, as if Batty had contrived the entire event. He rode off and, in another few minutes, the Bastard Stewart was riding up in half-armour, his face pale but his manner determined. Seventeen he was, Batty remembered dully, fighting the blood-orange pulse of his senses. Half-brother to the wee Queen Mary, sired by her Royal da on Lady Margaret Eskine.

The Bastard Steward, biting his bottom lip, nodded to Batty, asked about the guns in a distant way and then left while his men – French among them by the banners Batty saw – went tearing into the English, driving them back to the water's edge; horsemen with lances rode among them and they looked like the Border riders he knew well.

'Time for us,' Ewan Fraser suddenly announced, standing up; his men grouped round him like a dog-pack and he looked at Batty and raised the big two-hander.

'Last of the Lovat,' he said and loped off, trailing his hounds.

'Bigod,' Hans Cochrane said, shaking his head. 'I am glad I am on this side of him.'

Batty said nothing on how irritated he was that they were supposed to be guarding his guns and yet had gone off plundering. Later, in the blood-swirling retch of the foreshore, with the blinding cough of powder smoke everywhere, he and the others manhandled the rabinets down on to the turf above the shingle, where they could shoot fist-sized iron balls into the flat-bottomed boats that had managed to push themselves off, back towards the English fleet and safety. Far out in the Forth, held there by the shallow inshore waters, the great ships loomed, magnificently impotent.

Batty had crunched over splintered bone and sloshed through bloody parts of what once had been men – his doing, he thought. No match with a slow match, that's Batty Coalhouse; out in the water, the frantic fled up to the neck. On the shore, vengeful men prowled – and Batty spotted Ewan Fraser with blood all down his face. Next to him was Huw, limping and reeling on the edge of falling down.

'I killed a captain,' he exclaimed with delight; around him, men moved to and fro, as if there was no enemy left – which might have been the truth, Batty thought, for he had come on none and was grateful for it.

'He was cursing me,' Huw went on, 'and I gave him steel in the teeth. He had ten silver pence on him.'

'Have we won then?' Ewan asked, mopping his face with a square of cloth, shaking blood from him like a dog coming out of a river.

'I dinna ken,' Huw growled mournfully and reeled away spitting blood, 'but, ochone, I believe I have lost.'

Batty helped with the guns, using a rammer to force the ball on to the powder bag, then a stiletto dagger thrust down the vent to poke a hole in it. The vent man poured priming powder in from a little horn, blowing on the linstock match to keep it glowing; Batty gave him a scathing look – if that spark landed in the powder horn they'd all go up. The vent man looked back at Batty, grinned and waved the linstock in a question. Batty nodded, the match went down and there was a moment of fizzing, then a loud pop.

Batty skipped out of the patch of the gun's recoil and stuck the rammer in the churned-up ground as he went on a little way, picking his way over discarded equipment and rag-doll bodies, trying to find someone to ask about how the battle was going; he did not want to have a sudden surge of vengeful English down on his guns – after what they had done to them, no quarter would be given.

He heard shouts and bangs and screaming horses, then heard someone roaring in what he recognised as the barbarous tongue of the Frasers, so he went towards it. The rest of the Frasers were in a knot with John Dubh towering in the centre of a crowd of men – and women, Batty saw – who were cowering and screaming. None louder than the man in dun and black, who had his hands raised as high as his voice.

'We are not of the army. I came with them to watch and offer spiritual guidance. I am a minister of My Master Jesus Christ. Spare my life.'

'Aye, weel – if you are a good one, your Master has need of you,' John Dubh replied in thick English. 'If not – the De'il take you.'

The sound of his sword was sickening; the man screamed, the women shrieked – one fainted – and a voice bellowed: 'Johnnie Dubh – are you killing men of God here?'

They all turned into the purpling face of the Lord of Wemyss, cantering up with a banner in one fist and steel in the other, his head bare and his wisped hair all wild; behind him came grim-faced, well-armed footmen and horsemen cantered out from behind him, lances poised. John Dubh merely grinned and wiped the blood and hair from his sword.

'Och, no, Your Honour. A wee Reformed cant – nae men of God here.'

Wemyss, rampant Catholic and bloated with victory, waved his sword in the air and lumbered off, followed by his loyal bodyguard and yelling 'Well done – carry on' over his shoulder.

The wind was blowing away the smoke, for all that Batty heard his guns fountain out more of it. The Frasers fell to looting the dead minister and gathering the women in knots like sheep.

'Are you done here?' Batty demanded, annoyed; he wanted the Frasers guarding his guns.

'No' quite Master Coalhouse,' John Dubh declared, squinting at the coins he had taken; he bit one experimentally. The women clucked a bit and then squatted, trembling whenever the guns spat – Batty realised they must be servants from Newark Castle and said so. Then he called out, asking if any had seen Will Elliot the steward, but had only blankness back.

John Dubh spotted Batty's jaundiced eye over the body of the minister and grinned. 'We will be back with you afore long, Master Coalhouse – this affray is over and we will let the Stewart's men charge about in the heat to finish it. I wouldnae mourn for this one much either – he is a shitlegged chiel of Reformist, which is flat-out Lutheran by the back door.'

Out in the bay, one roundshot had struck a crowded boat and the subsequent panic overturned it; the screams were distant, mournful threnodies which John Dubh glanced up at and then ignored. There were horsemen from the Bastard Stewart's command galloping exultantly up and down the shore, ramming lances through anyone fleeing into the surf.

'Losh, man these here are in no danger from us, but them prickers might cause them hurt. We will escort these fine Newark ladies to some decent shelter. I am sure they have mislaid their chastity and it is only chentlemanly to see if we can uncover it.'

Everything in Edinburgh was fevered – wee Mary, the Queen in swaddling, had been packed off to France and a betrothal to the Dauphin, which meant the English plan to forcibly wed her on to young King Edward was a poorer hand.

It also meant the French thought Scotland was their own and arrived to challenge the English hold on Leith, Haddington and everywhere else. The main English forces had scuttled back to Berwick, all save the luckless besieged, and everyone was *en fête*, from the official receptions at the slightly charred Holyrood, to street peddlers offering fruit and nosegays and the Egyptiani offering fortunes while they picked your pocket. You could not walk down a wynd or a cobble in Edinburgh that did not have acrobats, stilt-walkers or rope-dancers.

Goodwives looked on in astonishment at the women who came in the French train in their sumptuous dresses with wide sleeves and swooping partlet, teetering on perilous, unseen heels with a little dog under one arm and a coterie of *demoiselle de compagnie* and at least one footman in cramoisi or citrine satin. It could just as easily be a boy with a trained dancing monkey, dyed blue or yellow or bright green. And none of them were titled or even within a whiff of it, just ladies who came with the soldiery.

It was, Ewan Fraser, noted scathingly: '*pàrtaidh an diabhail.*'

Batty had no quarrel with the Devil's party it was and the taverns between West and Nether Bows did their best to turn into salons, vying with one another for the outlandish, for that was where the French gentleman chose to play cards for high stakes.

The best card game in the city was that of the Chevalier de la Tremoille, a young sprig of that French House. He served on the staff of the French army, as secretary intendant in the fiscal department where, as he said with a wink 'all the best money is'.

He was not short of it and presided over games in places of his own choosing and with his own 40-card deck. The one Batty attended was in Johnnie Lyle's Natural Wonders exhibition, a cramped four-storey house off a wynd up the Cowgate, full of the sinister and odd which customers could view for the price of a meat pie.

He had only gone there to meet the Strozzis and Lord Methven, Master of the Scots Artillery and was glad he had not eaten at all. They sat between glass jars of preserving fluids full of body parts – a lamb with seven legs, an infant with flippers instead of arms, a two-headed cat – and were served wine by blackamoor dwarves dressed in not much more than coloured scarves and palm fronds.

De la Tremoille – dressed as a woman, which was his habit when off duty Batty learned – dealt to a select group which included the Chevalier d'Antone, who gambled for a living, Ewan Fraser – claiming status as a 'lord of the Lovat' – and the Comte Saintgalles, who swore he had the secret of winning at Primero and, incidentally, immortality.

'But you lose,' de la Tremoille pointed out when Saintgalles brought this up – yet again boasting about how gaming had sustained him for the last hundred years of his own life. Since he seemed to be only in his thirties, that secret was worth more than winning at Primero Batty thought and said so.

'You may think it,' Saintgalles said diffidently, briefly studying him from under an arched eyebrow, 'but maintaining one's style in all that time is essential. Otherwise, it is just an eternity of *ennui*.'

He certainly seemed to have the monies to preserve the style and neither he nor d'Antone were much good at gambling, for all that Saintgalles claimed he had the secret of it and d'Antone insisted he was a professional. Fraser played recklessly and de la Tremoille laughed at his losing scowls.

'All Scotch are the same,' he said. 'Your Regent Arran should be here, since he plays the same way with his name, his sword, the lives of a few thousand Scotchmen and the fortunes of some faithful gentlemen.'

'The ones from the north fight naked underneath dresses, I hear,' d'Antone said, frowning at his cards and then offering Lovat a winning smile. 'Which is why you esteem them well, Chevalier de la Tremoille.'

'That and their barbarous tongue,' de la Tremoille answered non-plussed and slid a card from the pack as he smiled at Lovat. 'Speak it to me, sir.'

Lovat said something in Gaelic and de la Tremoille clapped his hands with delight.

'Liquid gold, is it not, gentlemen? What did it mean. sir?'

'Yes, pray tell Master Fraser,' Saintgalles demanded laconically, knowing full well that it had been insulting, even if he did not understand a word of it.

'You are a skilled practitioner of the cards and a gentleman of honour,' Fraser replied and Saintgalles scowled.

'Skilled, certainly. He has dealt me a hand like my very foot. My very foot, I swear.'

Batty learned later that Fraser had actually said 'You are a perverted idiot who would take a diseased cock up the arse'.

Up at Holyrood the great and good – D'Esse the French commander and Arran the Scottish Regent among them – were sitting with Mary of Guise listening to Sermisy's *Au Joly Boys* and Scott's *Lament On The Master Of Erskine* set to music, which was all refined and polite.

Down here the only music was the chink of coin and the play was brutal – Batty watched since he was not allowed in the game because he did not have the stake, nor the style of a gentleman to be permitted credit.

He said nothing and eventually discovered why he had been summoned here when he got head to head with the Strozzis and Methven, all of them close in a corner and stared at by a goggling foetus of something which reminded Batty of a fish-eyed boy he had seen once, out along the Solway.

'Admiral Seymour is away back to London with his plumes in draggles,' Methven said, chuckling fruitily. 'The business at St Monan's was a disaster and cost him one of his fleet of fifteen warships, foundered in the shallows, not to mention a wheen of sojers.'

'His other ships failed to prevent the French taking Inchcolm,' Leon Strozzi added, 'and the spiriting of the wee Queen away safe to France. He is much reduced and at the mercy of his enemies.'

'Aye, his plumed hat is on a shaky peg,' Methven agreed. 'So also will be the one of his brother, the Lord Protector. I am sensing a change in the wind, gentlemen.'

'Perhaps – but it is an impasse at Haddington,' Piero Strozzi declared, scowling and spilling wine down his front in an attempt to get as much down his throat as he could.

Batty could sympathise; he was trying to kill the pain in his leg, shot through the fleshy part of the calf when he had gone to site artillery against Haddington not long since.

'Not for the English,' Methven answered in a growl. 'They cling to it like misers with a fist stuck in a hole – the only way to get loose is to let uncurl the fist and let the gold fall and they will not do so. The rest of the English are fleeing south, hanging on to what fortalices they think they can hold. Most of them are deserting.'

By now everyone knew the baby Queen of Scotland had gone to France to be married on to the French throne's heir, Batty said, so there was no more need for a war to force a union with her and Edward, now king. Besides, the great will and heart of Henry had died with him; no-one had stomach for the fight anymore.

'Least of all the Lord Protector,' Strozzi agreed in his thick accent and grinned, raising a horn cup to Batty, 'whose nose you helped bloody at St Monan's.'

Batty acknowledged the honour with a deprecating nod, wondering if this meant there was coin coming with it. There was, to his surprise and then dismay.

'Sandilands had his wee fortalice at Newark spoiled,' Methven said, his beard ruffed like a badger's arse and his glare as if Batty had ordered the affair.

'I was next to it,' Batty pointed out gruffly, 'pinching the embers out of my beard.' Methven patted his good arm soothingly, then brought up a bag which chinked loud enough to turn the head of Saintgalles.

'Sir James Sandilands also lost a few tenants and his castle servitors,' Methven went on, 'including his steward, Will Elliot. I am aware you ken him.'

Which was a slurry of old, reeking memories where Batty's cunning plan to free Will from a cage on the top of Hollows tower had blown half the tower down and Will with it. He had lived but had never been the same again.

Methven saw some of that in Batty's face and nodded. 'I heard you gave the Border fire and sword to rescue him and Sir James has asked for you to help Will again. Sandilands values him, even if the man cannae hirple without a stick, I hear. His mind is sharp and he keeps matters in order.'

Batty suspected Will was dead; if he had been dragged off into a boat with other prisoners, it would be for ransom and Will was not much attraction when viewed in a better light.

'Ransom it is,' Methven said when Batty hoiked this up. He shoved the bag at him.

'Forty pounds in good shillings – no coppernoses or clips. A great sum for such a wee lord as Sandilands, who also has Newark to refurbish, so you know the depth of his regard for Will Elliot.'

He took a long swallow of wine; nearby, Saintgalles flung his cards down with a gilt-strip Gallic curse. Methven plucked a roll of seal-dangled paper from inside his doublet.

'Here is a writ of safe travel signed by Arran and wee Georgie Hume, who lies sick to death after being run through at Pinkie. His wife surrendered his castle to the English, but Georgie is yet Warden of the Scottish East March and the Hume name still carries. Intelligencers tell me a deal of prisoners have been taken to Berwick.'

Batty eyed the bag, then the face of Methven, which was no less pouched.

'You want me to ride to English-held Berwick with a bag of silver and a Scottish safe pass, down roads where deserters crawl like lice, find Will Elliot and offer forty pounds for his release.'

'I told you he was man for task,' Strozzi said, beaming. Batty gave him a sour glance.

'You can have those Scotch from the north who guarded your guns,' Strozzi added. 'Good men in a fight, I am told.'

'We will keep Cochrane and the other gunners,' Leon Strozzi interrupted pointedly and his brother acknowledged it with a weary flap of hand; he did not sleep well for the pain and fatigue was limned in every line of his face.

'We will need them more now that Batty is gone,' he added with a mollifying smile. 'If the French don't find a way in to Haddington, then we will need to knock the stones out and make one for them.'

The Lovat Frasers. Batty felt sicker than ever and the foetus goggle added nothing. Methven let him stew for a minute or two; he knew of Batty Coalhouse, who hunted out those who had ignored arrest warrants – bills – for robbery, plunder, murder or worse declared by the March Wardens on either side of the divide. There had been little March Warden work since the English invasion and Methven had been told of some quarrel over a horse that had led Batty to blow up a powder mill.

He'd known that when he summoned Batty to Edinburgh and got him working with his guns. No match with a slow match, that was what he had been told and Batty Coalhouse had lived up to the reputation; with all he had done, you had to consider Batty Coalhouse was not the beaten-up one-armed old soak in bad clothing that he looked.

He grinned and Batty scowled back at him.

'You will not be going with just a band of carlins in saffron skirts,' he said. 'You will be part of the entourage of Harry Ree. You ken him I am told.'

Batty knew the Berwick Pursuivant, Henry Rae, a cunning and efficient messenger who rode back and forth from London to Edinburgh in his Herald's coat carrying this and that for one side or the other. Murder and mayhem might wash the land, Batty thought, but it stops at the hem of the gaudily embroidered armorials on that coat. Unless someone wants rid of him for the English spy he truly was.

'I ken him,' he said and made it clear he did not want to know where Harry Rae was headed or on what mission. It was enough to have the protection.

'Berwick and beyond,' Methven said, as if Batty had asked and then leaned closer, so that Batty smelled onions and wine from his breath. 'The beyond is no concern of yours. He is sent by the highest in the land, to seek the highest in the land and bring an end to this... unrest.'

'Your part in it,' the elder Stozzi said, easing his leg with a wince, 'is no more than one of mercy for the Lord Sandilands who wants his Steward back. Besides – this Will is an old friend, so you will help I am sure.'

Batty stared, seeing it like the flush from a drain. Will Elliot had been crippled by the Armstrong Laird of Hollows because of what Batty had done to others of that Name. Crippled more when his cage was swept from the torn roof of the tower – it was a marvel he had survived at all.

He had once been Land-Sergeant at Hermitage for the Keeper of Liddesdale and it had been a wonder to Batty to hear of him as a Steward in some lord's musty hall in Fife, but he had been glad that Will had made a life.

Now it had been swept away from him again and that was not right. He saw a face in his mind, then – young, pale, pretty and earnest. Mintie Henderson of Powrieburn had been the instigator of it all, but it was no more her fault than God's own. If things had turned out differently, Batty thought, she might have been smiling her young, pale, pretty face up at the sun of Will's smile and basking in the glow of it.

He looked at the bag and the writ, then swept both inside his battered jack with a swift gesture of his one hand.

You can only play the cards you are dealt, he thought, in life as in Primero. The others watched him go and Ewan Fraser raised his head to listen to the tuneless singing as he passed. He did not know the song, but he knew mourn when he heard it.

'Departe, departe, departe—
Allace! I most departe
From hir that hes my hart,
With hairt full soir'

Chapter Two

November 1548 – Berwick-upon-Tweed

Grey of Wilton sat in the Tolbooth solar contemplating his supper with a jaundiced eye. Gruel was all he could eat and he hoped – prayed – that would not always be so, for he longed for a chunk of meat slathered in good gravy. He could not even drink brandywine, for it would taste of the slough from the roof of his mouth and sting like the worst liniment.

He was in the solar because it had windows whose thick, small panes allowed more light during the day for reading without having to unfasten a shutter and have an icy blast off the sea adding to his woes.

His mouth ached, a dull bone-deep throb and his ragged lip did not seem part of his body at all, seemed to be a loose, flapping affair that made him sound like an idiot. The pair opposite him offered no soothe on it. One was the bluff, broad-faced figure of Harry Rae in his Herald's cote, the other was a taller, grimmer apparition in a jack of rust and stain, breeches to match and knee boots that had seen better days. He had a face like an old sin garnished with a Turk's beard and had only the one arm – Grey of Wilton knew both of them, but Batty Coalhouse by reputation only.

'Pursuivant Rae,' Grey said and Batty heard the slurring; Grey of Wilton had got himself into the heat of the battle at Pinkie Cleugh last year and ran his face on a Scots pike. Went through his bottom lip, smacked out a tooth and stabbed into the roof of his mouth, Batty had heard. A year had not worked well on it, he saw, as Grey dabbed spots of blood from his lips.

'I am aware I should offer you all assistance,' Grey went on, 'but I fear the practical prevents me. There are sick and wounded lying up wynds and on floors all over the town, with little or no succour.'

'I have a residence,' Henry Rae answered and Grey looked sourly at him.

'No doubt. If it hasnae been broken into and taken over.'

'I do not think so and if I am wrong, the occupants will not be in residence long.'

Grey nodded, dabbed blood off his lips then made an ugly, wet churring sound and spat something out into his kerchief; Batty watched, fascinated.

'Slough,' Grey mumbled and looked bitterly up at the Berwick Pursuivant. 'It would be a personal obligement if you would find room for some of the sick and wounded and take them off the streets.'

Batty could sympathise. He had seen the trail of tears all the way down from Edinburgh – broken carts, dead bodies turned off the road into the ditches so as not to impede the way. They were all the poor, not soldiery of any kind for those lads were going over the moor tops, keeping off the road and banding together for safety – and, if they had decided to desert, to plunder those who had no choice in their fleeing. Batty knew the Border riders would also be out, snapping up the weak and sick for what profit they could take back to their mean homes on the moss. The war was done with but the grim on both sides was still shaking loose the Border.

It was a slorach of bad cess, as Ewan Fraser had said on the way down and no-one disagreed with him, especially the remaining Lovat Frasers – John Dubh, Malcolm, Red Colin and Big Tam – who were still slathered in grief from having had to bury Huw, stabbed through the belly. He had won his glory at the cost of a life, Ewan said at the grave; to Batty it sounded too much like chiding, as if it had been a misplaced cloak.

'I will do what is possible,' Henry Rae replied and Grey had to be satisfied with that, for he turned his gaze on Batty.

'You are part of the Herald's entourage?'

'I have business of my own,' Batty replied, 'involving ransoming a hostage.'

'Will Elliot,' Henry Rae offered helpfully. 'Steward for Lord Sandilands at Norham Castle.'

'Ta'en off the beach at St Monan,' Batty added and watched Grey's face darken; should not have summoned up that grave-shroud fight, he thought, then was surprised at Grey's reply.

'Is this the same Elliot you killed a wheen of Armstrongs to rescue? Or the one you chased down on Tinnis Hill and fought?'

'The former,' Batty answered warily. 'The ither had a double-T in his name and possession of a soul he should not have had.'

He had no idea how common was the knowledge of Queen Mary's kidnap and recovery, still in her cot, from the hands of Hutchie Elliott but it was clear Grey of Wilton knew something of it.

'Last I heard there were a number of Scotch held by Thomas Bui, a mercenary who has taken over the Dun Heifer for what's left of his Company. I would try there – though I would be circumspect Master Coalhouse. He is called Malatesta and your usual diplomacy will not serve you well – besides, if there is trouble anywhere in this toon, I will turn out the garrison and imprison you in the lowest wet I can find, there to lick the stones for relief of thirst until you are hemped.'

'Aye, aye,' said Batty mild and smiling, 'If so, I will at least get to see old friends – is Red Rowan Charlton still in charge there?'

'He went to Pinkie Cleugh,' Grey of Wilton replied blankly. 'Died there of an arrow in the throat.'

Batty was shocked, the more so at the sorrow he felt for he had never considered Red Rowan Charlton as more than an acquaintance to be cultivated so that a stay in Berwick's prison was made more comfortable. Poor Red Rowan, who thought of himself as much finer than a Berwick gaoler and finally discovered the harsh truth of derring-do and war. Perhaps Grey saw some of that in Batty's face, for his pain-lined face seemed to soften a little as he shoved Batty's safe passage writs back at him.

'It would be a poor idea to cause ruction here,' he said and though it was gruff Batty could hear it was well meant. 'I ken what you did afore for the Wardens – I am now Warden of the East March myself – and there are those whose kin were on the rough end of your attention in the toon. That puts you in a poor light – and besides, you are a Scotchman, fresh come from the north and with a wheen of louts in saffron dress from further north again.

'Behave yourself,' he added, squinting at the gruel. Then he sighed and pushed the bowl to one side, looking back at Henry Rae.

'I widnae linger long in Berwick, Pursuivant. Since the Seymours have made such a poor fist of the war here, I am thinking London will be a fever of elbows looking for preferment. I hourly expect to hear of the Lord Protector's removal.'

Rae answered with a curt nod and took up his seal-dangled passes and conducts. Outside in the chill, wet air he sucked in a breath or two and Batty watched him scowl. He was short and slight and his paunch had swelled since Batty had last seen him. He still looked like a pox doctor's clerk wearing fine clothes stolen from his too-large da – all except the Herald's cote, bright with armorials.

'He is a pustule that one,' Rae muttered bleakly, 'and it is matter for great regret that the man who piked him never shoved it hard enough down his throat.'

Coming from an English, Batty thought, that is harsh and he wondered why Grey of Wilton was so disliked – then dismissed it. Plots circled one another like turds in a privy drain and Batty knew Grey bore the weight of being Captain of Berwick, Warden of the East March and more, besides his mouth wound. The Seymours were tumbling and all that had been firm was now morass. He said so and Henry Rae shrugged.

'No matter who Lord Protects the young king,' Henry Rae replied levelly, 'Master Ralph Sadler will still be on the Privy Council and I will be his intelligencer, among other tasks – you are welcome to the hospitality of my house, Master Coalhouse. If it still stands.'

Rae's sergeant, a Hume like the rest of his escort, cursed and growled and chivvied the carts under his command until they started a long, dark rumble down the Bridge Gate. Ewan walked this one, since riding meant he had to hitch his long mail coat up to his waist and the underserk with it. In order to preserve decency and some heat, he wore dark hose, which was shaming to a Scotch from the north.

It started to rain, fine as sifted flour and what few lights there were flickered wanly; Batty could hear the murmur and drone of those huddled damply in the wynds.

There were guards on the bridge, thankful that these carts weren't about to rumble out and across it. Out on the length of bridge were lights, bobbing to and fro and the guards told them there was a curfew in force because so much heavy ordinance and traffic had crossed already that the rickety bridge teetered on the edge of falling; men were out trying to shore it up in the dark.

Rae's house was a tall affair on the street itself, but that was the front entrance; the one for carts and deliveries was up a wynd on one side and through some double doors. It did not look right, as Rae said, dashing drips off his nose.

'No lights. Gate is shut. No porter. Davie Hume – take a couple of your lads and see if you can open those gates.'

'They must have heard us,' Davie Hume observed sourly. And, if so, Batty thought, they should either be out with lanterns welcoming the master or waiting to see who tries to get in the gate. He levered himself off Fiskie and patted the loyal beast while the Frasers, after a pause, did the same, handing all the reins to Big Tam, who had the muscle to hold them all firmly.

Davie Hume looked at the dismounted Humes, hitched his shoulders a little, then made his way to the gate and pushed it; it swung a little way and he turned.

'The bar is off. It's open.'

A wine-smelling voice spoke softly in Batty's ear.

'Two gets ye yin he is shot the minute he steps through.'

Batty would not give Ewan Fraser the odds for that, but indicated that he should get his kin prepared.

'Knives and guns,' he said hoarsely. 'Yon pigsticker you swing is little use in such a wee place.'

'Bugger off – this is our place.'

The voice was loud and shrill in the dark beyond the gate. Henry Rae raised himself in the stirrups and Batty could almost see the comb of him hackle up.

'This is the house of the Berwick Pursuivant, who is here. Vacate it immediately or be hemped.'

The reply was in an accent thick as clotted cream – Northumberland, Batty knew – and probably included references to the Berwick Pursuivant's birth and offered a destination for him to travel to. Davie Hume blew on the match of his long-barrelled pistol, kicked in the heavy double gates and rushed in, yelling: 'A Hume, to me.'

With triumphant cries the Frasers surged after and Batty sighed, looked up at the shadowed figure of Henry Rae, face blood-dyed with torchlight.

'Bigod, Herald, what part of not causing a stushie did you miss from Grey of Wilton?'

There were snarls and shouts and the clash of angry metal as Batty ducked through the gate; he did not want to particularly, but thought it only fair that he at least follow the mad Frasers. The courtyard was filled with dancing shadows and Batty could not tell one from the other, so he moved to the house and shoved open the door, stepping into a dim wood-floored hall and a curve of stair running up. It stank of sickness and sweat and fear. There were other doors leading off to both sides and they sprang open to spew out running men.

The figures materialised into two darker shapes and Batty reeled away from them – the closest of the fighters stumbled, almost falling over his own feet, so Batty pointed the dagg at him and squeezed. The wheel ratcheted round, spilling big sparks; there was enough time for the man to see it and shriek before the machine went off with a deafening roar, a great gout of blinding flame and a choking plume of smoke. Batty had time to see the shape become a man, wet-mouthed with fear, his eyes widely amazed, as if he had stepped through a portal into the land of Faerie.

The ball took him in the chest and he went backwards as if hauled by an invisible hand – Batty flicked the heavy dagg up and felt the burn of the barrel, then lunged forward at a second figure, swinging the axe-head handle at him.

The man managed a desperate parry with a backsword and fell back, trying for room to drag out a dagger, but Batty was having none of that and pressed home. The man's face was red and sheened, he had a goosegog pimple on one side of his nose and his eyes were bright with shock and terror.

They rolled up into his head when Batty brought the axe-head down on his collar bone, the snap audible. It did not cut through the heavy padding of a jack though it sliced the material to ruin.

But the bone-break was enough and the man collapsed, moaning; Batty kicked him in the head until he stopped.

There was a sudden, eerie stillness, a silence broken only by distant whimpers from the dark edges of the room, then a shape loomed up and reared back when he saw Batty with the axe.

'Good God,' Henry Rae said, looking round. 'Ye have slain two of them.'

'Aye, well seen,' Batty replied, feeling the breath rasp in him now; he wanted to sit down but dare not. 'Thank me efter.'

'The ones in the yard gave up without more than a yell or two,' Henry Rae replied bitterly. 'They are no more than sick and wounded.'

'Then these must be the sound ones,' Batty answered flatly and turned as Ewan came in, holding a sputtering torch high and peering round.

'A brace of them,' he said admiringly and Henry Rae scowled.

'I did not mean for killing to be in this.'

'Mayhap you should have thought of that before you let Davie Hume and the Frasers here aff the leash,' Batty said and watched Henry Rae stump off, bawling at people to sort out the mess. Then he bent to the man he had felled with the axe and saw that he was alive but in pain enough to turn his face the colour of spoiled cream.

'Half done is all good,' he said and Ewan Fraser turned the torch this way and that, letting Batty see the trembling huddle of women and bairns whimpering in corners of the once-fine residence, whose hangings had been stripped for blankets and whose furniture had been broken for firewood. He felt more sorrowed about shooting one of them dead now and said so.

To his surprise, Ewan Fraser sighed. '*An rud nach gabh leasachadh, 's fheudar cur suas leis,*' he said, then said it again in English – what cannot be helped, must be put up with.

–

What cannot be helped, must be put up with – Batty found echoes of that everywhere he went in the Herald's battered house. People were shoehorned into the outbuildings to allow room for the Humes and Frasers, the horses and the carts but at least they were all warmer and drier than out in the street.

Most of the folk they found inside were not soldiers, just ragged remnants of old lives, fled from burned-out homes and, to give him his due, Henry Rae did not turn them out, though he had the right and reason enough.

'That was a rosewood chair afore I left,' he mourned, pointing to the splintered wreck which was now feeding the fire in his cleared-out solar. 'I had books, too, but they have burned them also – bliddy wee Philistines.'

Like me they cannae read, Batty thought, so it was no great loss to them and the heat a great benefit. But he said nothing, for he could see the Herald had blood in his eye over it. Never mind his curtains and bed-hangings, the loss of his books seemed to set him frothing; Batty had seen this before and still could not understand it, as if books should be elevated above all. He could not read, but was wise enough to see that his views might change if he had the ability.

The one saving grace was that the cellar had been barred to looters by the servants who had not run off – the Herald's Steward, Will's Patey Hume, had fastened himself in it with three other servitors, preventing access to the food and, above all, the wine. They were, however, drunk as lords when released, which made Batty chuckle. Like Primero, you can only play the hand you are dealt he told the puffing Rae, who subsided gradually when it became clear they hadn't drunk everything.

The Herald raised a silver ewer and poured red wine into a blue glass, all of it recovered from the contrite staff, happy to return it as payment for a dry billet and some bread and hard cheese from the Herald's store. Henry Rae was happy, too, and drank to prove it.

'It is the wine that leads me on, the wild wine that sets the wisest man to sing at the top of his lungs, laugh like a fool – it drives the man to dancing… it even tempts him to blurt out stories better never told.'

'Never trust vows made in wine,' Batty echoed and raised his blue glass in salute. The Herald laughed.

'Shorter than Homer and lacking poetry – but that auld Greek would recognise the strength of it.'

'A man as good as yer auld Homer said it,' Batty answered, half away with the Faerie and the wine.

'Who?'

'Bunarotti,' Batty replied. 'Whom the world knows as Michaelangelo.'

'Ye ken him? From where? There is a story there and we have fire, food and wine, so speak on.'

Batty said little, simply told of being in Florence during the siege of '29 and how Michaelangelo was siting defences as an engineer. 'He likes wine and sculpture,' he added. 'There is no *terribilita* in paint, he would say. Carving is better and easier – you cut to the skin and then stop.'

He laughed softly at the memory, then lifted the cup in toast.

'I feel as lit by fire a cold countenance
That burns me from afar and keeps itself ice-chill;
A strength I feel two shapely arms to fill

Which without motion moves every balance.'

Henry Rae looked astonished. 'I had not heard the man did poetry also. There is a deal of love in that.'

Batty acknowledged it, but did not expound on it further since it was certain the Herald would not appreciate it. Instead, he murmured tunelessly, a verse of *The Lament of the Master of Erskine*.

> *'Fair weill, my lady bricht,*
> *And my remembrance rycht;*
> *Fair weill and haif gud nycht:*
> *I say no moir.'*

'Christ's blood, I hope you do say no more,' the Herald spat. 'I am heart sick of that bliddy affair for it is played and declaimed incessant at the court in Holyrood. The Dowager Queen herself has now banned it I hear – and Alexander Scott now wishes his poetry had never been set to music.'

Everybody wishes his poetry had never been set to music, Batty thought, but Mary of Guise's reaction is hardly a surprise when the verse is supposed to be the dying words of her lover, killed at Pinkie only the year before; every performance opened that wound raw.

They drank and cocked ears to the distant sound of raised voices; something smashed and clattered.

'Warden Grey will be busy,' the Herald noted then paused as the door was rapped hard, then Will's Patey stuck his mourn of a face round it.

'Yer Captain, Davey Hume, wishes a word.'

Wearily the Herald waved him in and the Captain entered, dripping over the scuffed floor.

'Raining is it now?' Batty offered mildly and had a sour look in reply.

'I cannae get all they wagons in the gate,' Hume said, 'especially yon moudiewart long yin. It will not be turned.'

'That's because you bought them without thinking,' Batty replied, which stung Hume into bridling, though he was stopped by the Herald's hand.

'Without thinking? We took them as bargain,' he said and Batty made an ambivalent movement of his head.

'Always look the gift horse...' he said, then saw Hume's face and sighed.

'You took what was left, for they were cheap and there was a reason for that,' he explained. 'Every wainwright makes his own wagons and most of what you have was never built in this land – they were brought by various Companies and discarded for the reasons you are now discovering. You have southern Italian wagons here, built for big loads – that's the great heavy affairs which you need a hand of fat-arsed horses with shoes to pull through the dubs of this country. You have ones from the Austrias, which are shorter because you need to work them round steep, climbing bends. And you have north Italian ones, the bugger that will not turn in the gate, made narrow and long because the bridges up there are not wide and there is no point to a wagon which won't cross a river, is there?'

The Herald bellowed with joy, then slapped Hume hard on one sullen, wet shoulder.

'Now you know, Davey Hume, and it takes a Scotch to set you straight. And those folk don't even do wagons, they use bliddy pack ponies, by God's balls. Pack ponies!'

If you rode over the tops of the trackless moss, Batty thought sourly, you'd see the benefit of pack ponies. Also across that shaky bridge – he was heart-glad he was not crossing it any time soon.

The Herald soothed Davey Hume with an offer of wine and laughed again. 'You should have regard for Batty here, who is well-versed in wagons of all sorts and the mercenary Companies that use them. He is late of the Sable Rose, after all and though half of them drowned in the Mary Rose, there are yet enough left in Kent for Captain-General Maramaldo to take to the wars.'

Perhaps he felt the chill, for he stopped, glanced at Batty's face and rubbed his own with a pungent curse.

'Ach, bigod, I meant to find a better time and way...'

'Maramaldo?' Batty demanded, feeling as if his face had been pulled from a snowdrift. The Herald sighed.

'Free from Dacre's prison and sent south to take charge of what's left of his old Company, the better to get it under some control.'

'Freed?' Batty echoed disbelievingly. 'He was to be hemped.'

'At the king's pleasure,' Henry Rae replied. 'The writ was only to be signed and the deed done – but auld Henry up and died, did he not?'

Batty slumped, marvelled and sickened all at once. 'The De'il looks after his ain.'

Davey Hume crossed himself and the Herald nodded soberly. 'The new young king was persuaded to release Maramaldo in order that he take charge of a wheen of men who might cause trouble. I hear the Company is to be sent to Devon or Somerset, where the common are set against gentlemen. They want the Latin mass and the recall of English Bibles, I hear.'

There will be little plunder in it, Batty thought, so Maramaldo will contrive to find some, even if it means levelling hamlets and vills to embers and ruin.

Maramaldo. He never ceased to maze me, Batty thought. Beyond that, he did not know whether to be glad or furious, but he set down the wine, which suddenly tasted of cloy.

–

During the day Hidegate's wynds were clotted with people passing up and down, dodging and elbowing and cursing in a funnel of space where you could reach out either arm and fingertip the rough, high house walls on both sides.

Masons, merchants and dancing masters, barbers and advocates, all met on the narrow passages with varying degrees of politeness. A douce goodwife, crushing her basket and trying to keep her hem out of the filth, would vie with a porter delivering coals, fishwives with their creels, the sweeps and the water carriers.

On the south side of it was the old Austin Friary, abandoned during the Dissolving some thirty years before and now mouldering to ruin – next to it, up another narrow twist of cobbles called Anchor Wynd, was the Dun Heifer.

Batty knew it was foolish to come here in a night made darker by a sea haar and a mizzle of rain, but he could not sleep and could not cast Maramaldo from his mind in order to allow it. The man who had cut off his arm had been sprung from a certain death Batty had helped arrange and Batty, who had come to a new way of looking at the old Captain-General, was ruffled about how he felt over it all.

The Anchor Wynd was darker than the Earl of Hell's back passage, so that even the lights of the lantern boys seemed to make little difference. They, knowing the way of it, were already lying in wait, rushing forward to offer their services and usually in pairs with one holding a great light on a pole, the other a bull's eye lantern for focusing on the ground.

There were a few lurkers, watching for opportunity and if they saw a one-armed man with a good belly as an easy mark they revised it when they caught sight of a jack of plates stained by war, a backsword and brace of fat wheel-lock daggs in his belt. That and the two dark pillars on either side of him, one dressed in a mail coat that came below the knee and fairly screamed 'mad Irish', the other a vision of Gallowglass save that his feet had shoes.

The curfew was imminent and the drum had sounded, giving folk a last few minutes to vacate the streets; the dying echoes of it slid into the night with the tramp of a garrison patrol, who would return soon enough to make sure it was upheld.

The arguments started at once, over who had hired what; the douce housekeepers in the tenements above used the noise and the drum as a reminder that they hadn't fulfilled a vital domestic function and began emptying nightpots and slops into the street, shouting 'gardyloo' as a belated warning. As a revenge for the racket it was stinking sweet.

'Haud yer hand,' voices bellowed back and someone announced that he was Thomas Loudon, advocate and cursed them roundly for ruining his second-best hat; 'my best was beshitten two days afore in this same pestilential place. I swear by the same pestilential wummin – if I ever get you in a court, mistress, expect nae mercy.'

'Mind yer foot, sir, or you will coggle doon…'

The timely warning clamped the advocate's lips and focused his attention on not being jostled down a set of steps; Batty hung back and let them go, aware of Ewan on one side and Red Colin on the other. He kept to the shadows under the tavern lintel until Daunie's quaver of voice warned him that the doors of the Dun Heifer were being shut.

'This tavern is not for the public, sir,' Daunie Dodd began and Batty thrust his face into the light.

'I am here to see Thomas Bui, known as Malatesta.'

Then he went past Daunie without waiting, stepped on to the uneven flags of the landing with the Frasers at his back; he heard the door close with a sinister grate. Lights bobbed and voices growled and muttered; somewhere, a woman laughed high and shrill.

The Dun Heifer was an old haunt for Batty, a dirty, mean den that needed candles on a dull day for anyone to see by. Everyone who was anyone knew the way to it without need of light or guides and, above the lintel on the inside, was the carved inscription *Lord, In Thee Is All My Trust*, the letters worn to shine by the touch of the superstitious, who wanted it to be true in a place such as this. Batty shouldered through into the kitchen.

Here he bowed politely to Mrs Dodd, as enormously fat and large as her husband was tiny and scrawny. She was swathed in her finest blue wool lined with murray over a sage-green underdress and had, until now, worn a headwrap as fat as any Ottoman Sultan's. She bowed to everyone who passed through, like the receiving line for Mary of Guise, but thought all was done with and stared open-mouthed at Batty, fancy head cover in one hand and her head shaved against the nits.

He left her, trailing the penny special smells – minced collops, rizared haddocks or tripe, a fluke of roasted skate and onions – into the dim noiseome den where usually lords, lawyers, ladies of ill-repute and the loathsome met and had their high jinks.

Not now, though. Now it was full of shadows and laughter, the odd sparkle of a geegaw, the high shrill of one of the gauds, a rill of Italian and a harsh of Germanic.

'Ho, Daunie, bring more light here. I cannot see these newcomers and I have a desire to – besides, my pastes are a mystery to me and I feel I have a decent hand.'

The voice was fruity and light but it came from a barrel with a square head, capped by grey hair to his ears, the chin carefully shaved. He wore a shirt in cramoisi which did nothing for the eyes sunk in violet ringed pools.

'You never have a decent hand and can never tell it anyway,' Batty said while the Frasers looked on, trying to be stolid and show none of the unease they felt; they were all aware of being surrounded by half-shadowed figures dressed like papingoes in bright colours, all slashed and paned and ribboned, stained with old sins. The women were bold, no less gaudy and no less stained.

The man roared and slapped the table and stood up.

'I need no light to know Barthelemie Kohlhase,' he declared loudly and Daunie, half-way to the table with a wax-slathered branched candelabra made a face and turned to go. Batty plucked the affair from his hands and stuck it on the table, scattering coin and cards; someone sitting in the shadowed end made an annoyed grunt.

'Barthie,' said the man with a wide, deep grin.

'Thomas,' Batty countered. They made no move to kiss cheeks or clasp wrists, but Thomas Bui thrust a horn cup at Batty and then gave Ewan and John Dubh the same. They sniffed, smacked lips and drank if off in one; there was appreciative laughter.

'At least now I know your attack dogs are Scotch,' Thomas Bui declared. 'No-one drinks brandy like they do.'

'They will drink anything,' Batty agreed, 'and have only one proviso regarding it — which I share — that it must not have been previously swallowed.'

He was aware of the men round the table shifting away, scraping back benches and stools to slide into the shadows and leave him and Thomas Bui alone. He sat down and Thomas sat opposite.

'What brings you here? Do not say chance.'

'The chance you have a man I seek,' Batty answered. 'Taken from the north scant days ago. Steward of a wee fortalice. His name is Will Elliot and he has poor feet which makes walking awkward.'

'He has missing toes and bad stab marks through the insteps,' Thomas Bui replied flatly. 'I had our barber look at him, thinking his wounds were more recent than they were. Hoping to get him to at least stand upright without a stick. I bought him from some *stradioti*; I do not know what Company they were in but I suspect they were leaving it at the time.'

Batty's heart spun a little and he tried to control his voice. 'Is he here still?'

Thomas Bui leaned back a little and contemplated Batty. 'What's your interest in the man?'

'Ransom, no more no less. Sent by the wee lord whose fortalice he stewards for.'

'I thought it might have been Maramaldo.'

Batty shrugged. 'I had heard he was out and away. Why would I care?'

'I hear you had him marked for a hemping,' Thomas Bui answered and Batty managed a laugh, though it sounded hollow even to him.

'The Red Bull Dacre had him on a gibbet, waiting the word of Fat Henry, who choked on it and died before issuing the writ.'

'So Maramaldo said,' Thomas Bui answered, 'together with a lot of cant about the Lord sparing him for better work ahead.' He saw Batty's face and how he would not ask the question that bothered him. So he provided the answer anyway.

'He spoke of you. He came here on the way south. Has a handful of Border horse – Charltons and not the best of them, mind – and a score of ragged chiels barely able to hold a pike the right way up. He was buying captives who could be indentured to him as fighting men and thought to get some old soldiers from me. Half his Company sank in the Mary Rose.'

'Did he take any?'

Thomas Bui shook his head. 'I had none by then. Only one thing stinks worse than fish after three days and that's guests who do not work and need feeding. I ransomed the English I had to some Scotch out of Carlisle. They take them for the delight of hanging them – hold a Fair Day for it and call it 'dancing on air'. I ransomed some Scotch to an English from a tower out in the wilds, probably for the same fate. I thought to add this Will Elliot to the party for he was no use to me.'

Batty knew that the distinctions between 'sold' and 'ransomed' could get you hanged, but the act was the same no matter the legals in it. He wondered who the English with a tower in the wild was and asked it aloud.

Thomas waved a deprecating hand. '*Niente è per niente* – 200 English shillings will get you the who. The where you must find for yourself.'

Nothing is for nothing. Batty had heard that many times before, but the price was steep just for a name and he said so. Thomas leaned forward a little.

'Only a tenth of that is for the name,' he answered, softly vicious, 'the rest is for me to forget Maramaldo's request to do you much harm as possible.'

Thomas Bui knew Barthelemie Kohlhase by reputation and some sightings. He knew he had been at the siege of Florence years before, helping Michaelangelo Bunarotti site defence works and guns. Before that, he had heard, Kohlhase had been a gunner for Maramaldo, who had something to do with the loss of his arm. He knew Barthie was a gunner much in demand. He knew the man was known as someone who was 'no match with a slow match'.

None of which prepared him for the sudden savage dig of metal in one knee under the table, nor the curl of smile over the sickle beard.

'I have adjusted this to take account of that being your left knee. How do you value your bags, Captain-General Bui? For if you do not part with the name and with us in good grace, I will blow them so far away ye could not find them with an almanac.'

Bui gave in and gave the name, then Batty stood, pistol still in his hand and backed for the kitchen, shepherded by the Frasers, watched by shadow men who scraped back

44

their chairs and waited to be let off the leash. Batty went past Daunie's now-scowling wife, then Daunie himself as he unbolted the door. Out into the rain-lashed street, a wind had scattered the mist and brought storm from the sea.

There was no-one around, which Batty decided was God's grace on a curfew. 'What now?' Ewan demanded and Batty gave him a scornful curl of lip.

'Run, ye bliddy fool.'

          -

They ran, though Batty's part in that was short and ended in a wheezing stumble. He was half-way up Hidegate, slithering on cobbles wet as a black whale's back, when he had to stop, one shoulder on a slimed wall, mouth open to suck in more air. Too auld, he thought fiercely. Too bliddy auld for this…

There was movement in the shadows and he remembered he still held the drawn dagg and lifted it menacingly; he hoped the powder was still dry.

'Stay clear, ye scullions.'

Then he heard the slap of leather and saw the figures coming up hard from the Dun Heifer; there were four of them and they stopped a loud shout away then one stepped forward. He had a lump of wood and a dagger and Batty had no doubt his friends were as similarly armed; they aim to do me damage, Batty thought, then drag me back to the feet of Malatesta.

Batty felt a lurch of panic, for he could not see any of the Frasers and cursed them under his breath. Run, he had said like a bliddy fool and they had obeyed him with all the speed of young legs.

'How now, Mynheer Kohlhase. You have played your hand, bully and now must suffer the cost.'

'I would concern yourself with your own costs ye lubberwort,' Batty replied and waggled the axe-handled dagg. 'This monstrance will cause your eyes to cross, or I am a Dutchman.'

The man's English was not up to the task and he clearly thought Batty was already a Dutchman – which is what he had been told – for he rattled off something in that tongue and then started forward, cudgel in one hand and a dagger in the other; his friends followed.

'Malatesta says I am to bat your bollocks into next week and bring you back, bloody but alive,' the man said, closing fast. There had been more from Malatesta, whose red anger had provided more glow in the dark of the Dun Heifer than any candelabra.

'Beat him, break his legs, break his one good arm, Panteleo. Do not fail me.'

Panteleo Vercellis did not intend to do that; he had seen what others who had failed suffered when Thomas Bui transmuted into Malatesta.

Batty cursed his luck, backed up to keep all of them in sight, for they were circling him like wolves; from a window, a woman's voice called out, querulous and shrill. One of the men barked back at her in German.

Panteleo stopped, close enough to swing and yet with pity in his face. He shrugged. 'I do not like it, for I have heard of you and it seems a great shame to have you damaged. There are people who will pay a lot to have you unsullied, so they can do that themselves.'

'Aye aye,' Batty said as level-voiced as he could muster, 'I will make you rich, nae doubt.'

He knew this man spoke soft in order to get closer, knew there was no soft in him at all and he hefted the dagg and aimed it casually from near his waist. 'No matter who gets to spend it on women and drink, one of them will not be you. Did you forget I had this?'

The man stopped and looked suddenly wary.

'Or did you not think I'd use it.'

'One shot,' Panteleo said, though he was licking his lips and Batty knew the hexagonal barrel must have looked like the entrance to a dark tunnel. 'They often fail,' he added hopefully.

'Mine never fail,' Batty lied. 'Move a wee bitty to the right. That way I can line you up with the chiel behind – at this range the shot will rip through your bollocks, out your arse and into him. Two for one...'

The man paused, then curled his lips and Batty knew it was coming so he squeezed the trigger, saw the wheel spin, saw the spark – and then nothing at all.

Misfire.

He cursed, reversed it and slashed the axehead just as the man ran in, making him rear back as he skidded forward; they collided, Batty thrown into the harsh harl of the building. The man lost his footing and fell to his knees – Batty did not hesitate, brought the axehead down on the cloth-capped head and heard the clang of the steel cap underneath it.

He cursed his luck and lashed out one boot, catching the man in the chest, throwing him backwards to the cobbles; the man lay there, dazed and gasping – but the others were closing in.

'Rush him,' one of them advised in Italian and the man next to him started to foolishly obey; there was a movement of shadows off to Batty's left and then a high, thin ping of sound; the man who had started to rush stumbled and fell, his head rolling free.

The others looked wildly around and one stared at the headless man leaking his life over the rainwashed cobbles. Somewhere a woman screamed. Ewan Fraser stepped out of the dark, cradling the huge sword and smiling.

'Ye have cut his head off,' one of the others cried out and there was no denying the truth, for the man was spasming his headless last in a spreading pool darker than the wet cobbles; lights and querulous calls came from all round.

Panteleo scrambled up, his knife still in one fist and his eyes wide with pain and shock; his feet sloshed and slipped in the blood.

'I will fillet you like fish,' he bellowed, but a big black-bearded face thrust out of the dark next to Batty – making him jump and cry out as loudly as the man with the knife.

'Losh, this game is rotted. Run ye bliddy fools,' John Dubh said and slashed the air a foot from Panteleo's face with a winking edge of backsword.

Batty gave Panteleo no chance to work out what to do next – he lunged, stamping forward on the front foot and slicing the axe in a flurry of movement.

Panteleo yelped and his sleeve turned crimson; the rest of his men were already slithering and sliding half-way down the Hidegate. Run, you cunny-licking harecop, Batty willed, but was surprised when the man's face twisted angrily.

'*Stronzo. Porco miseria*,' he said and came forward, the dirk slashing left and right. Batty fended the blows and the steel rang like bells; he heard more shouts, almost felt the lights on his back like a heat. He could not afford to stay longer fending off a dagger with an axe and crabbed

48

sideways, looking to head off up the street. Batty saw Ewan, walking casually as if strolling to a pie shop, hefting his bloody great sword and measuring distance.

'Dinna,' he managed, then flung up one good arm as the knife went up, only to find it a feint. The blow took him on the jack and he heard one of his horn plates crack – then the man lurched under the dull clanging weight of Ewan's blade flat on his head.

Panteleo went to his knees. Batty kicked him in the face and then went off up the street, stumping and muttering like a winter-woken bear, stuffing the pistol in his belt. When he had put a distance between himself and the furore, he turned and glared at the Frasers.

'I said run, ye bliddy fools.'

It was a long way back to Henry Rae's house and every wary step gave Ewan time to frown over how he had just murdered a man in a public street. He thought Batty might have had something to say on it, but the man hirpled along like a sailor on a rolling deck, singing softly and sounding like a cat mourning on the tiles for love.

'Fair weill, my lady bricht,
And my remembrance rycht;
Fair weill and haif gud nycht:
I say no moir.'

Chapter Three

Later, 1548 – Blackscargil

The wind blew squalls off the sea and brought gulls with it, crying like lost children. It made the Frasers uneasy, that sound, but all it meant to Batty was that there was weather on the way; you could taste the snow and Blackscarsgil was no place to be caught.

It was a rolling waste of tussock and copse, broken hill country under a pewter-grey sky. The whole country had such names – Muckle Snab, Bloody Bush, Blackhagg, Wolf Rig and more – but none was darker than Blackscargil.

'Then why are we going to it?' Malcolm Fraser had demanded sullenly, cold to the bone and fighting the spare horse and pack pony; being youngest he got the worst tasks.

'There is a tower in it and a man I need to see,' Batty answered tersely and all of the Frasers had to be content at that, though they did not like it much; they knew it already from what Thomas Bui had said, his lips stiff and dry. Batty did not want to tell them more, but when they stopped at the charred remains of a cruck, he had them halt and unsaddle.

The house had lost most of its thatch and the curved roofbeams were gone, but the walls still stood, blackened and frowning; there was a section at one end which had more thatch on the roof and they shifted gear into this.

'Where are the folk who lived here, d'you think?' Red Colin asked and Big Tam hefted off the pack-saddle and set it down in the mulch of old dung and straw.

'Deid as snails in frost,' he said flatly and no-one argued with him.

'How long are we here then, Master Coalhouse?' Ewan asked lightly and Batty scowled at him.

'Have you somewhere else to be?'

'I have not, other than a desire to be in a decent tavern with a leather of ale.'

'I am with you there,' John Dubh agreed, 'but you are paying, mind.'

Batty had heard the hardness creep into Ewan's voice and thought it best to curb his temper; it was unease at where he was going that made him contrary, he knew. That and having to trust these caterans from the north. He did not like any of it.

'We will be there by and by,' he said, trying for a smile and falling far short of it. 'I need to meet with the one who lairs in a tower just over the ridge. With luck I will find Will Elliot there, agree a ransom and we will be away.'

He paused, then hauled the leather pouch of coin from under his jack and handed it to Ewan.

'This is the ransom money. I will not ride in with it, so when I return will be as good a signal as any that the deed is done and we will all go with this pouch and fetch our man out.'

The Frasers saw the sense in it and if any thought of the money or what they could do with it, their faces did not show it. Batty added nothing that might throw an insult.

'Be watchful,' he added. 'They may work out where you are and almost certainly know that I am not alone – it would be a bliddy fool who rides in this part of the world alone. They may come down on you.'

'*Tha sinn nar seasamh deiseil*,' Ewan said sombrely and the others repeated it. We stand ready – Batty was unnerved by it, by the feeling that these were men ready to give their lives for this. For him. Bliddy northers, he thought trying to dismiss it, as equal likely to take all this coin and bolt back to their wee bog in the north. Up until their sombre 'we stand ready' that had been his worst fear and now he was thrown into confusion.

They had a fire lit, careful to feed it with anything that did not smoke more than faint blue haze, whirled away almost at once by the wind. They had oats and fish and made a decent meal of them both, washed down with wine, courtesy of Sir Grey of Wilton.

He had sat in his solar room and squinted at Batty and the Frasers, while Henry Rae looked on, standing hipshot and trying to act as if he did not care.

There was a lot about murder and a headless body and a lot from Henry Rae about the fourteen other killings in the town that night, over a dry spot or food or drink or women. None of them would be solved, he added pointedly. In the end they had been waved away and, outside, took farewells as if they meant it.

'Good luck with your venture,' Henry Rae had said, hitching a splendid fur trimmed cloak round his Herald's cote to keep the rain off. 'I hope we do not meet again.'

'Same back at ye,' Batty had growled. 'Watch out that your ain heid stays on your shoulders – where you are going is more dangerous.'

Batty was roused by Big Tam thrusting a horn cup at him, which he took and sniffed suspiciously – the strong whiff of it confirmed that it was *aqua vita*. He took it, sipped and swallowed, feeling the burn, raw and fiery. The Frasers laughed softly at his watered eyes, then Ewan held his cup up in a toast.

'*Uisge-beatha*,' he said, 'to remember *Blàr na Léine*.'

Batty knew *uisge-beatha* was their name for *aqua vita*, the water of life. He also knew *Blàr na Léine* was the battle that seemed to have doomed the Frasers, so he asked about it. Ewan was silent for a long time, he and all the Frasers staring into the fire.

'The chieftainship of the McDonalds of Clanranald was in dispute,' he said eventually. 'Our Laird, chief of the Fraser of Lovat, was the uncle of Ranald Galda whose cause he supported. We took four hundred of our best and joined with the Earl of Huntly, chief of Clan Gordon and Lieutenant of the North.'

There was a silence, then Ewan said: 'It did not go as we had thought.'

The others growled deep hooming sounds in their throats, a noise that hackled Batty up.

'We thought to crush the McDonalds and make Ranald the chief and went to Inverlochy and took Castle Tioram.'

His head bowed and he shook it, then drank. 'That was it, or so we thought. Ranald Galda was installed as the chief, Huntly went off one way and we started back for home. The treacherous skulking bastard MacDonalds fell on us in some wild marshland to the north of Loch Lochy – *Blàr na Léine* which means "field of bogs".'

'We did not need to fight,' John Dubh interrupted bitterly.

'In the end, we here did not,' Red Colin answered, 'to the shame of us all so we cannot go back.'

Ewan spat out *aqua vita* so that the fire flared like a dragon's breath.

'Everyone got killed save us,' he went on bleakly. 'The Lovat heidman is dead, so is his heir and my own from Beauly are all sent to the mud. I thought it best that some Lovat Frasers did not leave mithers to weep.'

'They weep anyway,' Malcolm added, head down. 'For shame.'

Mothers weep up and down the land, Batty thought. You need only look round at this wee cruck house to see tears; they are soaked into the walls. Yet they will come back if they live, he thought. They will creep back and build it again and plant again and move sheep and cattle out into the pasture and, if they are fortunate, will manage a harvest at least once before bastards that look like us come down on them again.

No matter that the war atween Scotch and English is trickling to a close, he thought; for the reivers it is just a better excuse to shake loose the Border.

–

He sat astride Fiskie while the wind circled and fingered, looking for ways into the cloak's ragged hems while it muttered about snow. Batty had seen the sky, pale milk where a sun fought to shine, grey as lost hope everywhere else. It did not add much to the pele of Blackscargil, a tall block of stone pierced with wan lights even though it was mid-morning. Surrounding it was a man-height drystone wall and a scatter of buildings, roofs slated or thatched.

'Who lives there?' John Dubh had asked when Batty set out to ride the little way over the rise to it.

Nebless Clem Selby lived there, though he was not the first to do so. Until recently, Batty had been told, the Tower had belonged to Dand Selby, known as Firebraes in his better days. His better days had been a long time before, but Grey of Wilton had mentioned how Dand had been married on to Eliza Graham from Netherby, a woman half his age.

He had said it with a sly sidelong look, for he knew Batty was a Graham, though not welcome with that Name anywhere save for Netherby; Eliza Graham meant nothing to Batty and his face did not flicker, which disappointed Grey of Wilton.

'Dand was failing,' he went on, 'when Nebless Clem arrived with enough men to overawe and enough kinship to be allowed to stay.'

The rest was familiar enough; Nebless Clem had proved vigorous, cunning and ruthless and his work at raiding and trading had put Blackscargil back on the up. Nebless Clem, deputy to the Laird of Blackscargil, had become the power, inch by sly inch.

'Then Dand died,' Grey of Wilton had added flatly. 'Now Clem has tower and the Graham wife both. No-one kens how Dand Selby died, but he was auld and sick.' He accompanied this last with another of his sly sideways looks that said how Dand Selby hadn't been old or sick enough for Clem – or mayhap even his wife.

'How did he lose his neb?' Ewan Fraser had wanted to know and Grey of Wilton had shot him a sour look.

'Poking it in ither folk's business, no doubt. Let that be a lesson.'

Batty knew little about Nebless Clem, but he had heard how he had lost his nose. He had boasted how he could smell out witches and did it loudly and often the day he rousted out seven Egyptiani women from his woods, where they were collecting herbs and, Batty thought, God alone knows what else. He left them dancing on the air once he and his men had had their sport.

The Egyptiani had had their revenge; they came in secret to the tower with all the other traders who slurried around the place, though they made sure to hide what they were. In the night they were gone and so was Clem's nose; they found him gagged and bound in his own bedroom, blood everywhere. That was a brace of years ago.

'Fortune smiles on him,' John Dubh had offered on hearing this. 'The Egyptiani stopped at just his nose.'

They stopped short, Batty was sure, because the Travelling Folk did not want more feud out of it, but the message was clear; his tower was no protection against the Egyptiani and the punishment was slight for the deaths of seven. He would sniff out no more witches.

Batty knew that secretive race well enough, especially the women; he shivered as he looked down on a strange scene, but it was nothing to do with what he saw and everything to do with memories. He heard them singing, soft and sweet, as they had when sent out by the Randy King to make sure the Armstrongs hunting Batty stayed at arm's length, for he had the hospitality of the Travelling Folk at the time.

In his mind he saw a woman on her hunkers, dress carelessly rucked back to her thighs and the dark mystery of her naked fork all exposed.

He had not felt a twitch at it. Not the way she was gralloching a man, to make sure he had not swallowed his wealth before dying. She was singing, soft and dreamy while the snow swirled and it was as if she did nothing more than stir the makings of a blood pudding in a bowl.

> *'There was a maid this other day and she would needs go forth to play; and as she walked she sighed and said, I am afraid to die a maid.'*

As she'd sliced and cut the Armstrongs who had pursued Batty, he'd heard other women, adding their sibilance of sinister chorus, saw them in the shadows working smooth and slow while the blood crept out to darken the slush and the steam of it misted them.

> *'For I will, without faile, maiden, give you Watkins ale; Watkins ale, good sir, quoth she, what is that I pray tell me? Tis sweeter far then suger fine and pleasanter than muscadine.'*

He shook himself like a dog from water and tried to concentrate on what he saw, though it was hard. What he stared down at looked like a Fair Day or a Truce Meet, but skewed, as if seen through wavering glass.

There were trestles under awnings that flapped like loose sails in the cutting wind. Smoke rose from cook fires, men and women chaffered back and forth, offered goods for sale, argued cost and quality while stamping their feet to keep warm. Pack ponies sauntered in and out in neat threaded lines and men stumbled after them, hands lashed and feet fettered enough to let them walk but not run.

Business was being done here and everyone was a trader – and not just of fabric, cabbage and small beer, Batty thought. He glanced at the uppermost room of the tower they called, simply, The Scar and saw the light in the single slit of a window mute to a peep behind closing shutters.

'One-armed and alone, though I have reports of him being with a handful of others.'

'Where is this handful, Mickle Anthone?'

It was said softly, but Mickle Anthone grew wary at once, for he knew Nebless Clem's ways well enough. He watched the long-fingered hand toying with the coiled whip and licked nervous lips.

'Nearby, sheltering – I suspect a few places and have sent men to look. He has come alone to make himself seem less of a threat. He has empty saddle holsters and no seeming weapons ither than a backsword, for the same reason.'

'D'ye know him?'

Mickle Anthone squinted and frowned in the dim of the top room. He knew Batty Coalhouse well enough – most of the Trotters did, for he had scoured out Sore Will and Red John for having fouled Bills a few years since. Red John had been hanged for it. Mickle Anthone did not say this, all the same and muttered only that he knew the man by reputation, all the while looking from under lowered lashes at Nebless Clem's face.

It was singular, that face, like a fierce dog fox, long and sharp snouted – though the snout was leather these days. The image was accentuated by the whiskers which stuck in coarse, thick red from just below his ears, joining the mass of russet hair round his head like a ruff save where it had gone bald. He covered his vanity with a rakish blue wool bunnet, which also hid the laces of the mask, a moulded confection that covered both cheeks and gave him a nose of leather.

'Only what you ken yerself, sir – he is known as Corbie for the way his victims can run and jink and hide only to look up at the last and see him there, like a fat crow on a branch, waiting to peck their e'en oot.'

Clem knew Mickle Anthone wasn't telling all, but it was probably nothing he did not know himself – the best part of it was that this one-armed man called Corbie was favoured of Netherby, which was where Megs came from.

'Well, he didnae come this far to stand and watch,' he said. 'Bring him in.'

Mickle John headed for the stairs and Clem stopped him at the door with a last word. 'The other business – who has pledged?'

'The Trotters of Till promise fifty, full-armed and horsed. The Grays of The Snab similar, Bangtail Heron of Eastbraes can bring a score. The Forsters at Owlrig are undecided.'

Mickle John waited until it was clear nothing more was forthcoming, then left. Clem fingered the ivory-inlaid butt of the whip and thought about the Forsters of Owlrig. Even without them he had enough riders for what was needed – but it was the fact of them prevaricating he did not like; he would have to slap them when all the rest was done.

–

Batty came up through the gazes, some of them hard enough to let him know that they knew him; he felt like a chick wandering into a nest of weasels, but handed his horse to a lad who gave him back an idiot, black-rotted grin.

'See to him,' said another man, stepping from the tower. He was short, squat and dark, his hair straggling into a bad beard which he scratched. What showed of his skin was flaky and pustuled.

'Anthone,' he announced.

'Batty Coalhouse. I have come to see Nebless Clem about a ransom.'

Anthone had started to nod, but his eyebrows shot up at that and he kept nodding until, finally, he led the way to the tower door.

The barmkin was parapeted and men walked it, stamping against the cold. Inside the tower's ground floor were the beasts which Batty had expected – horses all of them, for any cattle were byred elsewhere. There was a haulage sling for lifting heavy goods up to the next floor, the kitchen – Batty could see the glow of the fire and smell the baking bread.

A wind of stair went round and round, past other doors, all closed. At the top, he was ushered in with a brief pause and a whispered urgency.

'Never call him Nebless Clem,' Anthone warned. 'Not never.'

The room was unpartitioned, floored in planks which had had a sheen to it when new; years of nailed boots had scuffed it to ruin and the other marks showed Batty that it had once had tables and trestles and chairs. Feasting, he thought, though it would have been a poor meal for guests since the kitchen was so far away the food would have been cold by the time it reached here.

The walls had some ratty tapestries, almost certainly lifted on a raid of someone else's house and there was some furniture. Most of the room was dominated by a solid plank table littered with papers and a trencher with the remains of a meal. There was a good fire and Batty saw that it was fed with coal; well, wood would be scarce here, he thought – but where the De'il did Nebless Clem get coal?

The man himself sat behind the desk in a plush chair with ornate arms and back, though the gilding was scraped off here and there. Plunder, Batty thought. Nothing in this place has been fairly bought.

'You are Batty Coalhouse,' Clem said finally and he toyed with a coil of black whip, which Batty saw was fine with ivory work in the handle and the curled thong of it studded with black metal barbs.

'I am,' Batty answered and eased his stance, seeing he was not about to be invited to sit.

'What want you here?'

'Will Elliot if you have him. I am give to understand you paid Malatesta in Berwick for the man and I am here to ransom him.'

'Ransom?' Clem said and his eyebrows lifted at that. 'Is he kin?'

'I am here for the Lord of Newark in Fife,' Batty answered. 'Will Elliot is his Steward and he wants him back. He is prepared to pay forty pound in English coin for him, provided he is in good condition. I would needs see him afore we handseil the deal.'

Clem laughed. 'Would ye now?' he said, then yelled out 'Mickle Anthone' and did not have to wait long for the sore-faced man to appear.

'Fetch up the cripple,' Clem ordered and Anthone hastened to obey. Clem sat back in the chair and poured wine from a silver salver into a gilded cup; Batty was not offered any and took note of that. Clem began to speak then fell silent as someone entered the room; Batty felt the presence and turned, expecting Will Elliot.

Instead he found himself staring at a woman, who stared back at him. She was as tall as Batty, dressed in a simple wool skirt falling in conical folds and cut low to show the white chemise beneath. Her hair was long and brown, falling free to her shoulders and her eyes were grey, the colour of a storm at sea, Batty thought. She was shapely and lovely, though there was a razor's edge to her.

'Mistress,' he said and she acknowledged it, then drifted past him to stand next to Clem, who grinned up at her.

'Kerchief your heid,' he said shortly. 'You're indecent for a married woman.'

'My husband is dead,' she answered and Clem frowned. He took the butt end of the whip and laid it on her skirted leg, then dipped it until he found the hem of the dress and insinuated it upwards; she did not flinch.

Anthone came back, with a hirpling figure at his side. Batty and Will stared at one another while Will's mouth dropped open. He was unbound and unfettered – he would hardly be able to run in his state, Batty thought.

'Batty,' Will said hoarsely. 'Is that you there?'

'It was when I rose,' Batty answered, 'and hope it will still be so when the sun falls.'

'I had not thought to see you ever again,' Will answered and Batty thought he heard a tinge of bitter in that. Not a surprise, considering – everything Will had once been had been stripped away by the events around Hollows. Seven years since, Batty remembered suddenly.

'I am glad to hear you found some decent work at Newark,' Batty replied, awkward now. Will nodded and shifted his weight; Batty moved to the spare chair he had not been invited to sit in and scraped it over the floor to let Will sink gratefully into it.

'Aye – wee James Sandilands was good to me,' Will said. 'D' ye ever think on it, Batty, that sixty miles either side of the Divide is peace? I was brought up in the Border lands and all my life believed that was the way of the world

62

everywhere – murder, rapine, plunder, neighbour against neighbour. Yet ower in Fife there is none of that.'

'Allowing for a lack of English,' Batty reminded him. 'For here you are, taken in plunder, with Newark burned. But Sandilands has sent me with forty pounds English to bring ye home.'

'He is already promised.'

The voice brought Batty's head round to where Clem sat. The skirt was rucked up pretty far, far enough for Batty to see the hand and coil of the whip and judge where the handle was; he saw her wince slightly, then adjust her stance. Clem took his hand out from under and looked at the glistening butt; he grinned across it to Batty.

'Promised?' Batty echoed blankly. Clem nodded.

'So – since the sky threatens a deal of weather on the moors, you had best be on your way afore it occurs.'

'Promised to whom?' Batty demanded; he liked Clem a lot less than when he'd first laid eyes on him and had not been overly impressed then. Clem frowned.

'None of your concern.'

Batty saw it had all been set up to show Nebless Clem's power, from his welcome to the act with the whip butt. He looked at Will, who shrugged.

'I am no wiser than you.'

Batty turned back to Clem. He saw it was useless to promise more money and he thought, briefly, of dragging out his backsword and running it through the moulded facemask. Then he took a deep, dragging breath, nodded amiably to Clem as he sat, toying with the whip, the butt still glistening. And let his mouth run him down a blocked wynd.

'I would wager you wish you could smell that,' he said.

63

Chapter Four

Later still – somewhere else…

The building was burning and the roof had collapsed for the third time. He lay under the flaming beams of it, feeling the sear all over his back and struggling like a beetle to move, to wriggle free – to turn over, at least, away from the agony.

His breath laboured in short gasps and every one of them cauterised his throat. He saw the dark shadow, heard the familiar voice.

'Kohlhaas – you need to get out from under here. They are throwing shot at the Vecchio – David is in danger.'

David was in danger. Batty had seen Simoni's masterwork when he had first come to Florence, had marvelled at the breath-taking size of it, the menace of it, the smooth polished nakedness seeming to take a breath before striding out to confront Goliath. As long as it stood, Florence's enemies would fail at the walls, it was believed.

Michaelangelo reached down a hand and Batty felt himself being plucked and dragged, which only added to the pain.

'Hold him steady,' Michaelangelo said, but Batty could not see how he or anyone could hold the massive statue steady. Then he realised Michaelangelo was staring off into the flames and wondered if rescue was at hand – or at least someone shifting the burning balks off him. The ceiling fell in yet again, a great blast *of flame which washed over him and then was gone in a flurry of sparks.*

It wasn't Florence, Batty realised suddenly. Not the siege, with Michaelangelo fretting over his masterwork. It was later, at Kőszeg when that tiny fortress was being battered to ruin by Ibrahim Pasha and all the Turks of Suleiman I. It wasn't a church he lay burning in, but a counter-mine and it wasn't Michaelangelo come to save him but Baron Nikolas, his upturned sweep of moustaches smouldering as he gripped Batty's shoulders.

'It will do no good,' the Baron said in his thick Croatian English, 'if you harm, him worse — Netherby won't care for it and they are already watching and waiting for you to fetch a priest and marry me.'

That wasn't right, Batty thought. She said that while I was on the wet ground, with Nebless Clem standing over me and a crowd baying like slewdugs on a scent. Should have resisted throwing a flyte at him, he thought — but the snow blew his face stiff while his back flamed.

'Keep him on the horse, Big Tam,' said Ewan Fraser. 'We have a wheen of miles to go before we find shelter. If we do at all.'

'He's burning up,' Big Tam said. 'He will die…'

'Death is here,' Giovanni Loppe said and he should know, Batty thought. I watched him die in the breach at Kőszeg, one of the many heaps of rubble which had been solid wall a few days before. The trick to keeping the Turks from coming through the holes, Batty had told his men, is to creep out in the dark and lay pots of poisonous powder, the fuses all chained to one ignition. Poisonous powder was gunpowder and a mix of tiny iron pellets and broken pottery coated with piss, shit, salis armoniaci and the juice of scallions. When it went off, no-one escaped and where it did not kill it burned.

The true trick was, his men countered, to creep out there and lay them without getting shot down by arrows and hackbutts from the Turkish sentries. Loppe got careless and got a fusillade of both so that he fell on his pot with a lit slow match – the light was shrieking, the explosion loud. Mayhap Loppe saw it as the last trump and the Gates opening for him, Batty thought. Mayhap that's what happened to me; a pot exploded too early and got me in the back. Now I am lying in the rubble of the breach while the Turks come to wipe away this little pimple of a fort and continue on to Vienna, the Golden Apple…

–

He was called Thomas, a tall lean man like some ancient pole-sitter fallen off his perch. He had a neat-trimmed beard and hair cropped to his ears, all the same, so he was no nit-swarmed mountebank, which is what Ewan and the others always thought when they heard the word 'physician'.

Actual physicians were rare as teats on a bull – usually the ones calling themselves by the title of 'Doctor' were tooth-pullers or the sort who sold bone relics such as another big toe of St Anthony or the skull of Jesus when he was a babe.

This one had a wool overrobe with short sleeves which let him roll up the long sleeves of his undershirt so that he could delicately slather Batty's back with some ointment.

Ewan was, though he would not admit it, ruffled as a wet cat over the place they were in, which was all hefty cold stones and poor light – save for the one next to Thomas the Physician. The folk in it were no better, slippering around like monks though they were not and Ewan had set the others to finding out how many while they took care of the hobbies and their gear.

'A big stone,' John Dubh had whispered to him only a moment before. 'Give or take a peck.'

It was their way of tallying cattle – *aon, dhà, trì* right up to *fichead*, which was a score, at which point you put down a big stone. This one was a rock Ewan did not trust much – the dark and the sprawl of the place, ancient and crumbling though it was, could hide more.

On the bed, a half-naked Batty moaned and tried to move; Thomas patiently prevented him, then turned to Ewan.

'Could you help hold him fast? Best he does not roll over onto that back.'

Ewan obeyed before he even realised he had done so, but it was the mark of this Thomas that you did what he said.

He and the others, towing Batty on his own horse and trying to keep him from falling off it, had come up to this place in a flurry of driven snow, half-blinded and heading for Edinburgh. None of them, in truth, had thought to make it, but felt they had to try – discovering this blocky huddle of low, solid buildings had been a gift from God. Once, Ewan was sure, they had belonged to God; the place had old stones fallen from ruined walls that spoke of monastery in hushed tones.

Thomas finished his task and wiped his hands on a cloth. Batty, though still gone from his head, seemed easier in his breathing and made less sounds than before.

'Beaten,' Thomas said matter-of-factly. 'With something that had nails or studs.'

'Whipped,' Ewan corrected. He had watched it from the top of the ridge, lying on the snow-patched grass, peering through the frozen fronds of a tussock while they dragged Batty from the tower.

They had stripped him of jack and shirt, lashed him to the wheel of a cart, having to make a loop round the stump of his missing arm. Then the one in the facemask had stepped up and uncoiled the black whip, shouting words which made the watchers howl appreciation for this was good entertainment on a bleak day and in a place where hangings were no longer novelty.

The masked man stepped back a few paces, judged the distance and made the whip crack so that the gathering crowd went 'ooh' and 'aaah'. Then he swung it round his head and bent his body to give it full force before bringing it down; the smack made the watchers grunt and a couple of women shrieked.

Once, twice — six times. Then a woman stepped up to him, lithe and fine Ewan saw and not afraid of a man in the heat of bloodlust. She said something and the man stopped; he coiled the whip, breathing heavily. Then he shouted orders that brought men forward, one of them leading Batty's horse.

They started loading him on to it and the masked man spoke in short, panting rushes to about twenty surrounding men, all helmeted and armed. Ewan had an idea what they were going to do — ride Batty out and bring him round enough to tell where the rest of his party was. Where the coin was. He slithered backwards, then scurried in a half-crouch.

'Who did this?' Thomas demanded and Ewan blinked back to the Now, to the pool of strong light that only made the shadows of this place darker still; a snow wind got a finger in and made the light dance madly and the flames of the fire throw up embers.

'The Laird of Blackscargil,' Ewan said dully and Thomas frowned.

'We know of him here and he is no lord, just a dark heart with a stolen tower and someone else's gudewife, or so I hear. What did your friend do to warrant this?'

'Nothing but try to ransom an old friend,' Ewan replied. 'I think yon dark heart fancied to take the ransom and keep the friend. Nebless Clem, I am thinking he was, since he wore a mask affair with a leather nose.'

'Aye – it would have been enough for him to hand a whipping out if your friend had called him that. It was also wise that you all ran,' Thomas said, making Ewan glance up, hackling, but he saw it was no kind of insult, just a statement of fact. 'How did you spirit your friend away from them?'

'We fought,' Ewan answered, which was no lie, but not all of the truth. They'd known the men would track back to the cruck house, had seen them earlier when the light was better and the snow a lot less. So when they came up, all lances and squinting and cursing Batty for always wanting to fall off the horse, they got a Lovat greeting.

Two went down from latchbows, solid smacks of bolt that blew them off their horses and even if they were not stuck through, they were winded and gasping. Then we tore into them, Ewan remembered. He knew he screamed out '*A mhor-fhaiche*' and launched himself off a crumbling dyke like the wrath of God. A wee skip and a hop into the air, sword gripped in both fists and underhand.

The horseman, with his fine lance and his decent back and breast, his neat helmet and, Ewan saw at the last, his fine-combed beard simply stared. His mouth was open and his eyes held a look that let Ewan know he had seen that it was death coming down on him and was resigned to it.

The big blade skewered him like mutton on a dish, then Ewan slammed into him, making the horse stagger. Ewan landed heavily but upright, but the horse with the man on it gugging for breath from a torn throat, took a few steps sideways, tangled its feet and fell over, screaming.

The nearest after that was the luckless man who'd had the thankless task of keeping Batty in the saddle, but he gave that up to fight his own mount's shrieking fear. Ewan struck, felt the tug and heard the man yell out, then fall; his strike had been neat and deadly and the man had most of an arm missing, which Ewan found eldritch, almost Faerie, for someone who had been holding a one-armed man upright on his horse only moments before.

John Dubh went past him, wild breath smoking from his mouth as he roared. He had no targe but a decent broadsword that he hacked madly with as he went rolling into the rest of the prancing, yelling pack, screaming spittle and Gaelic.

'Well, you seemed to have come out with your man and no more than a scratch or two,' Thomas said, as if he had heard all Ewan was thinking. 'All's well that's well done.'

Ewan said nothing, but stared at the light and the fire. There had been a score of men at least, well armed and one of them had a matchlock pistol which he shot wildly as he careened away. They saw Malcolm go down holding his belly and yelling. Big Tam saw it, but no-one could stop to find out more, for they knew the men would recover and come back at them.

So they had left him and run. Same as we always do, Ewan thought miserably to himself, since the Battle of the Bogs. It had been a long, harsh misery of a ride to here and no-one knew where here was. He looked at the tall, lean shadow of the physician and asked.

'Soutra Aisle,' Thomas replied easily. 'Once a monastery and a hospital but now Reformed out of monks and left only as a refuge and infirmary for weary or sick travellers on the old road to Edinburgh. We are part of the College of Trinity in Edinburgh now.'

He glanced down at Batty and then nodded to Ewan. 'There is food – not much, but hot and filling. Likewise a room with a fire to keep out the chill. Tomorrow I will treat your friend's back again.'

'Will he be fit to ride?'

'Not for days.'

Ewan fell silent; he was sure they'd be followed and if he had stumbled on this place, it was likely pursuers would as well.

–

They sat in the ruins listening to the crash of guns, feeling the shudders on the wall, hearing the noise of overshots like a gale in the trees.

'We will all die here,' Bocanegra said bitterly, his face a sheen of dirt-smeared sweat in the guttering light. Batty had no answer, but his back burned – so he had been caught by one of his own petards after all. So much for 'no match with a slow match'…

'This is because of Maramaldo,' Spinola added savagely. 'We shouldn't even have been here save that you thought he was here and followed him like a dog sniffing a blood sausage.'

They all agreed with angry mutters – Doxaras, Alvaro, even his second, Theodore Luchisi. All of the Company of Gold; Batty could hear the poor gilt of it strip away. Even if we get out of this, he thought, we are finished…

'Time to wake,' said a voice from the dark and Batty tried to turn his head, but it seemed to be fastened to the floor; he had not even realised he was lying on the floor.

'They are leaving,' shouted the Baron, his beard bristled and matte but his splendid moustaches still curled. 'They are leaving.'

They were. Batty could see them even though he did not know how he got to the last standing ramparts of Kőszeg, an unimportant little fortress a day's march from Vienna. Under a thick layer of dust, men, shields, flags, drums, horses and wagons, groaning laden camels and men all tramped away, back down the road they had come up. For more than twenty-five days, without any artillery, Captain Nikola Jurišić and a garrison of 700 local Hungarian peasants and a few mercenaries held out against nineteen full-scale assaults and an incessant bombardment by the full Army of the Ottomans.

Then the Pasha heard of an army forming up at Vienna to march on him and decided not to face it.

Batty heard the cheers of those who had considered themselves dead the day before. He watched the Turks trundle away, the sound of the whips loud as they urged their beasts south. Not ones with black-metal barbs – those were too cruel for valuable beasts. Only slaves felt the lick of them.

–

'Whips,' he said and a bright light scoured his eyes until a shape blocked it.

A voice said: 'There you are. Welcome back.'

It was a long, sheep-like face under a soft cap and it told Batty to hold himself awake, then scurried off. When the man returned he had another with him, a confident, neat-bearded man who said he was called Thomas and stilled Batty's attempt to get up.

'Don't,' he said. 'The best you will do is roll over on to your back and that will be painful beyond words. Here – I am about to lotion you.'

He smeared his hands with some paste and saw Batty's wary, glaucous stare.

'A mixture of eggs, oil of roses and resin from the terebinth tree,' he said. 'Soothes and heals.'

Batty had no complaints; his back was fired but not blazing and he found his mouth worked after a fashion. He asked the questions he needed answers to. When he was done, his throat hurt.

The sheep-faced man gave him small beer in sips and Thomas wiped his hands clean, nodding with satisfaction.

'You would have roared a deal,' he explained to Batty, 'given what was done to you. Six strokes, I jalouse. If it had been more, you would be deid of it.'

She stopped him, Batty said, remembering the voice, soft and low and hissed at Nebless Clem. The biggest wonder in it was how Clem had heeded her and coiled his whip – Turk, Batty thought dully. I recognise the work for I picked up two or three in the litter left by them when they had gone. And *janissary* hats, made to look like huge sleeves and with a spoon-holder sewn in; Batty had such a spoon to this day and was no wiser about why they had one in their headgear, nor why they venerated cooking pots or why none of them was even Turkish.

Ewan and the others came when they heard he was awake and broken from fever, huddling around and twisting caps in their hands while Ewan told what he knew.

'I am sorry for your dead,' Batty managed when all was said and Ewan shifted in frustration and bitterness. *Magairlean* he said aloud before he had even realised.

'Aye, you have it right – bollocks it is. Hands will wag above Lovat graves right enough,' Big Tam added mournfully and Batty knew he spoke of the restless, discontented dead.

Batty's croak brought them back to the moment and some sense; who else was in Soutra Aisle other than the ones who were supposed to be. Was there any sign of pursuit? Was there any word on Will Elliot?

His throat was raw when he had finished, but Ewan had answers – only a packman and a carter carrying coals to The Scar were in residence, both caught in the bad weather.

'The carter's stot is lamed,' John Dubh added with a grin, 'so he will not be going anywhere for a whiley.'

Batty did not ask how the beast came to be lame, but his eyes fixed on Ewan, who shifted from foot to foot.

'I heard,' he said slowly, 'one of those moudiewarts before we sprang on them, saying as how they needed this business done with for they'd be off to Carlisle with the cripple the day after next.'

Carlisle? Batty could not fathom it. Why would Carlisle pay ransom for Will Elliot – and more than Batty himself had offered? Was he wanted on some fouled Bill?

Ewan finally stopped shifting and plucked a bag from behind his back which he placed on the bed. The ransom, intact and safe.

Batty eyed them one by one, then nodded.

'Soon as yer honour is able,' John Dubh said, 'we should quit this place. I am sick of eating dock pudding.'

'Tomorrow,' Batty said, which made them laugh.

Chapter Five

Last day of Advent 1548 – near Carlisle

They ate dock pudding before they left – with no bacon in because it was Advent. Still, the mix of Passion docks and nettles, oats, onions and egg let them ride far on that first day, westwards on a rolling waste leprous with patched snow.

When the light went under clouds and the horses started stumbling, Batty called a halt at the Beef Tub near Hawick; he did not want to frequent a place where other travellers came and went, but everyone needed rest. Nane mair than me, Batty thought, feeling the fiery tug of the stripes on his back and the way the world shifted and rolled like a sea.

He had not been fit for this ride, but lied about it, more fretted at staying longer in Soutra Aisle; riders would come looking for them and he wanted away before that. He groaned with everyone else at the Advent lack of meat in such a named place, but the Beef Tub offered a gruel of winter vegetables which they ate at a board set back in the dim, Batty watching the other faces and praying he recognised none.

That night he slept in the stall with Fiskie, the pair taking comfort from each other and the warmth of the other beasts welcome even if their staling fouled his breathing.

It reminded him of Powrieburn in the days after he had been shot off Fiskie and dropped a hundred feet down a gully. Mintie and Will Elliot had come out, found him and dragged him back; what happened after that did no-one any good.

The next day took them to an even worse place and Batty cursed himself for it; he had not planned on it, but there was snow tumbling from a leaden sky in flurries, with a wind that picked it up and drove it in whirling circles like starlings at dusk.

It forced them into Mosspaul Tavern, the horn-panel lanterns a lure that stumbled them into the courtyard, where ostler boys dragged their mounts to shelter.

'I will see the beasts are decently treated,' John Dubh said, shaking snow off his cap. 'You need the warmth and some decent food, Batty, afore you fall in the dung here. By God's Grace it will not be dock pudding or bliddy gruel as fare.'

'Take note of how many other beasts are stalled,' Batty said, urgent and low and John Dubh nodded. 'Look for reiver hobbies.'

It wasn't dock pudding. It was goose, considered a fish for fast days and Advent, the roasting smell of it a firm beam for the ale and farts and sweat of the place to rest on. There was a whistler and a hurdy-gurdy player laying out firm, foot-stamp tunes – no soft love songs here, Batty saw. He also recognised the tune as a *branle*, a French dance and the hurdy-gurdy had the buzzing bridge of a French-made instrument.

He mentioned it, casual as asking for goose for four and the woman wiped her hands and smiled. She had started the day neat in wool skirt and partlet and even a kerchief for her hair. The latter was long gone, leaving the tresses to draggle free, while the partlet was mostly unfastened and heaved a considerable bosom out of a stained underserk. She smelled of sweat and the musk of recent sex.

'The Frenchies are everywhere noo,' she answered. 'Annan has fell to them and they are up and doon the road to Graitna, looking for advantage and hoping to get intae Carlisle, which is still held by the English. These players are not Frenchies though, if you are looking for same.'

She squinted at Batty a little, slantwise and considering. 'If you are Scotch I wouldnae try to get in Carlisle these days – they have closed the gates.'

A man yelled at her – the innkeeper, Batty imagined and kept his bonnet pulled low, for he was sure the man would know him. For the same reason he had his cloak draped round his left side, to hide what was missing.

The woman scowled back at the innkeeper. 'Nae work until Plough Monday,' she said bitterly, quoting the law on Advent.

'Save for the tending of beasts,' Ewan threw back, 'so I suppose that applies here.' He grinned and that made her smile back at him; she still had decent teeth to make it winsome, Batty saw.

They ate well and drank decent ale, with their backs to the farthest wall and stitting at a board set in the shadows because the place itched Batty. The other three saw it and looked from one to the other, then pointedly at Ewan. So eventually he asked.

'This place is where folk from the Debateable come,' Batty answered in a low, terse voice, having to go close to their heads to be heard above the music, 'which is the most lawless place in a lawless land. The ones that are reivers are mostly known to me – or me to them, since I probably dragged a deal of their kin back to face the Bill they'd fouled. A few of them were hemped as a result.'

'By God, Batty,' Big Tam marvelled in a mocking rumble. 'If a man is known by enemies, you are a byword for certain. *Èisd ri gaoth nam beann gus an traogh na h-uisgeachan.*'

Batty didn't understand that much and said so in the same breath that he hissed at Big Tam to be done with the Gaelic so close to the English. John Dubh leaned in, smelling of small beer and goose. 'Listen to the wind upon the hill till the waters abate,' he translated.

It was good advice, but keeping a low profile was no longer an option, Batty thought. He kept his lip fastened tight on the main reason for his itch – that Moss Paul was close to the Armstrongs at Hollows, who actively hated him. They had cause, of course – he had blasted their powder mill and ruined their tower, killed more than a few of the Name including the Laird's wife and humiliated the Laird himself.

It was where Will Elliot had been held, hung up in a cage on the crow gables like a bauble for the Christ's Mass – Batty suddenly realised it was around this time of year it had happened. He wondered at it. Years since and now it was risen like some dark beast that would not be killed or ignored.

In the end, the warm and the food and the ale eased the clench in him and he laughed once or twice when the Frasers made a weak jest, careful to keep away from the Gaelic.

Ewan had wriggled out of his long mail coat in the stable and was fretting that it would still be there when he got back to it. Batty was sympathetic; he had saved his weapons, but his jack of plates was gone, stripped off him before he was whipped and now lost. Apart from the protection and the front-fastening that let him get it on and off one-handed, it had held his knitting and needles inside. He had one sock and now would never have the other – I should have concentrated on mittens, where one would be a use, he thought.

Big Tam asked about his back and Batty lied, saying the bedesman at Soutra had done clever work and it did not hurt at all, while all the time trying not to lean against the wall and drive fire into him.

It was all pleasant; there was an upstairs with two or three rooms but they were not for sleeping and the rent was included in the cost of the whore. Ewan eventually gave in to the lure of it and went upstairs with the woman who smiled. She handed out bread and ale and cheese to the hurdy-gurdy man before leading Ewan away.

The hurdy-gurdy and the whistle broke into 'Ding-dong merrily on high' in honour of the season and everyone joined in, stamping and smacking tables. They rocked the roof and fluttered the lights – and hid the sound of horses arriving in the courtyard, then men coming through the door in a blast of cold air and snow.

The music dribbled to a halt as people stared at these newcomers, weighing them up; Batty saw the innkeeper's hands drop below the slice of fronted oak that formed a serving top for drinks and food. Ca' canny, Batty thought. Make a move with a cudgel and they will show you why they favour those flanged maces dangling at their belts.

There were six of them, dressed in loud colours, puffed sleeves showing from under mail coats cut for riding, hats of all kinds, never without a plume. They bristled with weapons and beards.

Dressed like the Turks they fought for preference, Batty thought. *Stradioti*, mercenary prickers from the Balkans, almost good enough to take on the Scots reiver horse – but these weren't taking on anyone. They reeked of marinaded grease and woodsmoke and blood, but their faces were patched as old mutton with cold and hard travel.

There were mercenaries of all sorts – called 'furriners' by the locals – because Fat Henry relied on them since his main army of English faced the French in the south; one fourth of the Royal army was mercenary these days, Swiss, Landsknechts, Balkan throat-slitters and crowds of light horse to try and take on the reivers swamped the Border – but the ones who had arrived were not any of them.

Still, they tried for swagger and failed by such a long way that the hurdy-gurdy man struck up again, the whistler joined in and people went back to bawling out the words and thumping the tables.

'Barthie.'

His heart flipped and his stomach joined in, like a pair of mountebank tumblers. He saw the man who had called out and knew him at once, cursed him wordlessly. If he'd had any second sight to see with, Manolis Voicha would have shrieked in horror at the way he was casually consigned to the Ninth circle of Hell.

Instead he stepped forward, grinning out of a mass of grizzled beard. 'Barthie Kohlhase – it is you there?'

You can only play the cards you are dealt, in life as in Primero…

'It was this morning, so I am supposing it is still. What brings you here Manolis Voicha?'

Beaming at having been remembered, Voicha fell into Ewan's empy seat with a clatter of ironmongery, then eyed up Big Tam and John Dubh, nodding warily to each of them. Batty introduced them; it was all smiles.

'A long time, eh?' Voicha began; behind him his comrades were negotiating for drink and what food was left. 'Piedmont, was it not? When our Company fell to pieces.'

'When you all left you mean,' Batty replied sourly, but Voicha merely broadened the smile in his big square face. When he hauled off his cap, grizzled curls sprang up.

'Well, you were done by then, Barthie. Drunk most of the time and even when you were not you were taking contracts that chased Captain-General Maramaldo at the expense of profit.'

He cocked his head sideways. 'I hear he is in this land. Did you meet him? If so – is he dead? I imagine one of you would be.'

'Where are you headed?' Batty countered and Voicha shrugged.

'South. Carlisle, where the Company of Theodore Luchisi is assembling. Fewer than we were but still to the fore. I hear we are bound for further south still, to fight rebels on behalf of the new young king.'

Batty had thought Luchisi was dead in Piedmont. It had been a vicious struggle between France and Spain, barely noticed by Batty save through a haze of wine and worse. In the end, he had woken in an empty and looted camp and lurched off, cursing Luchisi, whom he believed had taken over his Company. It took him a few months to realise the truth, but he'd heard Luchisi had died of fever or ague or plague and considered it only the due of such a treacherous bastard.

Voicha did not hang round long; Ewan came back and stood over his seat, reclaiming the great two-handed sword from Big Tam and leaning on it. Voicha eventually pretended that excusing himself and joining his own was his idea; Batty wished he would leave off calling him 'Barthie Kohlhase' in every effusive farewell sentence, but he suffered it.

He had no relief, all the same. There were faces trying hard not to look at him and one in particular that he recognised – a weather-worn mask of sleekit, white lines fretting the sides of the eyes and showing what colour it had once been before wind and woodsmoke got to it. His hair straggled untidily to the shoulders and was gone from the top of his head entire. He had a bowl out of which he spooned gruel and his grizzled moustaches dripped; he did not use the other hand to wipe them clean all the same – that one never moved from protecting the fat pack next to him.

Needle Tam the peddlar. He had silk thread, good needles, ribbons, buttons, geegaws and other joys for women in that pack – but the true secret was what he carried from the English Wardens to the Scots Names and back again.

And he knows me, Batty thought. He was there when Blind Dog Pyntle emptied out the bag of left arms I had cut from Armstrongs and sent to Hollows as a dire message. The owners had been left tied to trees by the one arm, but two had died and the rest walked around as a shrieking reminder of Batty Coalhouse's vicious.

Later in the night, the doors were barred, the innkeeper and ostlers and women dragged themselves off to sleep and the rest nudged each other for space closest to the fire without actually falling in it. Batty tried to look and not be seen looking, particularly for Armstrongs. There was a fearsome tally of Armstrongs laid out by me in the pursuit of the rights of wee Mintie Henderson of Powrieburn, he thought.

It seemed a different age, but it rose up and swirled like smoke from the fire. It did not surprise Batty, raising his head in the night to look around like a questing owl, to find Needle Tam was missing.

–

She watched from the tower merlons, right up on the crow-stepped gables and slated roof. Watched them load a body into the latticed cage, to be hauled up and left to rot down to bone as a message; she did not see who it had been and was glad of that, at least. She was not entirely sure the occupant had been completely dead when he was hauled up and abandoned.

Mickle Anthone laughed at something Clem said and then looked up at her, as if he'd known she'd been there all along; which might be true, she thought and shivered. All her husband's old retainers had been quietly scoured out of Blackscargil and she had no-one now she could rely on. Yet there had been a time when she hoped – prayed – for better.

She waited for Clem to come up to the room below, then went down to meet him. She said his name and waited, but he was staring out of the unshuttered slit; it was cold and snowing and somewhere came the sounds of music, loud voices, laughter and the smell of cooking.

There would be a Christ Mass feast in the big hall inside the barmkin, which had once been a byre until Clem had it cleared and cleaned. Now it was a place where his retainers slept – save for tonight, when it would be the feasting hall of some great chief.

'Must you hang that up?' she asked and he turned, saying nothing. 'It's a boy and still living.'

He said nothing.

'I don't understand you,' she said.

'He was an enemy. Now he is not.'

'What of the old man with one arm whom you scourged? Is he an enemy? The crippled one?'

'I let you talk to me the way you want,' he answered, 'up to a point. And not in front of the others. Best if you stay in the top of the tower here when I am gone.'

'If you say I stay, I stay,' she answered and her tone was mild – but her eyes held his and hung on to them. 'Are you sure I will? No-one can be that sure, not even you.'

He took off the mask, easy as a pull on one of the trailing ties. The ruined face confronted her and she knew he was using it like a club. She let him be disappointed in how it had failed and wanted so much to tell him why that she had to clamp her lips tight until she could speak without betrayal.

'Where are you going?' she asked eventually and he frowned.

'No business of yours.'

'Will there be anything there like a minister or a priest you can gather up?'

'There might be, but if not, what of it?'

'Then I will leave,' she said. 'Return to Netherby as a widow.'

He took her arm, high up on the muscle and, despite herself, she gasped at the pain of his squeeze.

'Tomorrow I take the cripple to where he must go. When I return I will find you here and I will find the

84

men in the cages still hanging. I will bring a man of God. Or I will not.'

His mutilated face was close to hers now, so that she could see the slight bubble in the still raw-looking cavity form and burst with the passion of his breathing, even though most of it was through his mouth.

'Is that understood?'

She nodded. He started to fit on the mask and she went close to him, almost lip to lip, feeling the heat of him as she knew he felt hers. She tied the mask at the back of his red head, staring unblinkingly into his eyes and the mask.

I did that, she thought. Me. Eliza Graham of Netherby, not shrinking in a corner now. Not pressed into a wall. Not spatchcocked on a table.

Chapter Six

Christ Mass Day 1548 – Carlisle

Batty told them of Needle Tam and what his missing would mean. 'They will come at us,' he said flatly. 'Needle Tam will spread the word of me as far as he can – it is a mercy to us that he is too mean to own a pack-pony never mind a decent hobby so his is the distance he travels on his auld legs and with a muckle pack on his back. But he will know where to go to find Armstrongs.'

'Is this not close to your own kin?' Big Tam asked, racking up the girth as he kneed the recalcitrant hobby in the belly, to stop it puffing out and loosening the strap. It tried to bite him and he cuffed its nose, off-hand and gentle. 'The Grahams, isn't it?'

Batty nodded thoughtfully. 'Aye, they might hear of it too. They might not. And even if they do they might do nothing – kin is too strong a word for me and them.'

They rode through a bird-silent land where trees, stripped bare, seemed to crouch and shiver in the slicing wind; the road was patched with snow and empty of travellers; it was the day of Christ's birth and distant bells marked it; anyone of sense stayed cloistered and filled themselves with what decent meat and drink they had.

They came down through Graitna, a place of closed doors and huddled buildings, shuttered blindly. The only sign of life in it was the border post, where armed men stamped and blew and looked warily at armed riders. Well they might, Batty thought, being a mere custom post for taking tithes from drovers. Yet they are now the only sojers between the Scots and Carlisle.

Grey of Wilton's writ got them through without fuss and they skirted the Solway sands, where the wind blew skeins of snow and grit up like smoke. Here was where Auld Nan's cottage was, Batty remembered. Somewhere ower that headland; he shivered at the memory of it, at taking Mintie to it and all the ruin that had fallen out of it since. No good deed goes unpunished…

Ewan grew uneasy over the mood and the bleakness. 'Give us a song,' he demanded of John Dubh, who cleared his throat, spat and then launched out loudly enough to have Fiskie throw up his head with alarm.

> 'Last night I dreamed a drearie dream,
> Abune the Isle of Skye,
> I saw a dead man win a fight,
> And I think that man was I.'

'By God, John Dubh, I was thinking of something with a jig to it,' Ewan growled. 'To lift the moment as it were.'

> 'O I forbid you, maidens a'
> That wear gowd on your hair,
> To come or go by Carterhaugh.
> For young Tam Lin is there.'

The sick crow of it made everyone grimace. 'That's more of the style I seek,' Ewan said dryly, 'but a decent and true tune would be good.'

'Then sing it yerself,' Batty answered tersely and hunched himself into his cloak. They rode on in silence, down the long hissing-wind road and across the Eden to the Ricardgate of Carlisle as the day dulled down to grey and the trees seemed to swallow their own shadows. They saw no-one of note, but Batty itched.

The gate was shut and the guards gone; from the top of the gate-tower a blur of heads told them to 'bugger off'. Batty could hardly blame the gate-guards; it was the feast of Christ Mass and the law said the town gates would be closed at dusk. It was barely three-quarters through the day but already so dark that the rampart walkers were sparking up braziers and torches. That would be good enough for folk wanting off to enjoy good food and decent drink to call curfew and close up.

The Scotch Gate Tavern was nearby and surprisingly empty, but Patey Graham the innkeeper knew Batty well enough and explained it while the ostler boys hurried off with the horses.

'Folk knew the gates would close early, so they forsook drink and good food here for what lies inside. Besides – it's a quarter-day and they needs hand ower their rents afore it ends and while the collectors are this side of sober.'

He was a man built like a slab-side of beef hanging on a hook, not one who needed a dunter to help with the rowdy, but he was morose with lost traffic on a day when he'd gone to a lot of trouble to provide hospitality.

Batty thought he'd be brighter now that four customers had arrived to help eat at least one of the pies he'd had made, but Patey put him right on it.

'Aye, I have good food and decent drink,' he answered softly, 'but the word is out on you – I had Willie Armstrong in here with a brace of no good out of Mangerton and I am sure they will be back. Besides – those with you are bare-legged skirt-wearers far too Scotch for them around here.'

'I have had better welcomes,' Batty answered tersely, but the others shrugged it off and concentrated on the Christ Mass pie with pigeon and goose and pork in it. There were some smaller – and cheaper – humble pies, filled with the off-cuts of deer slain for the rich folks, but Ewan and the others opted for a big one. There was ale and even wine, so a forced night outside Carlisle's walls looked like being a decent affair, even if they were the only custom in the place.

There were two women serving and half-hoping at least one of the younger men would purchase their wares for the money in it – and the other half hoping they could go at least one day without having to. Batty nodded to them and sat with his back to the wall facing the door; the women ignored an old, big-bellied man with one arm.

He sat that way for a while, eating slowly and drinking. After an hour or so of this, three men entered the tavern, paused briefly at the door, two of them looking his way, as if in confirmation of what they had been told. Then all three headed toward the nearest board and pulled benches up, calling for ale.

John Dubh, his mouth hidden by a wedge of pie, looked sideways at Batty and mumbled: 'What think you of them?'

Not much, was what Batty thought – especially when they all stood up at once and strolled towards his table.

Patey Graham saw it and called out, his voice was loud in the quiet room. 'Nae trouble, for the honour of the day.'

The men ignored it. The one who was clearly the leader stood in front of Batty with the others left and right. He was in middle years, his face bog-brown where it could be seen through the veil of hair and beard; he had a jack of plates which made Batty conscious of the loss of his own and he had a matchlock pistol shoved in the belt of his breeks, the slow match smouldering.

'I am Sim Armstrong of Whithaugh,' he said and nodded left and right. 'These are my kin, Dand and Davey's John.' He said it to Batty, who felt his bowels do a slow, cold turn. Whithaugh. He had done a deal of damage to that place and Sim Armstrong had eyes that showed how he was not afraid of killing, though Batty doubted he had done a lot of it. He doubted any of them were here because they'd been sent; they came because Needle Tam had told them and they looked to bring Batty's head back to Whithaugh in triumph.

Dand was an older man, short and with a belly that poked out from under the jack. He had a grey beard and grey eyes that told Batty he was unhappy with all this, no matter how tough he was acting in front of the others.

Davey's John was a younger man, sweating and shifting from foot to foot like an over-excited hound. Batty knew this was a youngling who had done nothing much and craved the attention and notoriety of killing the likes of Batty. He was too young and too stupid to see how his life would end.

'You are Batty Coalhouse,' Sim said. 'We have a reck-oning with you.'

Sim knew this wouldn't intimidate the likes of Batty Coalhouse, a man whom he had never met but whose reputation had been with him forever, but was taking a chance anyway. There are four of them and only three of us, Sim thought, which fact Needle Tam had failed to mention when he told them where Batty Coalhouse was. Here was the slouching beast and it could only be better for Sim if the man's friends ran off.

'Our quarrel is not with you,' he added hopefully to them and one of the men – a real big bugger he noticed uneasily – gave a short mirthless laugh.

Batty sat motionless and stared back, then looked around the room to see Patey Graham, cudgel now in hand. The women were wisely elsewhere.

'Ware that slow match,' he said, nodding at Sim. 'It is too close to your serk and your ma will get shrill if she has to mend the hole.'

Davey's John broke in, his voice high and tight with excitement. He moved closer to Batty almost touching him across the scarred board table. 'Mayhap you could just get the fuck up on your hind legs, come outside and face your justice.'

Batty looked up at him and Davey's John tried hard not to look away but could not lock the gaze; finally, he looked down at the table, clearly embarrassed and took a step back. Batty moved his eyes back to the leader.

'Whithaugh,' he said. 'I have had dealings with that place afore.'

'Dealings is it?' Sim spat back. 'A wee word for the slaughter of the entire of the place, from the heidman doon.'

'Clearly no' all of them died and those who did kept coming at me. Like you do. Who is heidman there these days then?'

Sim floundered a little; this was not the way the conversation was meant to go, as he had seen it in his head before entering the place.

'Francie Armstrong,' he replied and Batty nodded as if he'd known, which was a lie. He had never heard of Francie Armstrong and fancied he had been brought in from outside, since the entire Armstrong heidmen at Whithaugh had died at Batty's hand, one way or another.

Davey's John whipped out a knife, so fast it had to be something he had practised every other day – but it was still too slow. Big Tam rose up and Davey's John shrieked at the crushing grip that ground knife hilt and the bones of his hand together. He was struggling to get free when something dark and huge arrived at the corner of his eye and blew his sense away. Big Tam let him fall, massaging his fist.

Ewan moved almost at the same time, while Dand floundered, taken by surprise for all that he should not have been, given the circumstances. He had time to shout and half-drag out his dagger before Ewan hit him between the eyes with the hilt of his own. Dand collapsed like a mammet with cut strings.

Sim pulled his pistol and found he couldn't. He tugged and wrestled, his eyes squeezed tightly shut. He slowed and finally gave up his struggle and opened his eyes. He found himself staring down the hexagonal barrel of a monstrous dagg – it had an axe head as part of the handle, he saw, and he raised his trembling hands.

'I nivver fired…'

'Pull out your pistol,' Batty said coldly, his spring to upright still rocking the table; Sim started to pop sweat.

'I nivver pulled on ye.'

Batty gave him a hard, weary look. 'The hook of the pan cover is stuck on your breeks. Take your time and remove it, else the match might touch it off and blaw your bags to bits. Besides – your serk is starting to smoke and if it catches flame…'

'I didn't shoot at ye.' It was a whimper now and Sim did not want to touch his pistol. He wanted to sink down and curl up; Big Tam gave an exasperated snort, stepped forward and wrenched the weapon out, tearing the breeks.

'My slice of pie is growing cauld,' he growled.

Both the other men were grunting and groaning, surfacing from the dark pit they'd been thrown in. They blinked back to the horror of their position. John Dubh took up the fallen knife and flicked it up into the rafters with a mocking sneer. It hung and trembled.

'Get away from here,' Batty said to the Armstrongs, then laid the pistol on the table feeling his back burning; something had torn when he had leaped to his feet.

It was a mark of Sim's obeisance that lived with him forever after, that he never even considered making a grab for the dagg on the table while Batty fumbled in his pouch and came up with a round shot which he threw at Sim, who winced as it struck him. Batty picked up the dagg and levelled it.

'If I see you again, the brother of that will come at you a lot faster.'

They went, limping and scuffling for the door, shouldering one another to get out. Patey Graham blew out his cheeks and put the cudgel back under the bar.

'The tales they tell of you are true efter all,' he said. 'Save that naebody died, which I am give to understand is unusual.'

He shouted for the women to fetch more drink, then turned back to Batty. 'What if they come back?'

Batty gave him a hard look. 'There will be bodies. You keep pigs don't you?'

Big Tam poised with his mouth full of pork, then set the pie slice down and swallowed what he had with a huge draught of ale.

-

Patey's wife, Joan, treated Batty's back in the morning, when she came down and saw the blood-streaks through his shirt. She had him lay flat and face down on a trestle, stripped to the waist in the shiver of a new day and being stared at unblinkingly by a black cat. There was a long, hard time of feeling old wrappings tear free, being slathered and re-bound.

'Christ in heaven,' Joan said sternly. 'Whit happened here?'

'Whit does it appear to be?' Batty countered, sullen with the nag of pain and everything that had happened the night before; he had spent the rest of it sleepless in front of the fire.

Joan was a Nixon from the English West March, a woman who filled a dress and had once done it with curves until they blurred with age. She was not put out by anything men did, not even Batty and said so.

'You look to have been lashed,' she said, 'which happens only to vagabonds or runaways from their lord's lands. Which is it with you?'

'Sport,' Ewan answered tersely. 'By the Laird of Blackscargil.'

'Laird my erse,' Joan Nixon spat back and then crossed herself. 'God forgive the blasphemy and on this day, too

94

– but that yin is nae laird, just a wee reiver who had taken ower the holding. I hear he has no nose, so the Graham wummin there is to be twice pitied.'

'For all that,' Batty countered, breathing out now that the worst was done, 'he still looks down it at everyone else.'

Patey laughed and poured them all lambswool, while Batty fished out more coin to keep Ewan and the others fed and comfortable while he went into Carlisle; they would not be permitted inside the town, Berwick writ or not, because they were Scots. The Master of Norham's bounty was diminishing, but it would never ransom Will Elliot anyway and Batty was sure he'd be forgiven for spending it when Will was eventually spirited away. He was strangely sure that would happen, though he had little reason for it.

There is more than one way to skin a cat, he thought and then caught the unblinking accusation of the black mog's stare and felt uneasy at it.

'A bad business, banning the Scotch from the toon,' Patey muttered. 'Some of those folk have produce for the market and in hard times like these, all of that is welcome.'

Then he smacked his lips and raised his horn cup in toast to his wife.

'To the maker of the lambswool,' he declared and everyone joined in enthusiastically. Batty took a long, savouring moment to enjoy the roasted apples, beer, nutmeg, ginger and sugar soothe on his pain, though it was already fading enough for him to get up. The cat yawned, showing vicious fangs, fixed its face with some deft paws, then moved langorously away.

Big Tam wiped off the white froth that gave the drink its name and offered Batty the peace of the day. It was only once he was outside, feeling the lack of his jack and his weapons and the biting cold and the fire striping his back that Batty heard the bells for St Stephen.

—

The rat watched him with a black, bright eye. It had already stolen his bread and Will was sure it had been in the bowl of gruel, front claws and snout. He did not mind, for he had no appetite. His feet ached, as they had done since the moment the Armstrong Laird of Hollows had rammed the point of a two-handed sword through both insteps, laughing as he did it. Six years since, he remembered and not a day passes that they do not ache.

His left hip ached in echo, because he put too much on it trying to climb stairs and the damp in this place did nothing to help the old wear on it. He scraped a notch on the wall of the dark place, squinting hard to see it since the only light came from a slit high up and there wasn't much of it. There was a breath of cold wind, bringing smells of cooking and the sound of laughter, so Will supposed it was either Christ's Mass or the day before it, but he could not be sure. Neither was he sure of how long he had been here since the day Batty had arrived and been huckled off.

Batty. He did not know whether to weep for gladness at the sight of someone he knew or sadness for it being Batty Coalhouse. Nebless Clem striped his back, he'd heard from the dark shapes who brought daily bread and gruel – sometimes with bacon in it, so he knew they were not going to starve him to death, that they wanted him in some sort of order.

He'd been astonished at seeing Batty, facered by it too, if he was honest, since it brought everything starkly back from the time he had been the upright Land Sergeant of Hermitage looking to woo Mintie Henderson of Powrieburn to the shattered remains of Will Elliot, brought low by Mintie's dark revenge on another, delivered by her weapon, Batty Coalhouse.

God hated him, was the truth of it, Will thought. I believed I had found sanctuary, escaped that band of terror and death that ribboned along the Borders – Christ's blood, it had taken most of his years to work out that life was not murder and raid and rapine anywhere else. Sixty miles away on either side and you could live in peace. Almost. He remembered telling Batty that like some evangelist minister, but aware that it was no revelation to him – besides, Batty inhabited a land of war wherever he went. His footprints were bloody...

Mayhap he's right, Will thought, for when he'd tried living in the backwater of Fife, war had sought him out and dragged him back – and here was Batty, once again. He felt a twinge through his ruined feet, as if the bones moved on their own, had their own memory of what Batty's rescue meant.

For a long time after he had been dragged onto a boat and sailed across to the other side of the Firth, he'd thought he would die, for sure. When the furrin paid-sojers, the ones Batty would have known well, had packed him like lumber all the way down to Berwick, he thought he would die. Even after that, dragged to some dank tower perched on the English East March, he'd thought he would die. When all the stars of our plans and ideals which we drape like a cloak on our own lived lives, have burned out, death is a monstrous, silent void. The only matter left is to silently accept this as our true identity.

Then the noseless man of Blackscargil told Will he was bound for Carlisle, not Hell so that he was whirled back into confusion. In the end, for no reason he could explain to himself, he knew Batty was in it somewhere and Will waited in the pain and the dark for the sinking that is death and the rising of what was coming.

–

Batty went through the town gate with no trouble and he'd probably have been able to do it without Grey of Wilton's wee script and dangling seals; the guards were swaddled against the cold and the soft flurries of new snow, the cullis was fully up and the big twin gates flung wide.

It was St Stephen's Day, a market, so Batty went with the flow of people carrying bundles, pushing loaded two-wheeled carts or trying to keep out of the way of the limping poor. These last were the threadbare patched, some hirpling on crutches, some of them pinch-cold children and all headed for the kirks, where the alms had been unboxed and would be handed out.

It was the Feast of Stephen and the cookshop stalls were savoury and huckstering, but Batty ignored them, making for the castle gate, taking a deep breath for this was trickier, even if he knew the guard here.

It was Dauney Nixon, who knew Batty well enough to warn him off.

'Nae Scotch allowed. You shouldnae even have got this far – are ye weaponed?'

'I am innocent as a nun's kerchief – besides, you're a Scot,' Batty countered and Dauney rubbed his nose with the back of one half-mittened hand, looking confused. It was true he lived with his kin on the Scottish side of the border when not in the garrison, which was a dangerous matter he did not care to have aired.

'I am not when standing here,' he declared.

'Neither am I,' Batty said and Dauney had to admit that was true. Neither Scot nor English, he had heard, but some money-sojer from across the sea. Well, there were a lot of them in the castle.

'Wharton will no' mind another,' Batty said, smiling, when Dauney spat this out.

'Wharton disnae ken whether he is on his erse or his chin,' Dauney replied. 'Carlisle looks to be the only fortress the Scots dinna have. Yet.'

Batty shook his head in commiseration, though he had none for the wily Warden Thomas Wharton, whose schemes had come to nothing and left a charred slather of burned holdings and lolling bodies. The war was over, all but the sealing of wee pieces of paper on it and Fat Henry was deid as old mutton.

Still, myself and Wharton had history, Batty remembered, particularly the Warden's younger son, also called Thomas, who had been left trembling with fear and cold after an incident near Hollows. All his men had died and one a gentleman, no less, whose brains had ruined young Wharton's doublet; the youth had never been the same since and Batty did not want Wharton hearing of how the man who was instrumental in that was in his castle. He fumbled out what he hoped was enough coin to prevent it.

Dauney made the coins vanish and let him in, closing the gate swiftly on Batty's back as if nothing had happened at all. Smiling, Batty, headed off into the inner ward, looking for the man he knew well and whom he hoped was still to the fore.

Wynking Gib was a man as big as Batty, with cheeks like a winter squirrel, stubbled so that they looked as if they could rasp rust off a blade. He was a Graham entrusted with the inner ward prisoners, those not important enough to warrant proper cells but not yet about to be set free.

He was stumping along in big boots and a jack – a front-fastener, too, Batty noted with yet another pang at the one he'd lost – but a split-brim bonnet instead of a burgonet. The helmet, fastened at his waist, clattered against the keys that marked his status as gaoler; it was regulation to have the helmet and Gib could easily clap it on if he saw importance coming at him. Batty thought the rust-coloured bonnet was ill-shaped because it was forever being crushed by the helmet – it made it look like an old ginger cat had found its way to sit on his head.

He said nothing of this as he made his way through the ward, busy with chaffering troops with nothing much to do but idle and spit; there were lean-to shacks along the cold, wet wall that looked like kennels, but the hounds in them were all prisoners.

Gib was astounded to see Batty and, from his quick look left and right, unsure of what to do with such a notorious appearing like a Devil in a morality play.

'Ho, Gib and well met,' Batty said and Gib gave in to the pretence, though he drew Batty to one side and spoke low and quiet, mainly about what he was doing here and did Batty know what would happen if an importance discovered it?

'Losh, Gib,' Batty replied. 'I am under writ to discover the whereabouts of one Will Elliot, soon to be delivered here. I am also instructed to ransom him if possible.'

Gib gnawed a finger and the facial tic that gave him his name flicked one side of his face.

'I am expecting such a person,' he admitted, 'instructed by the Warden and Governor himself to exchange him for another. I do not believe there will be ransom.'

Wharton himself, Batty noted and wondered idly and aloud, what Tom Wharton wanted with the likes of a wee crippled Elliot. Gib puffed out his cheeks, which was an alarming sight and coupled with the sudden spasm of tic made Batty think the man's head was about to explode like a petard.

He looked right and left again and Batty wished he would not, for it was as clear a sign of conspiracy as waving a large flag.

'The Warden wants Will Elliot as surety for the appearance of Rynion Elliot, known as Buggerback at the next Truce Meet. Said Will Elliot was recommended by Rynion himself.'

Batty knew Rynion Elliot of the Shaws and that he was called Buggerback because he would swive a knothole with moss around it. The fact that he had promised to appear at a Truce Day Meet was astounding enough, considering the crimes he'd be accused of, but he had contrived to get Will as hostage for his appearance which was cunning. Batty knew there was little love lost between Rynion and Will, former Land Sergeant of Hermitage.

More to the point – a Truce Day Meet? There had not been one for years because of the war and Batty said so. Gib shrugged and winked, but whether that was his tic or a sly indication of knowing defeated Batty. A thought struck.

'Who is to be exchanged?'

Gib, more relaxed now that he had spoken with Batty and all seemed to be perjink, smiled, winked and indicated for Batty to follow him. He led him to one of the lean-to shacks and Batty peered in.

At first he saw nothing, smelled a stable odour of staled straw and spilled gruel. Then the straw rustled and a head popped out, stalks wisping to spiked hair and beard. The head was followed by a familiar figure, swathed in a cloak which hid the haired body and stunted legs and a multitude of other sins.

'Master Coalhouse,' said a quiet, refined voice from the misshapen dwarf who pushed out of his straw home. 'Or whatever you are calling yourself these days. Well met.'

'Ape,' Batty said, smiling broadly for he knew now what Nebless Clem was up to. He hauled out his flask and handed it over to the Ape, the haired dwarf who was part of the Egyptiani entourage of the Randy King. On days when the daring visited the Egyptiani at a Fair, the Ape wore clawed mittens and taloned boots as the Beast, who was 'tamed' by Beauty, red-headed Megs massaging the Ape's prodigious member until the inevitable. It was lucrative draw and even women came to pay and watch, round-eyed and wet mouthed; one or two even clutched themselves when they thought no-one was looking.

'Are any others of your race held here?'

The Ape finished swallowing, stoppered the flask and handed it back; Batty saw Gib's eyes follow it and that he licked his lips.

'They are not, Master Coalhouse. All tucked up safe and sound in their winter encampment. I was unlucky. I lingered ower a wummin and an argument and was snatched up.'

About to be even more misfortunate, Batty thought, when Nebless Clem unfurls his whip and asks you where the secret winter camp of the Egyptiani lay. He plans a cauld revenge for the loss of his smeller.

He was distracted by a sudden flurry of laughter and movement, looking up to see some gaudy figures trailing through the throng, a swaggering of puffed sleeves and paned hose. *Stradioti* – Batty lowered his face lest he be recognised, but he saw them head for the short tunnel that held the wall-postern gate at the end of it. Gib saw him look and spat.

'Bliddy furrin sojers,' he growled bleakly. 'Afore they came naebody got in or oot o' that save by my allowance – noo they have a key and come and go as they please.'

'It leads to the water meadow and the Eden,' the Ape replied tartly, which let Batty know he had been considering it. 'Ye cannae get out unless you swim or have a boat.'

'They have a boat,' Gib replied. 'Row it across to a howf marked with a bush on a pole. It has drink and hoors and they row back when sober the next day. The key lets them avoid confrontation wi' guards and sich.'

He scowled at the Ape. 'I see you considering it.'

'I could join them in the boat,' the Ape replied scathingly. 'Mayhap they will think me a large rat and leave me be.'

Batty said nothing, simply handed his flask to Gib and then produced two coins which he rubbed together between thumb and forefinger. Gib choked in mid-swallow and then stared at the coins, the Ape and, finally, shook his head.

'Naw, Batty. Ye can scarce walk out of here with a prisoner as if you had the right of it. Especially one who looks like that.'

Batty took the flask and handed the coins over. Then he explained what would happen, while the Ape listened, head cocked to one side. Afterwards, the guards on the Ricardgate watched him walk in his rolling way, back to the tavern, trailing a song over his shoulder.

> *Janet has kilted her green kirtle*
> *A little aboon her knee,*
> *And she has broded her yellow hair*
> *A little aboon her bree,*
> *And she is to her father's ha,*
> *As fast as she can hie.'*

Chapter Seven

Later, on the Eden

They rode out over the bridge, now empty and with a cold brazier where the guards had once been; too cauld for those to stay here, Batty thought, up to their bollocks in iced winds.

They rode half-blind through the snow flurries, along the black slide of the Eden, squinting for any signs.

'Pole with a bush,' Big Tam muttered, easing himself so that his long-suffering mount grunted. 'Might as well play hoodman blind.'

There will be a light, Batty thought, for those coming across that black water by boat, in the night and with no moon will need something to row for, else they will end up in Solway's firth.

John Dubh spotted it, though it was little more than a wan glow, hung from the pole with a bush on it. He called it out and Batty admired his keen sight and then told him to keep his voice down.

'There will be four at least, mayhap five,' he told them. 'They will have horses stabled, for they will use this as a place to start patrols from if commanded – but they will be snugged up with drink and possibly a woman or twa.'

He looked round them all, dashing melting flakes off his lashes. 'I want no deaths. Fasten them up and find the postern gate key. Once we are back here, we can loosen one set of bonds enough to let him get free in an hour or so.'

'At least we have an extra mount for your wee friend,' Ewan declared and Batty put him right on that.

'The Ape might not ride and if he does it will not be done well. He walks or travels in a cart when with the Egyptiani, usually with the bears they have. He will have to be taken up by one of us – not me, who has but the yin arm and not Big Tam, whose poor hobby is sway-backed as it is.'

Big Tam wanted to know more about the bears, but the others shushed him and dismounted. Then they set forward, trying not to crack and crash through the under-growth and broken fence of the place. Batty moved slowly, painfully aware of the tugs from the healing scars on his back, more aware of the almost irresistible itch.

It was a low howff with shuttered slits and low-hanging thatch like a draggle's morning hair. There was only the one way in to a house as thick-walled as Carlisle Castle itself – through the door which huddled under the thatch.

They crept up to it, brittle on the virgin snow; Ewan pushed, felt the give and then the stop of the bar and looked inquiringly at Batty. Big Tam rolled his shoulders, but Batty stepped in, his fist full of the axe-handled dagg, freshly wound and double-checked. He rapped the axe on the door, then nodded to Big Tam.

There was the sound of muttering queries, the rattle of the bar being lifted and, just as the door started to open, Big Tam shouldered into it like a falling boulder. There was a sharp yelp, the sound of splintering and then Ewan and John Dubh forced past Tam into the place.

By the time Batty came in it was all over. Three men huddled in place, one of them blinking owlishly and bleeding from the nose, the others pinned in place by blades and now Batty's pistol. In the firelit dim a fourth man sat up in a rickety cot, a woman whimpering at his back; the place reeked of sweat, stale food, spilled ale and old sex.

'Now then,' Batty said. 'Who here speaks decent English?'

'We all do,' said the bleeding man, picking himself up from the floor and eyeing John Dubh's gleaming backs-word blade warily. The man squinted up at Batty.

'Is that Barthie Kohlhase there?'

Batty sighed, feeling shivered and hot at the same time. His back itched and burned and he felt weary, so weary he could not be surprised at the sight of Joachim.

He said the man's name and had nothing back. Not a surprise that he is struck dumb, he thought, since I was his Captain-General until he ran off with all the others.

'Joachim Sadoleto,' he said again. 'Who has the postern key?'

Joachim had been a boy when Batty had known him, peacock-proud of his ribbons and feathers and his *schwesche*, the gaudily painted drum he beat to move people out of the way of the lumbering guns, strutting importantly at the head of the column. He still had his ribbons and feathers, but now he was the oldest one there and a sergeant by his collar-chain. Still, Batty thought, he had run off with the others and that shows his character.

Joachim looked at him, then the blades surrounding him and gave in. He handed the key over and then, under the watchful eye of Batty's big pistol, allowed himself to be roped with the others. Big Tam would stay until they got back with the Ape, but the rest sorted out what they wanted to take and Ewan went to fetch the two-hander from his mount. It was a bad idea and Batty agreed with John Dubh when he said it; Ewan would not be put off.

'If I was you, Joachim,' Batty advised at the door, 'I would run for the Italies when we turn you loose. Theodore Luchisi will have to shoulder the blame for this, since you are his men and Carlisle's governor will want you hemped at the very least. They will say you are in on it.'

'Not the Italies,' Joachim replied miserably. 'There is famine and the Sweats there.'

'The Germanies then,' Batty answered coldly and Joachim shook his head.

'The war there has turned too religious for my taste.'

'Then go to Hell.'

Joachim cocked his head at Batty and closed one eye. 'You look a bit peaky,' he offered and Batty could not gainsay him, for he felt it; his back flamed and itched and he felt the sweat roll down and under his belly when he sat at the steering pole of the boat, for all that the black water of the Eden hissed with a snow wind.

Janet has kilted her green kirtle,
A little above her knee
And she has braided her yellow hair
A little above the brow
And she's away to Carterhaugh
As fast as she can go.'

He sang it soft in decent English, insidious and rotten as aloes until Ewan told him to stop. 'Bad enough I do all the rowing without having you with your crow-voice rasping in my lug.'

'I would row,' Batty offered mildly, 'if you want to turn in circles.'

'Hist, the pair of ye,' John Dubh whispered. At the same moment the boat grated and lodged itself on the bank; the oars were stowed and they scrambled up on to the sward.

It was an irregular patch of green used, in better weather, to turn out the inner ward prisoners for some air and exercise – they played at the football mostly and could not escape because the castle walls came down tight to the Eden at both ends. The only way to flee was to dive into the river and take your chances of getting across before a hot trod galloped round by the brig and dragged you back, bruised and bloody.

'Smart and silent now lads,' Batty said. 'Any noise and we'll be dancing on air and turning around.'

He went up slowly, feeling as if he didn't quite fit his own body and it took him three attempts to fit the key in the lock. When he rasped it free, the door shoved open as if on its own – but two figures were framed in it.

One was the Ape, who scuttled out, shivering in his cloak and shuffling through the snow in too-big shoes. The other was Gib, looking fearfully over his shoulder and winking so hard Batty was sure his eye would fly out.

'Ye need to give me a wee dunt,' he said and then his bravery cracked. 'Just a wee yin, mind, enough to make it seem as if I...'

The blow from John Dubh was meaty and smacking, laid Gib out flat; Batty checked his neck for the heart in the throat and was relieved to find it steady enough; there was blood on Gib's teeth.

'That was fierce,' Ewan chided and John Dubh grunted and knelt.

'If ye had wanted less you should have brought a lass to hit him – here, Batty, this is for you.'

He had rolled Gib out his jack-of-plates and, for a moment, Batty hesitated, then gathered it up, trying hard to hide the shame of thieving it by not looking at anyone.

'Follow us Ape,' he managed and they scurried back to the boat.

—

All things that pass must step upon the world, must stroke or grind some trail, move fresh snow, break ice or silence. There is nothing but the sibilant shush of her own blood in her ears, like the slow-beating wings of some giant unseen bird.

Or an angel, she thought, or the soft pounding of entwined hearts; she had once wished for that, as all girls do before they rush to Carterhaugh and Tam Lin. Now she had climbed the wall of all that back into the welcome darkness of the lost world.

Clem was ridden off with poor crippled Will and had left Mickle Anthone in charge – and to watch his wife, Gudwife Eliza. Now Mickle Anthone was snoring, victim of the drops she got from the Graham women in return for letting them forage for their rare herbs in the woods. It was a high price they paid, she thought, bowing her head with the weight that pressed her down. I should have killed him, not fed him the same drops and cut off his nose, but she had balked at murder. Nor should I have blamed it on the Egyptiani.

Now she was out and away. Netherby, she thought, though there might be little welcome from the heidman,

Dickon, since he was the one who had arranged her marriage to here originally. That was then and before Nebless Clem; she thought Dickon might be warmer towards her now.

The snow drifted and the wind sifted, keen as a blade. She turned the hobby towards unlit pastures, the black glades, boughs and trunks scrabbling for the moonlit sky. She blew out a cloud and heeled the horse into it all, feeling pursuers on her back and determined that nothing will find her but morning.

Chapter Eight

Morning near Blackscargil

The weather was going. Mist swirled, but the snow stopped falling and started to melt, leaving dark, wet stains; the moon was unclouded enough to make the patched snow glitter like diamonds.

It was wet and still cold all the same and Batty felt bad for Fiskie, who deserved to be unsaddled in the warm, rubbed down and fed barley in a bucket. He had none of that the first night they stopped and looked to have the same now. Mind you, he thought, I could do with warm and a bucket of barley my own self. He felt chilled and fevered at the same time and he knew it was no good thing and probably to do with poisons from that whip. Bliddy Turk affair, he was sure. Filthy with auld sins.

He was warmed by the knowledge that the others and the Ape were safe enough. 'Tak' the Ape as far as he will allow,' he told them, knowing the dwarf might want to keep the secret Egyptiani camp just that — a secret.

The Ape, lifted on to the front of Ewan's horse by Big Tam finished scowling at everyone for treating him like a wean, then reached out both hands and took Batty's single one in a double grip.

'I owe you,' he said simply. 'The Randy King owes you.'

'I will want to know how ye came to be caught,' Batty pointed out and that got a filed-teeth grin in return.

'Drink and women, Batty. Drink and women.'

Drink and women – Batty could use both now. He knew he was back at the ruined howff where he and the others had first laired, made a fire and some comfort; he did not want a fire now, for he was close to a ruffled Blackscargil, so he huddled and waited for morning, trying to keep his head from nodding off and knowing he would likely fail. Now we see how I stand in the sight of God, he thought before sleep took him, draping a blanket of balm over his slashed and itching back.

–

We all watched the clever drummer-boy treat the oxen, peering as if it was a Fair Day sideshow, though Batty was keen for the learning in it.

In a bowl Joachim took fluid from the lung of an ox which had died of wheezing sickness. Then he soaked small pieces of gun cotton wadding in the slorach of it, took a knife and pushed it right under the skin, a handspan from the root of the tail, till it came out at the other side. Then he inserted a piece of the soaked lint in the slot.

'I had this from my da,' he told them proudly and everyone nodded sagely, as if they also knew the recipe – which was a lie, though few thought it would work.

The beast got sick – then recovered after a few days and would never get the cursed sickness again. In many cases, however, the tail dropped off below the incision which at least let Batty tell his own beasts from others. Those who saw it crossed themselves and called young Joachim a sorcerer. Those Batty told to sod off and waved steel and pistols at them to show he meant business.

Luchisi squinted one eye and mused that if this worked on kine, it might work for, say, the Red Pox on men.

'Or just help them die faster,' Voicha growled. 'Besides – Batty won't want to lose his tail.'

All of this delayed the Company about two weeks, but they had a good spot beside a river, with good grazing and better water. A few lads, Luchisi among them, tried fishing but were no good at it, which made Batty laugh. Luchisi got annoyed and challenged Batty to a contest, thinking a one-armed man was no match even for an indifferent fisherman.

Batty, drunk and dangerous, waited until Luchisi was by the bank and casting before he hoisted the petard he had made into the river and watched it blow up while he howled with laughter. Luchisi went on his arse in the mud and was rained on by a cascade of water and dead fish; it was only by the grace of God that nothing worse happened.

Joachim helped gather up the fish but Batty remembered his look of reproach when he woke the next morning to find himself alone on the muddy bank, abandoned and sick with the afterclap of too much drink.

–

Almost as sick as I am now, he thought, struggling up and knowing something had woken him but not what. A ripple on his neck warned him, a tremble of the ground sending augers up his burning spine; he peered, he squinted, cocked his head and listened. Nothing but welcome darkness in the lost worlds – then Fiskie whuffed and got an answer.

She came out of the dark and saw him only at the last, a fell, dark figure with a huge pistol in his one hand; she knew him once she had blinked a few times to shred away the shock and managed a strangled little sound.

Batty grinned, for he knew how he stood in the sight of God and it was no lowly stature. The Lady of Blackscargil. He said it aloud and saw her blanch, then stare with bemused eyes at his singing.

'Just at the mirk and midnight hour
The fairy folk will ride,
And they that wad their true-love win,
At Miles Cross they maun bide.'

'Welcome to Miles Cross,' he added, grinning up and waggling the pistol muzzle. 'Light doon and take your ease.'

'I widna be so cantie,' she answered tartly, annoyed at having been so frightened to whimper before – he was, after all, just a whipped, one-armed man. 'If you bide here you will find yourself hip deep in men who mean us both no good.'

'How many?'

'Six at least – two out in front to track, more behind.'

'How far?'

'The two trackers are close, the others about an hour – I laid out Mickle Anthone to give me more time.'

'Laid him out how?'

She told him while he limped to his horse and painfully clambered on it. 'You are suffering,' she added and he agreed with a curt nod, reining Fiskie round.

'Would be worse if you had not held his hand from me, so my thanks for that.'

They rode out in silence for a bit, until an amorous dog fox yelped and seemed to break the spell that kept their mouths tight.

'Whither bound?' he asked. 'Or are ye just running? And why – I thought you were cosy with the man? Is it his missing neb?'

'His missing heart,' she answered and there was a wealth of bleak there that out-froze the wind hissing on them. She leaned forward yearning to bathe in moonbeams from the wintery glade where shadows met, flowed and vanished.

Her mind sloughed off pretension, the dreams auld Dickon had placed in her regarding marriage to the Laird of Blackscargil, the results of it, what she had done and what had been done to her. Tomorrow the ice on the well will crack and ripple under her red chapped hands, as it had when she was girl. Tomorrow she would again be that girl back in her home, tomorrow she would beat washing on stones and hang fish in the smokehouse.

'Take me home to Netherby.'

Batty rode in silence for another eyeblink or two. 'It was not always so,' he ventured and she hunched up in her wool cloak and said nothing for the longest time, while the moon darted from cloud to cloud as if ashamed.

'It was not always so,' she agreed eventually. 'Dickon made me wed on to the auld Laird of Blackscargil for the advantage in it and I was never mair pleased to see Clem Selby when he arrived.'

She stopped, smeared with memories, then took a breath. 'The thought was to wait, for he was auld, my husband and when he was gone, I would get married on to Clem.'

'And live happily ever after, God bless the house,' Batty muttered, sure that something noxious was running from his back. 'Did your husband suspect nothing then? Or not care ower much?'

'Clem killed my husband,' she said flatly. 'When it was clear he was not so advanced in years he would countenance being a cuckold. Clem felled him with a blow, dragged him to the roof with Mickle Anthone's help and threw him down. They gave out that he had fallen but naebody was cozened by that.'

'Least of all yerself,' Batty offered, 'but yet you stuck with it. Until you realised he would never wed you, since he had gotten what he wanted anyway.'

She hunched in her cloak, looking at the ground.

'A bad cess of nae good,' Batty added. 'I have felt your new man's cruelty mistress – is he among those on our track?'

'He has gone to Carlisle with your friend, Will Elliot and most of the fighting men.'

Good in one way, pity in another, Batty thought. They came up into a morning filled with moorhens paddling in pools that did not know whether to be ice, a roll of snow-patched bracken and gorse studded with copses of beach, hazel and oak. They skirted a huddle of buildings fired to ash long since, victims of the wars and here Batty drew up the stumbling Fiskie.

'Need to rest the beasts, else they will founder.'

Eliza fretted a little that Batty had lost the way to Netherby, but climbed stiffly off and said nothing on it. Batty fumbled a handful of oats from his store and fed both horses; they lipped his hand eagerly, looked woeful when no more came and fell to standing, muzzle to muzzle, breathing in each other's smoking breath.

She crouched, not wanting to sit but needing out of the hissing wind, which even the little copse of trees failed to break. It mourned between slender trunks, low and bitter. Batty envied her knees which let her perch like that.

'You think Dickon Graham will welcome you back?' he growled, knocking iced snow off a stump and sitting. He felt the cold seep up his hurdies and thought about what that would do to his nethers.

Eliza had thought of little else. She would wake tomorrow to the bustle of tasks, among kin who knew her, who would bring her a civil meal. But it will be down to Dickon Graham of Netherby whether the rest of them scratch her with worried looks, wonder at what she has done to bring her back.

'Yes,' she said and he didn't argue. There was a pause, then she asked: 'D'ye ken what Clem wanted with your Will Elliot that's worth dragging a poor cripple down to Carlisle?'

'Exchange for a stunted mannikin of an Egyptiani,' Batty replied, then stopped because he was not sure if the Ape was an Egyptiani at all, though he moved with them and was valued. He felt her looking, waiting expectantly and when nothing came, turned into her gaze.

'Clem wants to know where the Egyptiani winter, a secret place only they know.'

Her face turned stricken in the brief flicker of unclouded moonlight and there was something more there, Batty thought, than horror about what Clem planned to do with the knowledge – though that would be enough to strike you rigid. Mayhap she thought of the seven women hanged in a glade.

There was a sound, a tiny ching, soft as a Faerie bell and Batty's head came up at it. She huddled, afraid. Batty slowly drew out his monstrous axe-handled dagg and worked his stiff bones off the stump. She marvelled at him, softly singing.

> '*At the mirk and midnight hour*
> *She heard the bridles sing,*
> *She was as glad at that*
> *As any earthly thing.*'

'Ho there.'

The voice was rough, hoarse with fear and Batty was sure the man squinted into the dark, searching for the singer. Faerie, he thinks and then laughed; nae Faerie would have a voice like a badly cracked bell. He saw a bobbing red spark of match fuse in the darkness and knew where the man was.

'Turn and leave,' he said, then hirpled sideways, knowing what would come. The blast of light, the great roar blew out sight and sound, but the gout of flame spat a ball three feet to the left of Batty and let him see, for that lightning instant, the man who had shot the matchlock caliver.

He pointed the dagg, squeezed and heard the wheel spin sparks. Then it exploded and there was a shriek; he flipped it, feeling the hot muzzle even through the gauntlet.

From his right came a cracking, a crashing, a flurry of snow rolling like mist; the figure in the middle of it lunged at Batty with a big, ugly, notched broadsword, his mouth wild and wet and open.

Batty struck with the axe, missed but caught the blade on the rest of the pistol grip, sweeping it sideways and away from him – then the man stumbled forward and hit like a runaway stirk. They both went over in an explosion of powdered snow.

Batty rolled, gasping in a welter of blinding freeze but with his back flaming into agony. He scrabbled for sense, clawed for purchase to stand and realised he had dropped the dagg; then the man rose like a nemesis, broadsword still in one hand and his face snarling triumph.

Batty saw it all then, the way time and age wears you to a nub, the way you can go too often to the well and how life, however long it has been, appears only as a single, short explosion stretched out in slow motion, an explosion in which question has become answer, possibility alchemicaled to reality, time transmuted to eternity.

Then the man jerked and screamed, a blade tore through the rest of his throat and he fell away trailing rubies, leaving the dark angel called Eliza with a bloody knife, her kerchief torn free and her hair like Medusa.

'Help me up,' Batty said roughly, to tear her from staring at what she had done – but when she did, her eyes were dark and clear, with no shock; she had no strain in her at all and that made Batty more feared than if she had been a shrieking harpie.

The man she had stabbed in the throat was dead, eyes staring at nothing and already done with melting the snow, though the last heat of him made it look as if he wept for the bad cess of his life.

Batty found the one he had shot and it wasn't difficult in the dark, since he moaned and whimpered. The shot had hit his hand and, like all the cruel weight that flew from the hexagonal barrel of a big dagg, it had not been content with a finger or two, but had blown off the whole affair. There was a deal of blood, but Batty expertly looped a snare he fetched from inside his jack and wrenched it tight until the trickle went to a seep, then stopped entirely; he felt the woman's unseen eyes, the question she would not ask and answered it anyway.

'You'll not die here. Fetch your horse and ride back to the tower,' he said and the man moaned, flopped in the puddle his blood had already made. 'Keep that snare tight, mind.'

'I wulnae make it.'

'Ye will if ye ride firm and dinna fall,' Batty answered firmly. 'It will be the only way of saving yourself, to find someone there who can treat this. Are ye a Ker by any chance?'

'John Forster,' the man gasped and Batty patted him soothingly.

'Well, ye can forget your right hand from this moment, for it is no longer a part of your world. Learn to be Ker-fisted. I am right sorry for it, but that's the price the likes of us pay for the life we lead.'

'Help me...'

Batty helped him up, boosted him to the saddle and held him there while he found a balance. Then he looked at the man, hard as cold iron.

'When you get to the tower,' he said, 'tell them this and no more. Tell them Batty Coalhouse is coming.'

He nudged the horse hard enough to make it move and watched it amble a few steps, pick up a pace, then went back to the dead man to find his axe-handled dagg. Blood had made a dark hole under the man's head and his tow hair looked moonlit bright against it. Batty blew snow off his precious pistol and, when he turned, the woman had both their horses held ready.

Eliza followed in his wake, no longer concerned whether he knew the way to Netherby, though she was rasped by his singing.

> 'Nae living man I'll love again,
> Since that my lovely knight was slain.'
> Wi' a lock o' his yellow hair,
> I'll chain my hert for everymair.'

—

Wharton sat behind a table littered with papers and the litter of a meal. The ornate butt of a wheelock dagg peeping shyly from under a sheaf of bundled reports and a dagger with a jewelled hilt was carelessly thrust deep into the scarred wood.

Across from him, lounging against the shutters, his son Henry had a pinked and slashed leather jerkin and a black sword belt and hanger over a red doublet and red hose with a prominent codpiece. It was altogether too German for his father, who preferred a plain shirt, though his overrobe was deep blue and trimmed with wolf fur; it was needed, for despite the fire the wind fingered through the shutters and fluttered the candles. Carlisle was a snell place, even in summer.

Near the fire, which was clearly too mean for his liking, stood an individual with his back to them all, heating his hands and growling softly. He was short and slight and paunched a little, his head drooped like a withering willow and the entire appearance was of a pox doctor's clerk. He wore a fine lawn shirt and heavy leather riding breeches and boots that came above the knee and looked as if stolen from his too-large da.

But when he put on the fancy embroidered cote that was slung, glittering the firelight, over a chair, he was a different beast altogether.

Henry knew why Harry Rae, Berwick Pursuivant, had come in the middle of winter, scowling at having had to do it. It made Henry sullen and unwilling to participate in matters with the other guest.

The other guest stood impatiently, hard-faced – well, what you could see of it under the tawdry leather mask that gave him a nose. He wore breeches and muddied boots, a jack of plates and a split-brim cap, all of them reeking of the moss and the moor. Wharton looked at him coldly.

Nebless Clem glowered back, measuring Thomas Wharton, the Warden of the West March of England and Governor of Carlisle. He was a lean man, age gnawing it to stringy muscle and wire tendons, his greying hair carefully cut to curl on the great, rough wolf-fur collar of the robe, his silvered beard trimmed all perjink. When he spoke he steepled his fingers together and closed one eye; the rumour was that his open eye was a sure sign he was lying and the one that let him speak the truth he kept always shut.

'It is a great shame,' Thomas Wharton said insincerely, 'that the Egyptiani mannikin escaped – but there you are. What can you do?'

'A great shame to Carlisle,' Henry Wharton put in pointedly and his father pretended to ignore him.

Clem thought that the younger Wharton dressed like a hoor, but you had to take into account his resolve in fighting out of the treachery of the Master of Maxwell not long since. Wharton had reached an agreement with the Master of Maxwell that he would join them with at least two thousand men, giving ten hostages as a pledge. Together they would attack the Earl of Angus, in support of Hertford's assaults in the east.

Henry was sent ahead, to burn Drumlanrig and Durisdeer, but the Master of Maxwell's men suddenly turned coat and joined Angus, chasing Henry Wharton into the mountains. Then the Scots force advanced on Dumfries and Wharton had to fight his way back to Carlisle with just his cavalry.

'Seems so,' Clem answered. 'Seems all too easy to walk in and out of Carlisle's fortress and free its prisoners. Well, I will find another use for Will Elliot and be on my way.'

'Not that easy,' the elder Wharton said softly. 'Help was given from inside as well as out – a gaoler is now in shackles and I would have the outside man join him. I believe you know him – Batty Coalhouse.'

Clem's face gave nothing away – one of the benefits of the leather mask – but his eyes flickered enough for Wharton to smile thinly and nod. Henry noted that the back of the Berwick Pursuivant straightened at the name.

'Aye, the man you striped,' the elder Wharton went on. 'I have heard he came to you trying to ransom Will Elliot and you gave him an answer. Pity you did not hemp him.'

Clem shot him a look. 'The law does not permit that.'

Henry Wharton laughed scornfully. 'Such legal niceties never prevented you from rapine, insight, arson and all the other crimes your band of rogues have stained the land with.'

'I will keep Will Elliot,' the elder Wharton went on, 'and ten of your men besides, as surety for the task you will oblige me with – namely, the apprehension of Batty Coalhouse. You may hurt him but bring him to me alive.'

The Berwick Pursuivant turned and made a slight coughing sound which made the elder Wharton scowl. He knew Harry Rae was pointing out how hangings were permitted only by writ of the Lord Protector, but he did not need to be told that. The Lord Protector was not here, in the Borders.

Clem bridled. He wanted to snarl at them but did not dare. He had no use now for Will Elliot, but he wanted to drag him out because Will was Clem's possession and he did not like to be robbed. He wanted, at the very least, to ride away and ignore the Whartons, but he was aware that four of the ten hostages the treacherous Maxwell had handed over had already been hanged; Clem was sure the ten men he'd be forced to leave would not be spared if he refused.

Yet an idea came to him through the red fog and blew the rage away in shreds.

'Will Elliot was once held by the Armstrong Laird of Hollows,' he said, 'or so I had heard. I also heard how Batty Coalhouse exerted all his legendary powers to free him, at great risk to himself.'

Wharton's head came up at that and he glanced sideways at his son. Clem almost grinned; so it was true enough, then. He pressed his point.

'Give me Will Elliot and let that be known to everyone. When Batty comes to free him from yet another tower...'

He left the rest hanging. Henry Wharton stroked his bushed chin and looked at his wolfen father. 'Better that then thrashing about the moors searching for him.'

'He'll be with the Grahams of Netherby,' the elder Wharton replied harshly, but he knew the likes of Clem could not take the Grahams on with the men he had, though he was lunatic enough to try. He looked blackly at Clem.

'You will have Will Elliot. If you lose him or play me false, you will find Hell an easier sanctuary than this Earth with me hunting you down.'

Clem wanted to say that Will Elliot was his prisoner, to do with as he saw fit, but he knew the truth of possession well enough and did the only thing he could; he thanked the Whartons kindly, bowed at the neck and left, clacking his big muddy boots out of the hall, feeling the heat of Wharton scorn searing his back. Like Batty Coalhouse, he thought.

The Whartons said nothing afterwards, for it was all too raw. They had come recently from London and the funeral of young Tom, son and brother and even if it had been a merciful release from the pox and the mad fancies it was still a sore wound for them both.

A handful of years before this the Warden's son had been sent on what had seemed a simple enough task – fetch the wee Queen Mary from the hands of the Armstrong reivers who had stolen her. The wee Queen would be brought south to King Henry and married on to his young son, thus shackling the Scots to a different future.

Instead, young Tom had somehow fumbled it, had ended up in the hands of Batty Coalhouse and, though returned intact in body, had never been the same since.

'Coalhouse killed my boy,' Wharton growled. 'Retribution is overdue.'

Harry Rae offered condolences but he was only dragging the attention to himself. When he felt it, he fished out a sealed packet from inside his shirt and laid it in front of the Whartons.

'To save you going blind,' he said, 'here is roughly what it says – young Henry here's gallant gesture to fight a duel with Grey of Wilton is refused by the Lord Protector, who urges you both to reconcile your disagreements with the Warden of the East March.'

Thomas Wharton had been expecting it, but slapped an irritated hand on the table, stirring the packet. Harry Rae was unperturbed.

'The Marches will need unity among those charged with presevering the peace along it. The war with the Scots is all but done with and England needs no Border brigandage. You are both charged with using your influence to prevent that.'

Thomas Wharton looked as if he would choke. For six years his endeavours, blessed by the old king, had been bent on fomenting the family Names in the Border to fight one another for the furtherance of King Henry's aims. Now it was all to be reversed.

'This Will Elliot business,' Harry Rae said mildly, 'is a case in point. The Border does not need Graham against that cut-nosed horror from Blackscargil. Neither, the Lord Protector agrees, does it need more hempings. He is unhappy about what you did to the Maxwell hostages.'

'Batty killed my son,' Wharton answered. He wanted to say more, about how the Lord Protector Seymour should look to his own position these days, but did not. Besides, if the Seymours fell, Wharton would go as well.

Henry Wharton knew that his fecklessly weak young brother had died of the pox, but it was true that whatever had happened between him and Batty Coalhouse had coloured him for the rest of his life, in night terrors and waking dreams.

He never said anything, simply nodded curtly to Harry Rae and followed Clem out of the hall, to make sure the ten hostages were secured and Will Elliot delivered. He did not like it and agreed with Harry Rae – the Maxwell hostages had been hemped and now Gib the gaoler was dancing on air for his part in the freeing of the Egyptiani midget. There was altogether too much rope and tree for Henry.

We need to be making useful friends, not snarling at everyone, he thought. The war here is done with and we have lost it – if we are not cunning then we will have the French coming ower the border from Scotland as well as crossing the Channel into England.

Spending time and blood on an auld one-armed man was a waste; Henry was afraid, more than he would admit to anyone, that his father's grip was slipping, that all the cunning and plot he had used to shake loose the Border on behalf of his king was come to nothing. He had failed, after all, Henry thought and that might crush a man's mind and resolve.

Chapter Nine

Netherby on the Esk

His back was on fire and someone said 'keep him verra still noo.' The room was burning as it had been before, but this time someone was stabbing his flaming back, slowly and with relish, spearing it until white-hot pain ran straight down him into the red, molten core of his being.

He felt himself curling, heard the strange sounds he made. 'Move the light a bitty, ah canna see. By God, the fester in this...'

The stabs began again and the pain grew until it filled the whole world, until it seeped into his heart and flooded into his head. He couldn't breathe.

'Batty Coalhouse – stop fighting. Just for a wee minutey. Ye have a great hert for fighting, I ken, but just bide still.'

'If he had a foot in Paradise he would take it out to fight back on earth,' a man said. Someone else had said that to him once – Mintie was it? He could no longer recall. There was the smell of herbs, some of which he recognised through the red throbbing – feverfew, marsh woundwort. His ma had known them and more and if she had been one of the seven in Nebless Clem's woods he would have hanged her as a witch, too. Someone snuffed candles out on the skin of his back.

He felt himself being bound, swaddled like a babe, then they left him and took the light so the darkness fell like a balm. Yet soon enough the roof burned and fell on him again, buried him under a scorch of dream timbers and burning scarlet flames.

–

He came out of an ocean of grey gently, not like all the times before when he breached back into the world like a whale. At first he saw only dim light and pale blobs, like the outlines Michaelangelo did before he painted, then they slowly, slowly coalesced into faces he knew.

One was a halo of tow-coloured hair and a curve of yellow beard like a Turk's scimitar, perched on a lean body running hard through wiry too string. Once the yellow had been golden, but it was now near white, but he knew it well enough and the eyes were the same cool grey-blue, glassed as a summer sea and set in a seam of ruts.

'Dickon,' he managed and everybody muttered and nodded.

'Back with us then – well done Jinet Graham,' said Dickon and the focus of his attention beamed out of a flushed, chapped face and fussed with Batty's bolsters so that he could sit more upright without undue strain on his back.

'Here,' Dickon's wife said, thrusting a horn cup at him, 'ye will have a drouth on ye if all the piss and sweat you put on my sheets is a measure.'

It was small beer and very small at that, with just enough ale in it to make the water taste. He drank it down, for she was right and he had a thirst on him and when he was done, the other faces made more sense.

'Batty,' Dickon said, indicating the men round him. 'Ye remember Fergus of the Mote and Tam Graham of Kirkandrews, also kin.'

'I do,' Batty answered and his voice appalled him, scratchy hoarse and slightly louder than whisper. 'From when we first met at Powrieburn. There were ithers...'

'Arthur of Canobie,' Fergus answered bleakly. 'Ambushed and killed a brace of years since. Armstrongs did that in revenge for Hollows.'

'I am right sorry to hear it,' Batty managed, then looked into the parched desert of Jinet's face, the blue eyes bleak. 'And for Davey-boy too.'

She patted his hand, though it should be him soothing her for the loss of her son. She took the cup away and Dickon watched her go for a second, then turned and nodded to Batty.

'Sair days,' he said flatly. 'Ye did well by my lad, finding his killer and exacting Graham vengeance. Six years have not balmed it much, for me or his mither.'

Batty was too weary to point out that it had been Davey-boy's own cheap gun that had done for Hutchie, but revenge was revenge.

Dickon leaned forward a little. 'I am not forgetting that he was there at Powrieburn because of Will Elliot. Nor that it was all to do with yerself, the Firebrand who torches everything he touches.'

'Davey-boy went of his own accord,' Fergus pointed out and Dickon reluctantly admitted it with a flap of one hand. 'He went for his regard for Will Elliot, who was held hostage at Hollows; he wanted to be in on the rescue.'

'I ken it all,' Dickon said wearily, 'yet where Batty steps death and fire follows. His footsteps are fu' o' blood.'

'He brought me back,' said a voice and Eliza pushed out of the flickering shadows. 'He saved me from Nebless Clem.'

Dickon shot her a savage look. 'We will hear more on that bye and bye, lady, including how came your husband to die, the loss of Clem's neb, the hemping of seven Graham gudewives and mair. Nebless Clem has a deal to answer for and I will expect a peck mair truth out of you than has been forthcoming, Eliza Graham.'

He turned back to scowl at Batty, who was blinking owlishy as he tried to make sense of the revelation that Graham women had been hanged, not Egyptiani. 'I hear he treated you badly and you thwarted him ower that wee Egyptiani creature, the Ape. A new feud – just what the dales need. But Thom Wharton is no long back frae Lunnon, where he kisted up his youngest son. Sudden fever they called it, but everyone kens he was poxed and his mind was away with the Faeries. Night terrors and worse, I had heard.'

'From what we did to him at Hollows,' Batty finished bleakly, looking at Eliza, who studiously avoided him. She had told Clem it was Egyptiani women in his woods, Batty thought and it was likely one or two of them had been auld foes of Eliza from girlhood. That sort of patient vengeance has to be considered.

Dickon, oblivious to all else but the moment, spoke again.

'We rescued a royal babe, but nae good deed goes unpunished and now Wharton wants his revenge also, for what you did in freeing the Ape. Wynking Gib has been hemped, which was the price for your clevery with the Carlisle postern. More will follow, certes. Well – you are a foul byblow of a Graham who has set the Border alight from Berwick to Carlisle, just when folk were thinking the war was done with. But you are still our byblow.'

'And, besides, the Grahams still want Blackscargil,' Batty replied, stung and watched Dickon's glowering face melt and reform.

Jinet patted Batty's shoulder. 'Sleep noo. When ye awake, ye will be stronger.'

She was right; Batty was stronger when he woke the second time, enough to sit up unaided and have Jinet tut about what that did to her stitching. The room was brighter, the shutters opened to let in the light and a cold breeze that scoured out the fug. From where he craned, Batty could see distant hills clear of snow and surmised he was in the top of Netherby's fine tower.

'I squeezed a deal of pizen oot o' yon wounds,' she scathed, 'which was no fault of the wee learned gown at Soutra, but all your own doing by being up and dashing aboot too soon. I had to cut a bit and stitch a bit and if you persist in your legendary stubborn, all my perjink darning will go to waste.'

'Aye, aye, you are right as all wummin invariably are,' Batty replied mildly, 'but you are forgiven for unlike all wummin you make a fine barley broth. Or so I have heard.'

'I will slap yer lug,' Jinet replied but her stern glare was mitigated with a smile. 'I will fetch some soon enough, with fresh-made bread besides – but after Dickon has had a word.'

Dickon bustled in with four at his back; for a moment, Batty thought they were Fergus and other kin until he saw the familiar grinning face of Big Tam, Red Colin, Ewan and John Dubh. He felt a flicker of panic, quickly quelled because they were smiling, but Ewan saw it.

'Dinna fash,' he said. 'Yon hairy wee mannie is safe with his ain folk.'

'Ah saw the bears,' Big Tam threw in delightedly.

'They let you stay, then?' Batty asked and they all nodded.

'Fine hospitality,' Red Colin added. 'Good food, good drink… and mair.'

Batty could imagine the 'mair'.

'So you know where the Egyptiani lair for winter then?' he asked and Red Colin nodded enthusiastically.

'Aye, aye – up by Dumfries…'

He broke off when Big Tam dug an elbow in his ribs, hard enough to drive the breath out. Then realising what he had done, Colin clapped one hand across his mouth, eyes stricken.

Batty shook his head with mock sorrow while Ewan glared at Colin. 'They are moving away efter Lady Day,' he said, 'so will probably be safe.'

Batty wondered why they were here at all, thinking them either safe with the Egyptiani or back in Edinburgh and when he said so, Ewan told him they had been in both and then thought of coming here to see if 'Batty's kin' had any news.

That made Batty look alarmed and at Dickon. 'How long have I been here?'

'Too long, give or take,' interrupted Jinet, sliding expertly through the throng of men with a savoury bowl. She shot a hard glance at her husband. 'Dickon here thinks all guests are like fish – after three days they start to stink. Here's the barley brose I promised ye.'

Too long, right enough. The year was running towards a turn and the hills Batty saw were green with new growth and empty of snow – small wonder the Egyptiani were stirring, for winter was done with.

The war wasn't quite done with, according to what Ewan and the others had to say, tripping over one another to tell their news from Edinburgh. The French were still hot for it, there was dissent in Norfolk and Kent and everywhere else, so much so that the English were already calling it 'the year of the many-headed beast'.

'Nae matter all of that,' Dickon interrupted suddenly, his voice like a slap on a table. 'Nebless Clem is still loose and looking for ye – he probably already kens you are here, but I have set watchers and he will no' make a move that I dinna find out.'

'Then we'll be away and leave ye in peace,' Batty said, putting the bowl aside; Dickon laughed harshly.

'Too late for that, Batty. Besides – as you have said, I have my own reasons for facing him.'

Eliza Graham and her claim on Blackscargil, Batty thought but he stayed quiet on that and on his thought on what she had done and was not telling. He did have something to say, all the same.

'This is not your fight, for all your claims of kinship. You are right, Dickon – the world is closing in on Batty Coalhouse. All sins fly back to roost.'

Jinet made an exasperated huff of sound and took the bowl.

'This and everything else is done for love of my son,' she said and there was nothing anyone could add to that; Batty remembered the limp little form, bloody as wound-rags, robbed of all weapons.

'When you are ready to ride,' he said to Dickon and left the rest unspoken. It would be soon, he thought, for it was almost Candlemas and after it Riding became too much work for too little gain. But this was different…

Jinet tutted, shaking her head and unworried by almanacs.

'If you rise from that bed to go on the Ride,' she said firmly, 'then you undo all I have done and Hell slap sense into you. But we all know that, if Batty Coalhouse stepped one foot into Paradise he would remove it to fight here on Earth so I have few hopes for you.'

They left, one by one and Batty sank gingerly back against the pillows, while Jinet gave a last fuss to them. At the door, she gave him a scathing look, knowing he would not listen to good advice about rest until the poison in him had finally seeped away.

She was not soothed by his soft, rotted singing and knew the song was called Barthie's Dirge; she shivered.

'They shot him dead at the Nine-Stane Rig,
Beside the Headless Cross,
And they left him lying in his blood,
Upon the moor and moss.'

Chapter Ten

Netherby on the Esk

Dickon had slaughtered a cow and split it. One half went for pot stew and pies, the gralloch was made into humble and the remaining half was prepared for the spit. There was a constant buzz and movement, like a beehive, as folk got ready for the Lady Day feast, which was Dickon and the Grahams of Netherby showing their style and wealth rather than regard for the Virgin.

Not that you could anyway. Fat Henry had decreed that the Virgin was no longer the one you lit the candles to, only Christ was to be so lauded, but some of the women of Netherby snapped fingers to that, wearing blue cloaks in honour of the Lady. Even the minister, brought from the kirk at Arthuret to lend solemnity to the rammy, dared not question the women of Netherby.

Batty kept out of it as best he could and the weather kept his movements slow and few – the garth was a great puddle and everything was moved into the big kitchen, now laid out as a feasting hall. There should have been a balefire to mark the end of one year and the start of the next, but it was too wet for that.

Ewan and the others helped cut wood, fetch, carry and spar good-naturedly with the Graham lads.

Batty spent his time in the stall with Fiskie, who was warm and happy and fed so that his whuffs and puffs were all joy. Batty was less joy. He asked for any old leather flasks, big ones for water or ale and got three which had started to seep at the seams. He asked for powder and got it and he and the smith, Jock's Richie, struck up a friendship while they scoured the forge for discarded tailings of ruined nails and other pieces of sharp rusted metal.

Eliza came to him as he stuffed the flask with powder and lethal points. She brought him ale and a slice of freshly made humble pie, all savoury steam; he eyed both of them suspiciously.

'What?' she demanded.

'Have you residue still in that bottle you gave your husband?'

She pursed her lips. 'If I have, why would I be wasting it on you, here and now? Are you in need of being laid insensible?'

Batty wadded the mouth of the flask, feeding a length of match through it while she watched, fascinated.

'Are you content here, then? They have welcomed you back, it seems.'

She rubbed Fiskie's nose and then sat. 'I am back, but only because Dickon needs me to stamp the Name on Blackscargil. He wants Nebless Clem out of there and me back in it – at which point he will find a new Graham man for me to wed.'

Batty started on a second flask, but paused long enough to cock his head at her. 'You had better not treat him as you did the last,' he said softly and she glared.

'I treated him well enough…'

'Dickon kens what you did,' Batty answered, 'and soon you will needs tell him all of it. Did you lay your old husband out with potions, then help carry him to the roof? You did not get yer wee alchemical from Egyptiani – I have seen the wummin here, including Jinet, grinding herbs for my back and other medicals; I am sure if they lived beyond Netherby they would be burned as witches, the pack of them. It was them made you the stuff you fed to your man, I am thinking. And the price was to let those seven women forage in your wood for herbs they could not find elsewhere.'

He stopped, put the flask between his knees and started to fill it.

'There was no Eyptiani in it. They were all Graham women frae Netherby, but Clem didnae ken that, did he – was it you or him who decided they'd be safer dead?'

She started to speak, then her head fell, her poorly pinned kerchief allowing her hair to fall round her face. It would not hide anything shown there, she thought miserably.

'Two were Graham women. The ithers were from across the border – Forsters and Charltons. All of them were cunning-women who met now and then...'

A coven, Batty thought trying not to shiver at the idea. Usually, these were just the wee healers of their own folk – but if anyone cared, they could hunt them down as witches and destroy them all. Like Clem had done.

'Clem's own idea,' she whispered. 'I did not want it to happen. We went into yelling at yin anither and he...'

Called you names and said things he could not after- wards unsay, Batty decided. Particularly the one about marrying you, which let you know that you had conspired to murder yer husband and that was all Clem had needed.

Blackscargil was already his and he did not need marriage to seal it. You did not, all the same, tell him that the women in the woods were Graham and so the train of all this blood and slaughter lurched on to a new road.

She looked pools of anguish at him and was on the brim of telling how Clem had really lost his nose when someone bustled into the stables, breaking the spell.

'Och, here ye are,' said Jinet, then looked sharply at Eliza. 'Help is needed in the kitchen – and cover yer hair.'

Eliza rose and left, scathed by Jinet's following glance.

'Are you sweetening that?' she demanded of Batty when no-one else could hear. 'Have you some interest there?'

Batty laughed and, eventually, she saw his seamed face and silvered beard and was mollified enough to remember why she had come.

'Here,' she said and thrust a ball with some sticks in it at him. For a moment Batty stared and she took it as being overwhelmed and beamed.

'I heard you knitted, a marvellous thing to see with the yin hand. I heard also that you lost your needles and wool – so here is a replacement.'

Batty laid the flask down and took the gift, smiling at her so she would be pleased. The truth was that he had knitted less because it seemed God was contriving to foul his one remaining hand by slow degrees – his finger joints were stiff and pained and he did not enjoy knitting as once he had.

Jinet never noticed, slathered with the deliciousness of news.

'The carts from Carlisle are here,' she said, beaming, 'with all that we need to complete this day's feast.' She peered out, squinting into the garth; the rain had stopped, but the eaves dripped and the yard was slorach of mud through which folk moved on raised clogs and women daringly showed their shins to keep dress hems dry. She called out to them, laughing.

> *'If Candlemas be dry and fair*
> *The half o' winter to come and mair*
> *If Candlemas Day be wet and foul*
> *The half o' winter gane at Yule.'*

They laughed back and plootered on while Jinet beamed. 'I will go and make sure they brought the proper candles wi' them.'

Wax, Batty surmised. Expensive, but Jinet would honour the Virgin and Dickon would smile like a rictus and dig deep in his purse. She was all Eliza wanted to be and never would.

'Just as well they made it through the wet,' she went on ducking the drips above the door, her voice trailing after her like smoke, 'for there's bread and the like on those carts, too, enough to feed the dozen or so riders who came with them. Scared the De'il out of the Graham watchers, who thought it was a raid.'

It was not a raid, as Batty discovered. It was an escort of twelve riders on decent shod horses – *demilances* of the English army, probably from the Lord Protector's own men. They were dripping and their fat flag with a red rose drooped on its pole, drenched to weary flapping. For all that, the Netherby Grahams looked on enviously at their German armour, the *harnasch*, which was a back and breast with lobster-tails down to the knee to meet the great boots. They had burgonets and hooded red cloaks and the sullen air of men who knew all the metal would need cleaned before it started to spot with rust.

In the midst of them, swaddled in a waterproofed leather cloak, was Harry Rae, the Berwick Pursuivant, being welcomed out of the weather by Dickon and Fergus and others; it seemed to Batty that there were a lot more Grahams than before and that the Lady Day feast was a good excuse for gathering them.

He found out how good an idea that was when Harry Rae stood with his hurdies to the fire, his fancy coat discarded on the table in front of him, high in the solar of Netherby's tower. It took Batty aback to find out how hard he breathed and sweated climbing all the way up to it.

'Batty Coalhouse,' Harry Rae said when he hirpled in. 'You look fine enough for a man who has shaken loose the Border, been whipped like a Turk slave and swam the Eden with a wee man on yer back, if stories have it true.'

'Harry Ree,' Batty answered, sinking gratefully on to a bench seat. 'You look as usual – sleek and full o' secrets. Is your hoose in Berwick still intact and free?'

'I will find out soon enough – that's where I am bound, save I stopped off.'

'What brings you here?' Dickon asked, while Fergus and others leaned forward like eager hounds, their faces blood-dyed by flames. Henry Rae, Berwick Pursuivant, did not like the look of them at all, but he was here for Will Elliot and reminded himself of the fact.

'I have been in Carlisle,' he said, 'and am now headed across to Berwick. The pestilential weather drove me here – and it was Lady Day, so I thought to avail myself of some legendary Netherby hospitality.'

'Granted,' Dickon declared expansively and nodded to a figure, who started pouring wine into horn cups.

'By God, Harry Ree,' Batty said wearily, 'you use that mooth of your like one of the hoors around Carlisle. If ye had wanted Lady Day and the dry and the warm, you'd have stayed in Carlisle, I am thinking.'

The Berwick Pursuivant bristled like a routed boar pig – but only for a moment. Then he forced a short laugh.

'I should have remembered you, Batty – you could start a fire in a closed white room.'

Then he turned to Dickon. 'I left the Whartons in Carlisle alternately raging and weeping over Batty here. They watched young Tom being buried not long since and they lay the blame for it at Batty's door – and the Grahams who helped him.'

'That's nae secret,' Fergus broke in. 'We have been keeping one eye cocked for anything they might do – but they got tangled up in the war and Maxwell's recent treachery gave Henry Wharton a sore neb.'

'He got out of it,' Henry Rae pointed out. 'Now they are doubly angered at Batty and his caterans having lifted yon Egyptiani dwarf out of the Carlisle prison.'

He paused, then looked daggers at Batty. 'I am told that Nebless Clem has been given Will Elliot back in exchange for ten hostages, who will be freed only if Clem brings Wharton someone he needs.'

'Rynion Elliot,' Batty put in, remembering what he had learned.

Henry Rae snorted derision. 'He can be a thorn up the arse of anyone he chooses, but Rynion of the Hill is not worth sheep droppings. If he fails to show up and be judged at a Truce Meet, someone will be found to fetch him.'

Batty waved a dismissive hand. No' me, he thought wearily. No' unless I play him at Primero for it.

'Naw, it is little to do with Rynion,' Henry Rae said flat and hard. 'It is for yerself. Wharton will hemp up Clem's men unless Clem brings you alive to Carlisle. You should have kept your auld heid low, Batty.'

That snapped Batty awake. Will Elliot would be of no use to Nebless Clem now that the Ape was gone and could not reveal the secrets of the Egyptiani winter lair. He said as much and Dickon nodded thoughtfully.

'He will dangle Will from The Scar tower and wait for you, Batty,' he said, waiting for an answer. When none came he frowned.

'There is a limit to what we can do,' he said and Batty nodded.

'As I said afore – it is not your fight, Dickon.'

'Aye but it may be,' Henry Rae put in, 'since Clem and ithers have been heard to say that, afore they go after Batty Coalhouse, they are coming to free the Lady of Blackscargil, back to the loving arms of her husband.'

'Did they say that?' Dickon replied mildly. 'Jesu, the lie in it – husband is he? Well, I have already put the question to Eliza Graham but I have no reason to doubt her word that no man of the cloth has set foot in Blackscargil since the Flood.'

He rubbed his face, blew out his cheeks. 'Besides – I ken Clem Selby. From a long time since when I had dealings with his da. They were coal-hewers, did ye ken that?'

He shook his head. 'A wee pick an' shovel boy from a shit-smear vill. He fled soon as he was able and took up the outlaw life – until he had enough men and gall to cozen Dand out of his tower.'

144

He shook his head again, his face showing amazement. 'Imagine it – a black-slathered wee thief raising himself to Laird. On what is rightfully Graham land. The presumption of it.'

As if Dickon was any better, Batty thought, but stayed quiet on it. Clem will come all the same, once Lady Day was done with, for he has his own obligations to that feast day. He muttered as much, feeling dark at his own lack of strength after climbing the winding stair of Netherby's tower.

'And we will be ready,' Dickon said tersely, then beamed. 'Until then, there is ale and beef and a great tart of rice and eggs. Go forth and enjoy it.'

'*Nunc dimittis servum tuum, Domine,*' Henry Rae answered, steepling his fingers.

–

There was beef and beer and bread – and the huge tart of rice and eggs, with fruit in it to make it even more tasty. There was cheese and wrinkled winter apples and as good fare as anything Fat Henry had enjoyed at his own feasts, or so everyone agreed.

The minister sat quiet in a corner, having done his duty in the procession of candles for the Purification of Mary – except that now it had to be Jesus in these reformed times – and keeping his eyes lowered on what the girls with their uncovered hair were getting up to in the shadows. There was music from drum and whistle and a singer who let loose with a thumping song which had gudewives tutting disapproval even as they wriggled in their seats at the words.

'When he had played unto her
One merry note or two,
Then was she so rejoiced
She knew not what to do;
"Oh, God a mercy, carman,
Thou art a lively lad;
Thou hast as rare a whistle
As ever carman had!"'

The minister tapped his toe to it until he realised and then shrank a little, since it was altogether too lusty. By the end of the evening he was flush-faced and thumping the table while, out in the muddy garth, a brace of Grahams set at each other with fists and feet, howled on by a crowd.

Batty slid off, his ears tortured and his head bursting with it. He was table-messed with the Lovat Frasers and did not think they noticed his place was empty, but he was wrong.

He went to the stable and Fiskie. He had a perfectly good bed, surrounded by the Frasers in the crowded confines of Netherby, but he preferred the quiet and Fiskie appreciated it – until Batty saddled him.

He was sitting with a horn lantern, working filched wax seals round the wadding and slow match of his *granado* when he became aware of a soft shuffling and a new set of dancing shadows. When he turned, all the Frasers were there.

'Unless you hate that beast,' Ewan said lightly, 'and want it to suffer all night with a saddle, I am thinking you are leaving.'

Batty worked the wax for a bit, then laid the black-leather flask to one side.

'Prudence,' he growled. 'Come the hour afore first light, I am thinking Dickon Graham will have word that the Selbys are on the move. He will move to ambush them if he can, keep them away from doing damage to Netherby.'

He picked up another of the flasks. 'If not this morning, then the next – but no later.'

'And you did not think fit to tell us?' John Dubh persisted. Batty sighed.

'You have done your duty as Wemyss saw it and paid for it. This is not your fight – you can go hame to yer wee bit glen and burn and take my warm thanks with you.'

'We canna do that,' Red Colin answered softly, bitterly and Ewan agreed.

'We ran, Batty. We are considered deid only because considering anything else is too much shame and hurt for those who have lost brothers and sons, husbands and lovers. Three hundred at least died – if I walked through the door of my auld home noo, it would break my ma's heart.'

Ewan fell silent, looking at the floor. Big Tam laid a meaty hand consolingly on his shoulder.

'So ye see,' John Dubh went on, 'we are tied to you like a wee dug to a blood pudding – besides, our contract was to see Will Elliot and yerself safe back to yon scorched wee fortalice. That's not yet done.'

'There might be death in it,' Batty said and Red Colin grunted a short, mirthless laugh.

'Nae might about it – but we are already deid, Batty. And I have heard how one of our ain hangs from yon tower, black and rotting. I am telt how Malcolm was still alive when it happened, but he was left to die in the rain and cauld.'

That would be spur enough, Batty thought, if they were not already slathered with the shame of their own running. Truth was he was glad they'd be with him and listened to them moving softly with creaking leather and the clink of bit and bridle, saddling up their own mounts.

They followed his example and left the girth loose, then sat and said little, listening to the wild music and shouts. None of them wished they were there, all the same, for if Batty was right the arriving morning would be no time for a bad head and bokking.

So they listened to him sing, so softly it wavered in and out of the carousing, until they dozed, waiting.

'She bathed him in the Lady-Well,
His wounds so deep and sair,
And she plaited a garland for his breast,
And a garland for his hair.'

Dickon had them routed out and back to the hall and Batty, stiff and shivering, felt the cold rain-wind as he sloshed across the wet garth to where Dickon, Fergus and the others were all gathered, festooned with arms, helmets in one hand. Batty felt fey, misted.

He had no idea what time it was, but it was likely to be this dark well into what would be morning. Dickon looked up and round them all.

'Watchers say the Selbys are on the move,' he began, 'hoping we have been heavy on the drink and feasting and can be taken unawares. The trail he is taking will take him ower the Newhope Water, which isna deep, but has steep sides and is too wide to hop a hobbler. The crossing everyone here knows well and we shall ride hard to be there first and catch them wet.'

'How many?' someone asked from the dim.

'A few score,' Dickon replied, 'all lanced and well mounted.'

Later, as more heidmen crowded in to hear how the Ride was to go down, the Frasers huddled round Batty and he could feel the nervous intensity of them like a heat, even above the fireplace where the ashes of the spitroast flames still trembled the air.

'I have nivver done anything like this,' Ewan breathed, in awe of what was happening, in awe of all the bearmen in their grim intensity and wargear. Batty hoped he would not ask about how it was, for the truth – as Batty was painfully aware – was that he had never been on a wild Border Ride either. In all the time he had been in these lands he had hunted solo, dragging men back for judgement on something they had done on such a Ride as this.

Dickon, his boots already muddy from the garth and no doubt wishing he hadn't worn his fur-trimmed cloak in the hall, laid it all out for them as he sweated.

This was not for stolen kine, nor loot. This was to stop the Selbys committing outrage on Netherby, revenge for the murder of Eliza's man and Clem Selby's treatment of a Graham woman. This was to seize and hold Blackscargil.

'When we put a cinch in the Selbys as they cross the water,' he went on, 'they will turn and flee. It will be oor job to run them away from Blackscargil. Fergus – it will be your job then to take your two-score and make for the tower with Batty and let him do what he does – blow in the doors and gain entry. There will be few men left to defend it and, once the entrance is breached, none will stand. We will have our rightful tower – and Will Elliot besides, for Clem will not bring him out on his Ride.'

Round-shouldered, bearded like a rampant badger, Fergus nodded his balding head. He was scarred on the left side of his face and had two fingers missing from the hand that clasped a horn cup of wine, tossing it down his neck in toast. 'Never forget,' they bawled and, out in the garth, the impatient men and fretting horses echoed it back.

Never forget. The cry of the Grahams – it even started Big Tam into growling until Ewan nudged sense into him.

'Aye, he is something is he not?'

They turned into the sweating beams of Jamie Graham, one of Fergus's men. 'Dinna be fooled by his gentle wit and jest,' he went on. 'He killed a Ker once just for spitting near him.'

The minister had been prevailed to bless the company and their endeavours and had stumbled through it twice, once in Latin and was aware that not only his mortal soul was endangered but the rest of his person in a devoutly Reformed England.

They rode out into the teeth of a wet wind, into a land blocked out by deep shadows each time the moon, like some naked virgin flitting from cover to cover, was shrouded.

Batty did not know where they were or where they were going after a while, but Fiskie followed the horse in front and everyone behind followed Batty, snaking in between slender trees which might have been real or the shadows of others, picking a way across the drenched tussocks; now Batty admired the skill of the reivers and how they found a way simply by knowing.

In the end, after too long a time, the horse in front of Batty stopped and backed up alongside him. Fergus leaned forward, thrusting his beard, the colour of burned fields, into Batty's eyeline.

'Here we hold and when we hear the stushie from our ambuscade, we head off to Scar Tower. I hope you have brought yer big baubles, Batty, or we may have trouble getting in the door.'

'I am never without my big baubles,' Batty replied and one of the Frasers laughed. Fergus simply nodded and moved his horse quietly to the man next to him and spoke, low and urgent.

'Whit noo?' Ewan demanded and Batty told him.

'Wait until told different.'

'We don't fight?' Red Colin asked, truculent and disappointed.

'We wait. Quietly. But dinna fash – there will be war enough even for you.'

–

They came down a narrow, steep gorge with a trickle of feeder stream that led to the Newhope Water. It was a darker slash on a grey-dim land and Clem stopped at the bottom of it, where the two streams merged.

He sat like some monarch at a review while the riders filtered down, lances unhitched, some with latchbows out and the breath of men and beasts smoking in short, hard gasps from effort and tension. It was cold and even under the mask, it bit into the rawness where Clem's nose had been.

About sixty men, Clem reckoned, with Bells and Charltons, Forsters and Robsons. Not as many as he would have liked, nor as many as he had requested, but enough for what was needed – revenge on the Netherby Grahams.

He remembered them from years ago at Auldshaws, when he was a boy and Dickon Graham just a youth, trying to exert himself in the eyes of his da. He had arrived with only eight men but needed no more – Auldshaws was a huddle of cruck houses, no more than a score. There were no fighting men here, but determined ones and with picks and shovels from where they dug out coal from the Pit.

War had washed over Auldshaws and, as the heidman tried to explain, it did not matter whether they were Scotch or English, they had looted, pillaged, raped, burned and robbed the place. Including the black rents.

Dickon had leaned on the front of his saddle, scowling. 'Including the rents?'

'Exactly so,' the heidman agreed mournfully.

'You should have hidden them better,' Dickon said and shot him. The boy watched from the shadows as his da flew backwards and the people moaned and drew back.

'Sort yourselves,' Dickon went on, 'elect a new heidman and when I return for the next rent, have it ready. You are nae use to me ither than for your blackmeal and a peck of poor coal.'

Clem stared into the darkness and saw his da being lifted up, lolling dead and dripping blood. It was then he had vowed to make the Grahams pay, but his life had been one of a thief and robber, a Broken Man relying on others he gathered up and dependent on none but themselves.

They'd had a long, hard life of it in the Debatable, but found a way to increase and some riches. Finding their way to auld Dand at Blackscargil had been a God-gift. The man had been a power in his day but it was long gone and his younger wife – a Graham from Netherby, no less – was clearly looking for a way out. While Dand snored, Clem took her on the table and was afraid at the end of the business, her intense silence and lack of any fear for him unnerving.

It was an unease redoubled when she brought up the thought on what to do with her husband and the idea that Clem, married on to her once she was free, would be master of Blackscargil.

By the time the old man was pitched off the roof, Clem had come to realise that he already had Blackscargil and did not need Eliza Graham. Still, he had not given her leave to go and wanted her back, as he wanted every one of his other possessions. She was a Graham and he had a savage longing to humiliate that Name.

The wind wheeped under the mask and into the hole in his face. He hated the mask because it did not let him wear a helmet properly, but he needed it because otherwise the cold caused him a shrieking ache and made him dribble, which revolted him.

Once done with this, he thought savagely, I will deal with the Egyptiani. Once done with this, I will have Eliza back where I want her and she will go on her knees and take the butt of my whip wherever I choose to place it. That reminded him of Batty Coalhouse, the one-armed man who seemed to have had even less fear in him than Eliza. Another Graham, he had since learned and wished he had known that at the time he'd strung him up. He'd have flayed the back off him and left him for crows.

He heard someone laugh as they passed him and snapped back to watching the trail of men crossing; the lead elements had heaved out the far side and fanned out, standing hipshot, talking in low tones. The others crowded down into the narrow ford, confident, without doubt; balked they waited patiently to move forward like a forest of lances.

The man nearest Clem gave a grunt and lolled sideways like a half-full bag of grain; the horse, annoyed by the imbalance, took two steps sideways to correct it and the man toppled off into the stream; the men nearest to him laughed.

Then another man gave a yelp and clutched his leg, a horse shrieked and Clem saw the fletchings of a big war arrow sticking from its neck; it collapsed on the muddy bank, kicking out more chaos. When the night was cracked open with the noise and flare of a caliver, he knew what was happening.

The dark erupted with bodies, most of them dismounted and screaming 'Never forget.' Clem heard the great bull bellow of Tam Forster, shouting 'Tarset and Tyne – to me' and he knew the Forsters were turning and running, knew that it was all rotted. He saw all his plans, all his dreams whirl off into the dark like wisps from a carding of wool.

He wrenched round the head of the hobby and beat a path through the frantic throng of his own panicked men, using the butt of the whip.

Up behind the trees, Batty heard the shouts and the shots, saw Fergus take the bridle of a horse nestled up to his own and yell out: 'Follow me, bonnie lads. Never forget.'

Then they were off and it wasn't until Fiskie, jostled and bumped to stumbling, caught the rear haunch of the horse Fergus was leading that he realised who as on it. The thump made the figure cry out and jerk, so that the hood fell back as she turned, angry and anguished.

Eliza Graham.

Chapter Eleven

Blackscargil tower

They rode, watching the moon get dressed and undressed by clouds. A fox squealed amorously and then, suddenly, they were circling some dark, dank ruins, hauling to a halt and looking down on the garth and the tower. The garth was surrounded by a tall timber stockade with walkways – there's where all the local timber went, bar one copse, Batty thought.

It was studded with buildings and, off to one side was the tall bulk of the tower itself, like the hunch on a twisted man's back; there was pale light spilling from the upper shutters. The garth walkways blazed with torch-light, flaring and flattening in the wind. They are on alert, Batty thought, and Fergus growled it out, tense and terse.

'They will see us, soon as we move. Sim, Buggerback, Richie fetch the ropes and climbing irons. Batty – get your wee baubles unfettered. When we go down, they will start a hullabaloo and shooting. We will gie back what we get, but the only way in is through yonder timber gate and that's your job, Master Coalhouse. If ye can do as ye boast.'

'Aye, aye,' Batty answered, less mild than he would have wished. 'Tell ye what, Fergus – I will keep yon wummin company here and you run down to the gate with a flask of black powder and a slow match.'

He felt the Frasers at his back, all wanting to know the one thing. Batty knew why she was there, but he asked just for the Frasers.

'She is to be put back like a dove in the nest,' Fergus said flatly. Then he raised his sword above his head and bellowed: 'Never forget' so hard it rang Batty's ears.

'Watch out for Will Elliot,' Batty shouted as the Grahams shrieked out of cover and spilled down, sliding horses almost to their haunches and then, as they neared the stockade, hurling themselves off and shooting bows and latchbows and the few calivers they had.

'He'll no' be in the garth,' John Dubh offered as they slithered towards the stockade. 'He'll be in yon accursed tower – Christ's blood, look you. You can see the cage where Malcom still dangles.'

'Are you well enough for this?' demanded Ewan Fraser and Batty scowled back at him. 'Your humours do not look good.'

'Physicker now are you? I have been slathered in the blood of Christ and drunk from the Grail,' Batty said, which was true enough if you believed. He had a momentary glimpse of a lined, seamed comfort of a face and hoped Sister Faith and her charges had found peace.

Ewan did not understand, but he nodded, reassured by Batty's vehemence. The Frasers formed a huddle round Batty and they went down to the timber gate and war.

It was a chaos of shouts and flying bolts, the odd arrow and the even more rare pistol or caliver blast, splitting the rising dawn with a brief, bright sun. Mostly, the defenders waved blades and shouted at the attackers who were waving blades and shouting back at them.

A shape lurched towards Batty and he hauled out the axe-butt dagg, knowing it was empty save for the priming

– but the man was Jamie Graham, panting out demands from Fergus while things hissed and spat in the dark.

'Ye are to blow the door, soon as ye like. Sooner, Fergus says.'

'Imagine,' Batty said, aiming for blithe calm and falling far short; it seemed to impress the Frasers, all the same, who grinned feral fangs at him. 'I had not considered that at all – run back and tell Fergus to get ready.'

He moved to the foot of the gate and felt himself struck on the back by something heavy enough to make him gasp at the blow and the fire it flared on his old wounds. He fell flat, felt a hand under his good armpit and was hauled up into the bright, mad grin of Red Colin.

'Aye to the fore,' he said, then indicated the lump of stone nearby. 'They are chucking stanes at us, Batty. I wid hurry.'

Batty got to the lee of the door, started to dig out the dirt at the foot of the double gate, where the slight gap showed the join. He saw a barrel poke through – someone with a caliver thinks I am trying to raise the bar. He stood up and stamped on the affair, heard the shriek as the butt slammed up into someone.

Then he unfettered the first of the black flasks from his waist and stuffed it in the hole he had made, scraping the dirt back over it, all save for the portion with the dangling fusse. Someone yelled from up above him and he risked a look to see a figure half-bent over the walkway, trying to get a decent aim with a latchbow.

Red Colin cursed. Big Tam picked up the stone thrown at Batty and hurled it up two-handed, so that it bounced on the sharpened point of one of the timbers, flew up close enough to make the man with the latchbow rear and lose his balance. He gave a short, pungent curse as he toppled over the parapet and fell with a sickening wet thud into the clotted earth near where Batty crouched; the stone hovered in the air for a moment, then arced back down and struck Big Tam between neck and shoulder, a sickening crack that let Batty know something had broken.

The man who had fallen moved and moaned, so Batty found Brother Curve from his family of daggers and slit his throat with it. Then he stuffed it back in its sheath, hauled out the axe-butt dagg, pressed the trigger and watched the wheel spark and flare on his slow match. He blew it to a soft sputter of orange embers and started to scuttle away, round to the left, to the lee of the other timbers.

He saw Red Colin hauling Big Tam by the shoulders, but he was a dead weight and Colin wasn't strong enough. He struggled, inch by inch, a man's length from the middle of the gate.

'Leave him,' Batty urged, seeing the horror that would unfold. 'Get tae cover man…'

'Almost there,' Colin gasped and Batty should have gone to him, should have helped, but the slow match itch was all over him and he knew there was no time.

'Drop him and run…' he bawled.

He knew Colin would never run, not ever – not again. The flask blew with a harsh, coughing roar. Blew the doors wide open, blew a slew of sharp metal inward – and some back out, despite Batty's attempts to minimise that with the covering of dirt.

Red Colin seemed to jerk, rise up like he wanted to fly. He gave a long shriek and fell on Big Tam; the next moment they disappeared from view amid a storm of bodies, all stamping and shrieking their way into the garth.

Ewan and John Dubh elbowed into them, then stood like a breakwater on the tide, two big men with scowls and big swords; the Grahams slid right and left of them, then suddenly were gone.

Batty got to the fallen pair, but it was clear both were dead – Red Colin had part of an old door hinge in one cheek, something else buried in his chest and a peppering of nails and worse all over his back where he had tried to shield Big Tam.

Tam looked untouched, until you saw how his head was cocked at a strange angle; the stone which had rebounded on him and cracked his neck and his life, so he was already dead when Colin had started dragging him to safety. There was something witchy and strange about it all – a man killed by his own thrown stone and another killed while saving a dead man? God and the De'il, Batty thought morosely, who rule the world turn and turn about and nobody notices the difference.

Ewan and John Dubh stared and said nothing. Neither did Batty – what could you say? What could you do? There were other ragdoll shapes lying around, all of them Grahams felled while waiting for Batty to let them through the timber gate. Beware of war and witches Batty had been told more than once; it was all too late for that now.

'Will you wait with them?' Ewan asked John Dubh. 'Make sure anything of value remains with us. When this is done with, we will kist them up along with Malcolm.'

John Dubh nodded. Ewan looked at Batty. 'There is one more door to blow open.'

They went into the garth, stepping over the litter of splintered wood and another body torn to shreds by Batty's metal; the wee man wi' the caliver, Batty thought, who shoved it through the door gap and tried to shoot me. His ma would not know him now.

The garth, studded with buildings, shadows in the rising dawn, boiled with people and shouts and one of the loudest came from a big man, helmet off so folk could see and hear him better; he had black hair like crow wings.

'Buggerback, ya moudiewart bastard – drag that smoulder out of the thatch afore it catches. This is Graham land now – do not burn, rape or loot anything or you will find yer neck in a cinch. And spread the word lads – the heidman wants nae black flag here. Nae black flag – d'ye hear? Round up The Scar's people and guard them – but nae deaths.'

Fergus appeared, still mounted and dragging the bridle of Eliza's hobby. He grinned down at Batty and nodded admiringly to the red-head.

'By God Pate's Davey is fine, though is he not? What d'ye think Eliza?'

Batty thought she looked scared witless, but she sat, pale as winter and said nothing while Fergus snarled in what he thought was winsome at her.

'Consider him well,' Fergus said, 'for this will be your new man when the smoke has cleared from here.'

He leaned forward so that Batty could barely hear the next. 'If he catches as much as the snotters, or falls off a low stool, ye will find Dickon less accommodating to your tale of it.'

He glanced down and seemed surprised to see Batty and Ewan there. 'Get on, Master Coalhouse. We need the tower as well.'

When Batty and Ewan crouch-walked, looking warily around, they could hear shouts and shots, but just from around the tower – the rest of Blackscargil was cowed.

To the left, Batty saw shapes darting back and forth, aiming big warbows and latchbows to keep the defenders on the roof from firing. There was at least one caliver up there and the men on the ground would not stand still to be shot.

They had to provide cover for the hookmen, who had three-pronged *grappin* tied to long ropes; the whirling of them sounded like some huge unseen bird flying hard through the night on a hunt.

It was a long throw and most of the attempts clattered off and fell back, the throwers dodging backwards because they could not see in the poor light. One or two of the hooks had lodged and the arrows and bolts from below were to stop the defenders leaning out and cutting the rope free. Still, Batty thought, I widna be daft enough to skin up that even if I had two arms.

Instead, while Ewan put his head on a swivel and his big two-hander on guard, Batty knelt by the door. He knew, from the first time he had passed through, that there was an outer wooden door, well fitted and thick, studded with nails to thwart axes. Immediately behind it was a metal grille that slotted spikes into holes in the floor. It wasn't all that thick, but good enough to thwart any who had exhausted themselves beating through the outer door.

'Ewan – fetch me the sacks from that cart there.'

Ewan stuck his sword in the scuffed earth and did as he was asked; the sacks were heavy with winter feed, made worse because they had been carelessly left and were soaked. He brought them and placed them as Batty directed, then Ewan watched him burrow between them and the door with his last two black flasks.

He realised the sacks were to direct the blast inwards and soak up some of the spray of metal which would go out, so that there would be no repeat of the tragedy at the gate; he thought of Red Colin and Big Tam, of Malcom hanging on the basket. Slowly, bit by bit, God was snipping the last threads from the hem...

'Get in behind me,' Batty yelled and Ewan realised the match had been lit; he scurried to obey while the men hurled their little anchors like the thrum of wind in the ratlines. Something flared from the top of the tower and Ewan flinched, but it was the caliver and no-one screamed, so it had missed.

He realised he had left the two-hander and started back for it, only to be hauled up short by Batty's strong hand.

'Leave it. Use a knife. If you are lacking one, I can lend you one of the Brothers.'

'I have another decent sword,' Ewan said, appalled at what he had been about to do. Batty looked dubious but said nothing.

The flasks detonated, almost together and Batty's face was a rictus of smile in the sudden flare and bang. No match wi' a slow match...

The sacks shredded and blew back, but the effect was enough. Ewan heard the crunching ruin of timber and the shriek of stressed metal and, when Batty moved, he followed.

Batty kicked at ruined planks; Ewan tore at them and then they saw the metal yett, leaning drunkenly to one side. Beyond it, two bodies writhed and there was blood on the stair, dark and viscous in the sconce light.

'Never forget,' Batty howled and the cry was echoed; suddenly, Ewan was being elbowed to one side by snarling, wide-mouthed men with vengeful steel, who battered through the remains of the timber and flattened the yett to the floor in a shriek of tortured, broken hinges.

Batty watched them go with a jaundiced eye and caught Ewan's sleeve as he made to follow.

'Will Elliot,' he said. 'Let's find him afore these wolves bite him as well as everyone else.'

The noise woke him and, for a moment, he thought he had fallen asleep in his chair in Hermitage and was appalled enough to scramble upright. There was a faint flicker of light from the dying crusie, one of the luxuries he had been given but only as long as the reeking fish oil in it lasted.

But the wall it hung on was a damp mould, slick with running water and the cold sluiced him so that he shivered. He heard shouts and what seemed to be the ringing of bells, then worked out it was steel on steel; there was a fight going on.

He had a wide bowl of water, the second luxury he'd been permitted and he went to it, aware that it was too heavy to lift and that he'd have to lap from it like a hound. Which was part of the humiliation, he thought.

When he bent to it, an apparition goggled back at him in the poor light, a floating face with a ragged beard and matted hair, lips chapped and braided to a tight line, cheeks clapped in, the eyes like small creatures hiding in the caves of the face.

He lurched upright and staggered on his ruined feet, stretching out one hand to steady himself on the slick wall. If he stood as straight as he could, he could reach out the other hand and feel the opposite wall with his fingertips.

'Will Elliot,' he screamed. 'Will Elliot.'

There was no answer, not even an echo; the mouldy walls sucked up the sound and he had expected no less

– but he did it every so often so that he heard the sound of his own name, hurling itself at the black stones, the door, to remind himself that he had once been Land Sergeant at Hermitage, second to the Keeper of Liddesdale, later Steward to Lord Sandilands in Fife.

He grew angry and lashed out a kick, then recoiled in horror at the sick pain of stubbing his foot. There were toes missing there, but the pain came from the instep, driven through by a sadist with a two-handed blade; the other foot was the same.

He had called on God and all the saints he could recall but now he knew the bitter truth. We live in ignorance, make up stories to find sense, to make the thunder the wrath of a falling angel, to make the sunrise a gift from a deity to brighten our lives and take us from darkness. We tell ourselves stories that make us the centre of everything, invent knowledge to prove it. It is all noise and flummery. I have let God go…

–

Batty led the way up the wind of stairs, stepping over the first lolling body just inside the ripped-open doors; the man wore only a doublet so the spray of metal from the blast had shredded him to bloody pats; one of the enemy, Batty decided, since all the Grahams wore jack of plates and had helmets.

There was another further up and round – another defender, it seemed, run through the body and leaking little rivulets down the steps. Up yet again was a door to the left, covered only with a brocade curtain against the draughts. It should have been torn free to allow anyone coming up to see in and it let Batty know the bitter truth

– none of the Graham men were thinking, only charging for the topmost room and killing anyone in their way.

'Watch right and left,' Batty warned and Ewan nodded, then moved to the curtain and tore it free; Batty snaked in to the room, going left so his good hand with its length of steel was ready.

It was empty, windowless, with a trestle table and benches, a cold brazier with a scuttle of coals next to it and a nightpot, which Ewan stumbled into. While he cursed, Batty decided that this was the neat warm cubby of the luckless two outside, the doorwards.

They came out and went on up to where the noise was greatest, a snarl of shouts and clanging metal, shrieks and pleas.

Another doorway, this with a plank door set in it on leather hinges. Batty nodded to Ewan, who ostentatiously shook his piss-wet foot and scowled – then booted the door.

It flew open and – nothing happened. Ewan took a step forward, planning to shoulder the door fully open and a length of steel whicked out, making him rear back with a yelp. Batty had been waiting for something like it and he struck the blade, hard, with his own; the clang of it seemed deafening and the blow clearly affected the unseen swordsman, for he gave a curse and drew back his arm.

Batty put his armless shoulder to the door and pushed – again the steel flicked out, this time with a gauntleted hand in the basket-worked hilt. Batty could not get his own sword into play and roared his frustration out.

Ewan grabbed the gauntleted wrist of the man and hauled hard. There was a grunt and a crash as the man was pulled off balance and struck the door, slamming it almost shut on his own arm at the elbow. The sword fell free and Ewan, snarling viciously, relaxed and hauled again, slamming the man into the door again. And again.

Batty took the chance to sheath his sword and haul out the axe-handled dagg; it was empty as a Monday morning church, but Batty wanted the axe end of it.

He shouldered the door again and this time there was no resistance, since Ewan had let the arm go. They piled in, to see a man flailing on the floor, growling and snoring hard through a battered face, broken and bloodied by repeatedly meeting the door.

He was scrambling upright, but Batty gave him no chance; he moved in, stamping on the front foot, slashing with the axe while the man scrabbled away, raising one hand as if it was a shield. It was not; Batty slashed ruin into it, making the man howl and curl up.

He was aware of Ewan on his right side, sword poised to stab – there was no room to use the slashing edge in the room – but hesitating. Batty did not. He knew the man, had seen the lard bulk of him, the thin hair plastered to his scalp. Mickle Anthone, Clem's right-hand man; he brought the axe down hard, hard as a man leaning into making blows with a whip, aiming for the head and falling short by a foot at least.

He only stopped when he ran out of breath and stood, axe dangling bloodily in one fist, half bent over. His heavy head swung all of a piece towards Ewan, who thought he looked like a panting bull about to charge.

Batty wanted to excuse himself, wanted to say how hesitation would kill you in a business as hot as this, but he knew it was a lie and was shamed of having beaten the man to seeming death, even if it was Mickle Anthone. In the dim light of a reeking crusie the man's blood moved sluggishly out from under his head and chest like a black lake.

Ewan stared, unable to speak and call Batty a bloody-handed killer, though he knew it was the truth. Knew also that it had always been so and it should have come as no surprise after all this time.

'Will Elliot. Will Elliot.'

The muffled shout broke the moment and Batty squinted for the location. Ewan pointed to the dark shadows further into the room and Batty now saw that it was no more than another porter's room, windowless and sparse – but this one was for the gaoler and the cell lay beyond.

'Will Elliot...'

The bellow was wavering, the door was barred by a single balk on their side, so Ewan lifted it free, while Batty stuffed the dagg in his belt, took the crusie and stuck his head and the lamp into the cell.

He saw an apparition, squinting against the scarring of the light, a mad-bearded figure running with tears and shuffling forwards like a sleepwalker.

'Will Elliot,' he said and the relief he felt, the great rush of emotion almost made him drop the lamp.

'Batty Coalhouse,' Will said hoarsely, stumbling out of the cell. 'It's always you.'

Batty gave him a weary glance. 'You're welcome.'

–

Someone shouted and a horn blew – our turn, Batty thought. Get them off the fortifications of the Prato Gate or they will take it and Florence will fall. He got up and started moving through the smoke which was an oiled smear that made the world into charcoal and slate. He caught sight of Fernan Lippe, his face like flour paste, his mouth a dark knife slice.

'Black flag.'

Batty heard it; everyone heard it and it seemed to leap from head to head and chilled to the marrow. Black flag. No quarter. Now the affair would be to fight or die.

'That isn't right,' Batty said, but Buonarotti was gone to the foot of a scaling ladder and climbing like a mad monkey, slathered with hatred for those who dared climb all over his creation.

Batty started to follow, heard the clatter as something landed, saw the little black ball of it career and roll. Knew what it was.

He hurled himself down, turning away to put his back to it — there was a loud bang and a sudden slather of pain and then oblivion…

—

He surfaced like something crawling out of an old barrow and when he opened his rheumy eyes it was to meet the pinch-lipped face of Jinet, scowling back at him. This was not Florence, then…

'I warned ye,' she said. 'Dinna exert yerself or suffer the bad cess of it.'

'Ye did,' Batty managed to mumble. 'How bad is the cess?'

She told him and it was bad enough. Some of the whip-scars had opened up and leaked. They needed stitching and she made it clear that hers was a perjink hand for hems and darning socks, but she was no clever doctor. He was also running a fever and, in answer to the question he had not asked — long enough to miss a wedding and a wheen of funerals.

'And every time I see you now it is efter you have been carted back like a bag of dung and dumped,' she added, then her frown looked forged. 'This time, though, there were black flags in it.'

He saw she was concerned about the idea of no quarter having been called on Blackscargil, but Batty put her right on it, so she eased the arrow between her brows, though a smile was nowhere close, he saw.

He lay one one side, feeling the heat on his back and thinking on the bastion at the Porto Gate. Black flag. He had not heard that term in an age or two and it bothered him how trivial things unleashed the blocked drain of his memories.

She bustled out and when she came it was with a bowl of broth, a hunk of bread and Dickon, looking fierce as as a Turk.

'You should be rolling sweat and dying of wound fevers,' she said and he thought she sounded disappointed.

'I drank from the Grail,' he answered and she looked uneasy at that and finally counted it as simple blasphemy.

'Ye missed the wedding,' he said brusquely.

'I was not in the mood for dancing – I take it Eliza is now a perjink wife.'

I hope, he added to himself, the new husband knows what he has taken on…

Dickon perched on a stool and stroked his curve of beard. 'Patey's Davey is now Master of Blackscargil, but we missed Nebless Clem,' he said sorrowfully. 'Chased the Forsters and Charltons back to Hell, but missed Clem.'

'He'll be back,' Batty warned and Dickon nodded.

'He'll be back to being the moss trooper he was before, a man broken from his Name and roistering up and down the gorse and whin with a band of other scabby bastards, hiding out on the wastes and calling themselves "Clem's Bairns" or "The De'il's Ain".'

Clem wouldn't like that, Batty thought, but had another, more pressing question.

'How is Will Elliot?'

'Better than yerself, limping ower the garth and making himself a nuisance and scaring the weans with dire mutterings about nothing anyone can see sense in.'

He shifted his weight and levered himself off the stool. 'I will send men with you and Will to Berwick. After that you are on your own – that's my thanks for your work with the *granados*. If it hadna been for them we would never have got through any of the gates. The good news is that the ride to Berwick should be soft as baby hair – the war is done with. Everyone has sealed an end to it.'

He stayed for a while longer, walking and waving his arms as he gave out what details he knew of the end of the war. Wharton's reward for all his cunning was to be removed as Warden of the East March, replaced by his old rival Dacre – but he remained as Governor of Carlisle and commissioner for the division of the Debatable Land. The Seymours were finished and now Dudley, Earl of Warwick was Lord Protector, mainly because of how he had handled rebellion in Norfolk the year before.

Batty wished Wharton fortune in the task of dividing the Debatable, since neither country had ever wanted responsibility for it. Dickon eventually left when the Frasers arrived. What's left of the Frasers, Batty corrected and felt bad for not having attended the kisting of Malcolm and Red Colin and Big Tam. He said as much and had a sombre nod from Ewan.

'Nae matter – you were not yourself. The task is done and they are gone to their Maker as perjink and proper *léine-chneis.*'

Batty knew that the personal household warriors were known as *léine-chneis* – 'the shirt next to the skin' – of the chieftain. Men who would die for him, stand in the way of a blade or a ball. He remembered Red Colin, tugging and panting – just anither minute.

Now Ewan and John Dubh were all that was left. 'What will you do now?' Batty asked.

'See you safe hame with Will Elliot,' John Dubh said.

'Then go back to the glens and kill MacDonalds,' Ewan added.

Batty felt a weariness that had little to do with his fever. 'Do you hate that much?' he asked. 'Is there true injustice in what they did? Is that the truth?'

Ewan stroked his beard – worked to a neat point, Batty saw. Like Dickon. Or even myself, he thought suddenly.

'Aye, they will say they were defending their wee bit glen and chieftains as were we,' he said slowly, 'but when injustice wears the same MacDonald face, you make connections, do you not? It is not truth. It is a muddy field strewn with the Fraser dead. It is simply how the heart works.'

John Dubh came forward with a bundle wrapped in Batty's cloak. 'You of all should know the justice in revenge,' he said, then laid the bundle on the truckle bed.

'When they stripped the jack and shirt away, it was a marvel that all the belly you had was not belly at all. You have been reduced Master Coalhouse.'

Batty knew well enough how much fat he had shed in sweat and pain, but when he twitched back the cloak he saw what had replaced it under the jack – a scarred leather bag of coin, remains of the ransom. A rickle of wool and sticks. Sausage-shaped wraps of prime corned pistol powder. A spare serk, no cleaner than the one he wore. He had not realised the room he had found inside the jack had been because of his own shrinkage.

'Yer waist is like the cheeks of the squirrel,' John Dubh said and laughed.

'At first light we leave for Newark,' Batty said. 'Make sure you and Will Elliot are ready.'

He seemed suddenly awake and alert and Ewan remembered the strange claim that he had drunk from the Grail. He could believe it was true of Batty Coalhouse. He and John Dubh left, trailed by the soft, sinister fingers of Batty's singing.

'She bathed him in the Lady-Well,
His wounds so deep and sair,
And she plaited a garland for his breast,
And a garland for his hair.'

Chapter Twelve

Kershope, the next day

The earth was mottled with new green forcing up through the yellow wither and patched snow, the trees still bare as poor hair; along the gills and burns the reeds whispered and the willows clacked bare branches like wry applause. A fish jumped ripples into the Kershope Burn.

Hen Graham of the Mote led the way, with twenty riders coddling Batty, Will and the Frasers like swaddling round a bairn. It came as a shock of unease when Batty called a halt at the Kershope water.

'We will cross here and make our way to Hermitage,' Batty said. Hen Graham looked astonished.

'You pass within a spit of Canobie, in the Debatable which is full of the Armstrongs who hate you.'

'The Armstrongs are everywhere,' Batty pointed out, 'and where you lead us has Charltons and Forsters and Dodds, not forgetting that dark nightshade that is Clem Selby. His nose is the only good part of him.'

'I was tasked to take you close to Berwick,' Hen persisted stubbornly and Batty laid his hand on the man's arm.

'Keep riding for a night and a day,' he said, 'so that those who follow think you still have your charges. That will give us a chance.'

Hen did not care for it, nor the idea that he was being followed, though it should have come as little surprise. Most of all, he did not like having to go back to Dickon and tell him Batty had gone off on his own He watched the four men urge their horses into the shallow black slide of Kershope Burn, picking a way across the rocks which made the water gurgle about how it wanted to be ice; he did not like the idea of being followed and, without Batty and the others, felt suddenly naked.

In a few short strides Batty and the others were in Scotland, where Batty turned and raised his hand in a last greeting. Hen Graham returned it and then they rode their separate ways. Batty watched them go, feeling like the last untainted butter spread too thin on bread. Feeling like he was under all eyes.

He and the others rode generally east with a little north in it to keep them off the rutted trackway up alongside the stream. It started to rain, so Batty put on his horse-cloak to cover the saddle-holsters as much as himself, keeping the daggs dry. He took off his helmet, because the pattering robbed him of all other hearing.

It was that and his constant, slow deerlike scanning that made Ewan ask whose lands these were. Batty, peeled off his slit bunnet, scrubbed rain off his beard and looked around.

'Armstrong in the main. One or twa' wee folk – Littles and Bourne and the like. Hendersons, who pay black-meal to everyone else just to live in peace. If you squint hard with good eyes you might see a wee rickle of hill. That is Tinnis, the Faerie hill and cuddled at its foot is Powrieburn.'

'We will not be going there,' Will said determinedly. Batty glanced at him.

'D'ye think of her still?'

'Only every day,' Will whispered. 'And I will not go there.'

Neither Ewan nor John Dubh knew exactly what the exchange meant, but there was such a sense of loss in Will's words that they both decided it had to do with an auld love. They also recalled something mentioned, in a darker way, about Powrieburn and Faerie and curses.

Curses they knew well enough; Ewan remembered when the Lovat Frasers had left their homes to fight, encouraged by the shrill of women, the screams and whoops of bairns – and the clapping hands. Always that fierce rhythm when the clan women raged or lamented – or cursed. That time it had been curses which raised the hackles on Ewan and the others, for none of them had heard the like before. He had asked Auld Coull, who looked paler than death, what it meant.

'Means? It means the wives of the glen are cursing and banning the enemies of Lovat, wishing ill-luck to them. I have heard wives flyte in England and Scotland and even heard the Egyptiani, who have mastered the foul art of it, so it's nae marvel to me to hear it. But the ill-scathe tongues of they witches, wi' their gruesome demands that men should be slaughtered like sheep and that they may dip their hands to the elbows in the heart's blood of MacDonalds… it makes me feart and sick and they are on our side.'

It had been a seal on them, Ewan thought and though meant for the enemy, had somehow rebounded. Which is the nature of curses and witches. He remembered that he had made his escape by dragging the bloody remains of Coull on top of him as vengeful, uncursed MacDonalds prowled.

They came up on a huddle of three buildings seemingly crouching in the lee of a wood. Batty stopped and eyed it carefully; the others did the same, looking for smoke, signs of horses. There was nothing and John Dubh said so.

'There is thatch,' Batty pointed out, which did not make any sense to Ewan and John, but when they rode closer they saw the walls had a strange texture about them, were mottled like a collie dog. Batty put them straight.

'This is Redmoss, hame to Tam's Davey Little and his father before that. It has been burned out so many times the stones has turned like bone and you canna get the char out.'

He squinted carefully as he levered himself off Fiskie and then waved to Ewan to go inside and take a look.

'I ken the place,' Will said, slithering awkwardly off his own mount. 'Each time, the Littles would come back, fix the lost beams, fix the thatch and start ploughing.'

'They raised sheep,' Batty added, 'and could always rely on one or two of the clever yins running into the woods, to be rounded up again.'

John Dubh wondered at how resolute you would have to be to keep coming back after every raid burned you out and he said as much as Ewan ducked back out of the low door, spat and looked up at Batty.

'A man, a quine and two bairns. Deid a month I would jalouse. Not a mark on them...'

Batty went in, blinking at the transition from light to dim. He peered until he found rags and an old spurtle, made a torch and managed to get his firestarter on it. Once lit, he held it up so he could see better, envying Ewan for being able to see all he did in what was near pitch to Batty.

A man, a woman and two bairns, the man in a seat, the woman on a truckle bed with the bairns in either arm. They were gone to leather and sinew like rope, wisps of hair.

'Whit slew them?' John Dubh demanded, peering over Batty's shoulder. Batty heard the fear of disease in his voice, so he lied about what had killed them.

'Hunger,' he said and saw the pot with a few scrapes of withered boiled grass and roots. Saw the window shutters covered with blankets, to keep it dark enough to fool the bairns into sleeping and not wanting food. Saw the bow at the feet of the man.

'The whole of the country will be like this, worse along the dales and moss now,' Will said. 'The Border has been shaken loose.'

'Not a good death,' Ewan muttered. 'We are not staying here, surely.'

Batty agreed. He knew disease had a part in what had happened here, because the family had not tried to flee. It looked as if the man had come back – hunting, if the bow was any guide – seen the death of his wife and bairns and had simply sat down and waited for his own last breath.

'Or the Sweats,' Will put in darkly. 'Or the Bloody Flux.'

'Cheer us why don't you?' John Dubh flung back and ducked out into the drizzle.

'This land is cursed,' Ewan said, hunching in to the wet. 'Witches…'

Batty had no answer that would be a soothe, especially with night coming on. He had seen a witch, once, out in the Italies when he still had two arms and marched with Maramaldo. They were on some rutted trail, in wet such as this, slogging under dull grey lowering skies, shackled to guns and carts.

On the third day he saw the witch. 'Trailing her rags across the sky,' he said excitedly to the others. 'Her hair all wild and looking like snakes. Cursing, she were.'

The others all stared and then at Hordle Billy who led them. He looked at the priest, which no-one cared to see; Hordle Billy was in charge of five good men and shouldn't be seeming to ask a priest what to do, but old habits died hard. Back in his home town, Priest sat at the right hand of God and this one had more about him than most; this one was called Wilibald and had once led pilgrims to the Compostella shrine.

Witches was the province of priests, all the same and even those who doubted me, Batty remembered, had heard tales of a devil dragged out of the river two days from where they'd once lived, caught in fishing nets. The fisherman had beat the black, frog-thing until it squealed, but it tore free and ran off before they could kill it.

So witches was possible, Batty thought. If nothing else, the weather was hagged, for as the dark slid in the rain slid out, leaving the stealth of cold and a fat, gibbous moon. Riding weather, Batty thought, if it was the season for it – but everything was thrown into the air now that the war with England and France and Scotland was done. The Border had been shaken loose and everything was flying...

'That is what war is,' Will muttered, the first coherent thing he had offered since Redmoss. In truth, Batty was concerned about Will, who rode like a half-empty bag of grain and muttered about his soul, the world's soul, redemption and such.

'What is?' John Dubh asked and Will told him. That war always falls on the little people while those fighting it went about their business of glory and plunder.

Batty hunched up and shut his ears to it. He knew the truth of soldiers in war, which Will had never experienced for all his time as Land Sergeant at Hermitage. A few hot trods, the wild gallop across moss and whin in pursuit of people who only wanted to flee to the safety of the Debatable was not war. Will had fought once or twice and suffered injuries, which was not war.

Batty knew war. It was all he knew, he realised. He knew the fighters did not tally glory with their deaths; they died crying in their minds like bairns. They forgot why they were fighting, the causes they were dying for and died yearning for the face of a friend so they would not be alone doing it. They died whimpering for the voice of a mother, with their hearts sick for one more walk on the rutted track to the home where they were born, please God, just one more look. They died angry at the injustice of it being them and if they were truly blessed by God, they died faster than it took for them to say 'fuck' in that surprised way.

They knew what was important. They knew that life was everything and they died with screams and sobs at the one real and constant thought – I want to live I want to live I want to live.

They say if I had one foot in Paradise I would remove it to join war on earth, Batty thought. The truth is that Heaven will not drag the other foot out of the gore and let me in. War is all I know. If you tally up my life so far you will find a sorry list. Friends – few and usually tavern keeps or folk I owe money. Wife – none. Bairns – none he knew about. Prospects – none.

All he said aloud was: 'We will push on to Mickledale. It lies on a hill and folk have been there since God was a boy.'

'If they are watchful,' Will replied, 'then they will not let us in.'

Batty leaned in towards him a little. 'If you have no cheer to offer, offer nothing. These men around you risked life and limb to free you and return you to safety and you have done little else but grumble over it.'

Will nodded soberly. 'Yet you are in it, Batty, and every rescue you have ever done for me makes me worse than before.'

'Away wi' ye, ye ungrateful spalpeen,' Ewan spat. 'D'ye hear yerself? Every rescue Batty has ever done? What does that tell ye, Will Elliot?'

'Let us keep quiet and keep riding,' Batty said softly, so they did though the tension coiled like a hanging noose.

They made about twenty minutes before John Dubh called attention to the glow in the distance, though even Batty had seen it and his eyes, he was the first to admit, were not as they had once been. It was right where Mickledale should be.

'There,' Batty said and because it was almost too dark to see his point, he told them. 'The trees to the right. Move in and keep your mounts quiet.'

'Who would raid in this season?' Will demanded, almost outraged. 'There's nothing to be had from it.'

Aye, Will, you have forgotten nothing of your time in Hermitage, the guardhouse of the Liddesdale. This is the season where cattle are too lean and horses too out of condition. There is nothing to be had from a mad raid at this time of year save savagery and spite.

The riders were silhouetted against the moon for an eyeblink each as they passed, with no word and no noise save for the creak of leather and the shuffle of hooves. When they were gone, Batty let out his breath; there had been a score of them and that was a score too many.

Will stared at the flickering glow and mourned bitterly. 'Oh burn the house. You've murdered the husband, slaughtered the cattle, poisoned the well, raped the mother, killed the child – you must burn the house. It's mustard to your sausage. You are the bold riders of the Border, you must do your duty. Burn the house. Burn the fields. Burn the water…'

'Hist on that,' Batty snapped. 'There was enough burning of the water when Fat Henry was alive to demand it. The Border does not need you.'

'It does not need you nor the likes of you,' Will countered and it wasn't anger, just wistful and bleak. Batty ignored him, irritated – but he was right enough. The steading was a solid wee bastel house with a slate roof, the garth no more than a waist-high drystone dyke and the other buildings roughly made, with thatched roofs that had been fired by the raiders.

A milk cow lay with its legs stuck out like discarded bagpipes, a child sprawled, a wee rag doll in the blood-muddied garth, naked next to a dog shot by a latchbow. The reivers had run the wee milk cow through with lances and had stripped the place bare of anything small and portable, taking no cattle nor useful goods as was normal.

The main door of the bastel lay open, as did the iron yett behind it and John Dubh went inside like the vengeance of the Archangel, though no enemies were to be found. Instead, he came back spitting the foul from his mouth as he told them of the man sprawled in the undercroft, his wife upstairs, two other servant women and a youth, maybe the son, scattered and ill-used on both floors.

'The bairn heard the dog being badly treated and ran out to save it,' Will said, reading the sad tale of it in the mud and blood. 'She left the doors open and that was all that was needed.'

'This was not done for gain as I have heard it,' Ewan said. 'This was for sport and badness. Who would run a milk cow through with lances?'

They prowled, looking for stragglers and finding nothing but death – and worse. When Batty slithered stiffly off the back of Fiskie and went to the bairn he knelt and then straightened and spat to one side. He looked at the others, who went closer.

It had been a pretty girl, no more than ten years in the world before she had been stripped of her nightdress and the lash had ribboned her naked back open. The others were already too dead to be a sick joy for the man who had done it, but Batty knew him. They all did.

'Clem Selby,' John Dubh breathed and Batty's back seemed to flare at the sound of the name, each stripe like a new fiery brand. Ewan shivered all the same; the Selby men had passed close enough to be touched...

They put their horses in the stalls, leaving one empty. They struggled the bodies down to the undercroft and laid them in the empty stall, brought the dog in as well and laid it next to the girl. Will covered the naked, torn body with a ragged horse-blanket and sat for a while next to it.

The others went upstairs, found the cloth-covered jug of milk, the last squeezed from the cow before it was used for lance practice. They found oats and barley – too little of both which showed how the family would have faced a hard time if a harder time had not come to them in the night. There was cabbage and a hard, pale cheese, so with all that and a fire in the hearth, Batty got himself a full belly and a measure of sleep.

The morning came up on the plateau, showing where the old fort had once been, now no more than the mark of an overgrown ditch and some stones. Ploughing had cut away the rest of it and the road up to the house had sliced part of the old circle of ditch, making it look like a horseshoe.

Batty saw all this from the roof, cloaked against the chill but watching the riders come up. Eight men, with lances and helmets.

'Is it Nebless Clem?' Ewan called up and Batty came slowly down the ladder to join him.

'I suspect Armstrongs out of Whithaugh, since it is closest.'

Since they held Batty as an enemy, it was little comfort and Ewan said so. John Dubh merely laughed; he was in Purgatory and he knew it and Batty Coalhouse, with his beak nose and his bearded chin rising to meet it, fat-bellied, one-armed, and moving like a dung heap that had learned to walk, was one of the bigger imps in it.

'There are people,' Will said, 'who are born to rub others up the wong way; Batty Coalhouse was born to rub the whole world up the wrong way.'

Batty merely grunted and moved to one of the slit windows and unshuttered it. When someone called out 'Ho, the hoose,' he responded almost at once.

'Ho back at you. Who comes here?'

There was a pause. 'Is that Johnnie Little?'

'It is not,' Batty said, flat and loud. 'He is dead and his entire family with him, servants and all. Who are you who asks?'

There was a longer pause, with low muttering in it but Batty did not think any of the riders were surprised.

'Maurie Armstrong of Whithaugh,' the man shouted back, 'sent by the heidman to find out what occurs here. Come out.'

'We did not do this. Nebless Clem did this and left the youngest girl flayed by his whip. She is laid in the undercroft.'

Mutterings, which made it clear the riders were unconvinced.

'Who are you then?'

Batty sighed. 'Batty Coalhouse, escorting Will Elliot, former Land Sergeant of Hermitage, back to his home.'

It did no harm to lay out Will's old standing; Hermitage was a hard, short gallop away, but not short enough to beat a pursuit from here. All the same, Batty knew what would tip the scales.

'Batty Coalhouse,' said Maurie Armstrong and it seemed that his voice was as weary and resigned as Batty's own.

'The same. Innocent of this and wanting no trouble over it.'

'You may be innocent of this,' shouted a new voice, 'but of nothing else. We have riders coming...'

'You do not. The wee dug died afore it could run to you with whatever message was knotted round its neck. It's dying made the girl run out and leave the yett unlatched, sealing the fate of all within.'

Batty let that sink down on them. 'You came with a handful of men only to spy the land and if you met with serious resistance you were to gallop back and fetch the Whithaugh Name.'

'Thanks for reminding us,' shouted the unknown voice and Maurie shushed him with added curses to sauce it.

He does not like the idea of calling out Whithaugh for Batty Coalhouse and Will Elliot, Batty thought and then Will did a monstrous thing.

He opened both doors of the bastel and stood under the lintel in full view.

'Come and look at the bodies and see if we speak the truth,' he said. 'They were ill-used.'

'Only one of you, mind,' Batty roared out, stumbling for the ladder to the undercroft and cursing Will. Ewan followed and John Dubh stuck a caliver out of the window.

Batty arrived at the foot of the ladder, half-stumbling, the big dagg with the axe-head grip fearsome in one hand and a savage glower reserved for Will, who met it with a bland smile.

'A fistful of dagg is always better than a mouthful of arguments.'

The man stumping up on stiff, booted legs laughed and stood, waiting. He was red-haired and bearded, with a cast in one eye and barely into his second decade on the earth. He had a decent back-and-breast, a worn blue shirt beneath it, good breeks and fine boots which he placed carelessly in the dung and mud, as if he did not care. It might have been true, Batty thought, but the man was aware of what he was and had a decent length of backsword hung from his waist, a dagger on the other side. Both showed glints of gold and silver.

'You'll be Maurie from Whithaugh then,' Batty said, aware of the men with lances resting on hipshod horses beyond him.

'You'll be Batty Coalhouse of nowhere in particular.'

'Step in,' Will invited. 'Look at them poor folk and see for yourself no-one here could do it.'

Maurie made a neck movement, as if to look over his shoulder at the men, but he never did; it was a gesture to me that they were there, Batty thought. He wanted to shut the doors, but that would look too much like they taking Maurie hostage, so he left it, with a warning glance at Ewan to watch.

Maurie and Will went to each body, Will pointing out this and that. When they came to the whipped girl, Will knelt and made the sign of the cross over her, while Maurie stared. He did the same, however, to another slight form. That one is kin, Batty thought.

It was the servant girl who had her hair unbound but had a cream-coloured cap which still dangled round her throat by the ties.

'Libby Armstrong,' Maurie said dully. 'Sent here for the learning in it.'

And maybe also to flirt and sway at the son, younger than her but becoming aware of her body. A nice match. He said so and Maurie nodded.

'I see them ill-used. I see the youngest was lashed, though I can see no whip – but then, why would ye leave that out for me to see clearly.'

'We did none of this,' Will answered softly. 'Mercifully, we came on it too late, else we might have suffered the same. The man who did it does not care for us any more than you do.'

'Nebless Clem Selby,' Batty added and Maurie looked at him, then moved back to the door, ducking under Ewan's gaze.

He paused. 'Whether you did this or not,' he said – at which Batty's heart seemed to turn over and sink – 'it would be best if you came back to Whithaugh while it is determined.'

'And expect fair treatment from the Armstrongs of Whithaugh? I dinna think so.'

'Then face the consequences.'

Batty stood slightly to the left of the doorway. 'If you come at us,' he said, 'you will be answered. Ride away on a pleasant morning. This is a feud that has gone on long enough…'

'That is not for you to decide,' Maurie spat back. 'Will you let me back to my hobby and my men?'

Batty nodded. 'The doors here will be shut once you have gone. If we have to open them again while you are here, my fist will be filled with dagg.'

'Let us baith ride away from here…' Will began and Batty shushed him loudly, then nodded to Ewan; the wooden door closed, the bar went on and then the iron grille clanked shut with the finality of a tocsin.

'Ye should never have opened these,' Batty said scathingly to Will. 'If you do so again without my permit, I will fell you Will, for all I like you.'

'I thought to avoid war,' Will answered, not in the least trembling when faced with a jut-jawed frowning Batty, which Ewan thought very fine. 'It is always war with you, Batty, and I told you so when you ran like a wolf at the bidding of Mintie Henderson and could have stopped all the blood if you had chosen.'

'What do you know of war?' Batty growled. 'Land Sergeant at Hermitage. Twice a year if that, you turned out in a hot trod against reivers with cattle so the Keeper of Hermitage could take his tithes on recovery. You never whetted a blade as the Steward of Newark.'

'I know war is famine and death to those who want no part of it,' Will answered. 'War is what they call it to give the illusion of honour and law. But it is madness and blood and the lust to win even if folk like these lying in a stable die for it. It has always been thus and shall always be so.'

'God and the Devil rule the world by turns and you cannot tell me who is on the throne at any time, for they handle the world the same way.'

'The pair of you should go to be wee Lutheran cants and debate this every day at some German college,' Ewan interrupted. 'Mayhap you can turn those fine minds to working out how we get out of here.'

'We fight,' Batty answered morosely. 'Which is what they wanted from the moment they jaloused I was here.'

John Dubh stuck his head through the trapdoor. 'They are beyond the garth, in the lee of some auld stones. I can see the blue reek from a fire.'

They will sit for while, wondering what to do, Batty thought. They'll have seen me and two others in the undercroft and the muzzle of a caliver from above, but their imaginations will make more.

'He will not want to send a rider back for more men,' Will said as if reading Batty's mind. 'But he will in the end, because even with all he has with him, he will not storm a bastel like this.'

Batty heaved the saddle on Fiskie one-handed and started fumbling with the girth.

'Which is why we will run at them,' he said and they all looked from one to the other and finally worked out that it was the best way.

Chapter Thirteen

The bastel house at Micklegate

Maurie sat by the fire and chewed his lip. He did not want to send word back to the heidman at Whithaugh to send up more men, that he had Batty Coalhouse and mayhap three others trapped in Micklegate. Even as he said it to himself it sounded whining and afraid and he thought to sit for a while and see if the ones inside the house got worn away with fear and saw sense.

The others were grouped round the smoking fire, leaching heat as the sun came up, spearing rays that made their shadows eldritch. The horses, tethered to a rope line tied rock to rock, whickered with the new heat – and Maurie heard the sound of the outer door banging open.

He turned, expecting to see a man with one arm in the air and others following him with both hands held high. Instead, his mouth dropped open with shock.

Batty, flattened out along Fiskie's rough mane to avoid bashing his brains out on the lintel, came out at full gallop, axe-handled dagg held by the muzzle. The others followed, all bawling at the top of their voices.

By the time Maurie had managed to click his teeth closed, Batty was on him and he fell back, one hand raised in a futile gesture. His spurs caught and he went backwards over the remains of a moss-covered wall, landing like an upturned beetle.

Batty ignored him, ploughed on and let Fiskie crow-hop a low wall, then cut down on the rope tether. The axe wasn't sharp enough and the rope too loose; nothing happened save a little fraying.

Will scattered bodies left and right of him, rode straight into the rope tether which made the fastened horses jerk and squeal. Will came to a halt, barely hanging on – but the rope was now tighter and two blows from Batty cut it. The horses, freed, slipped away and galloped, pursued by a yelling Ewan.

John Dubh rode up and into an Armstrong who had sprung up, knocking him sideways to spin and roll. He lashed out with his backsword and Batty caught his breath, for he had insisted that no-one die today – but the blade simply cut the string of a waving latchbow.

Batty reined round and walked Fiskie back to where Maurie tried dazedly to get to his feet. When he had managed it, he found himself staring down the hexagonal tunnel of the dagg.

'By the time ye sort all this oot and send someone back to Whithaugh to fetch your cuddies back, we will be long gone,' Batty said. 'Let the heidman know how we took pains not to kill anyone.'

Not that it would tip any scales in my favour; it is no accident that those legal devices are known as an 'ambush' – as in 'lying in weight' – and start off against me, Batty thought as they rode away, fast and hard initially so that they were out of range of any bolts or arrows. Yet he felt Fiskie's mane lash his face and the wind in his beard and he almost laughed.

I have rode in a Ride and now I have led a cavalry charge. No wee feat for a man in his fiftieth year.

When he said as much, everyone laughed aloud and reined in a little to ease their blowing horses.

'Ye tell us ye have drunk from the Grail,' John Dubh answered with a dash of sting, 'so it is mayhap that making you so milkie about killing.'

'A danger in a man with a profession such as yours,' Ewan added. Will smiled.

'Batty feels shame, which has been a long time coming for him. Not about killing, mind. There is no shame in feeling bad about having to kill. The shame comes when you realise you no longer care.'

Batty said nothing and thought much. He wasn't ashamed – Will always placed his pronouncements as if he had plumbed the depths of a person, but always it was about himself and so invariably he got it wrong.

It's no small thing, ending someone else's life, Batty wanted to tell them. There should be some sort of uncomfortable weight to it and I feel it every time, though it has nothing to do with what I just did and everything to do with what I have just lost.

This morning I managed not to kill a man. Later today I might have to kill two. There were some he'd love to resurrect just so he could kill them all over again. And there were those not yet dead who deserved killing. There was balance.

Yet the weights were heavy and grinding, made more so by the increase of age. People, if they admire me at all Batty thought, do so because they believe I curl my moustaches at death. Everyone believes death is not to be courted at all – if they only knew that old age is worse…

Hermitage was a frown in grey, streaked black by rain, perched on a mound and glowering at the world. It was surrounded by a mottled fungus of domed tents and half-roofed stalls. People had come from Newcastleton and further with what produce they had, looking to sell or barter for the produce they didn't have.

There were hurdles with new lambs and a desperate clutch of bedraggled waiting by their only cow, tethered and bound for sale because they had nothing else.

'War,' Will said meaningfully as they rode up, but Batty's attention was all taken by the men at the tower gates and peering out the windows. Round metal hats and bills, spotted with rust, old leather jacks reinforced by latten chains. They were hard-eyed and leaned casually on the pole of their bills, watching.

They had always looked like this and Batty had never cared for the place, making a point of trying to avoid it wherever possible. To Will, this was his old home, a place so ingrained in him that he felt a pain in his chest and thought, for one terrible moment, that he would weep.

That was thrown from him by a voice which called his name. Then again and with some delight. The man who did it came over at a brisk walk, a grin on his bluff, bearded face. He wore the workaday of the Hermitage garrison – mud-coloured linen, dung-coloured jack, blue breeches and scuffed leather boots to the knee.

He beamed from under a split-brim cap and Batty saw the iron-grey hair straggled to the ears, but he did not know the man.

'Will Elliot,' the man said again. 'Would you credit it?'

'Do I know you?' Will asked cautiously and the man nodded so hard Batty thought his bunnet might fly off.

'Aye, mebbes. I was part of the garrison in your last year – Patey's Will Carruder. You wid have known me as Horse-Boy, since that's what I did then.'

Will thought he recognised the face, though it was young and cherubic back then, an ostler boy who had clearly risen far. With a lurch, Will heard him say he was the Land Sergeant; he felt Batty's consoling eyes on him and that made it all worse.

'Well done to you...'

'What brings you here?'

'Sustenance and shelter,' Batty answered before Will could speak, then told Carruder of the events at Mickledale, his suspicions regarding Nebless Clem and the arrival of the Armstrongs.

'I have felt the itch of them on my nethers all the ride here,' he added.

Carruder nodded sagely, then summoned a man with a sharp command and sent him for 'the Captain'.

'Keeper absent?' Will asked innocently and Carruder spread his hands in a Border shrug. 'He is abroad, I hear.'

Aye, well he might, Batty thought. He had backed the wrong horse, had Patrick Hepburn and now had a long road back to acceptance at a Scottish court – but he still had his lands. For now. Now you have a Captain, Batty thought, sitting patiently in the rain. Used to be that a Land Sergeant was enough, but it seems the lesson of Will Elliot's independent thinking has been learned – this Captain will be a sprout of the Hepburn brood and so more likely to do as he is told.

The Captain was taller than anyone else, even John Dubh. He was clean shaved, his fair hair curled neatly at the ears but allowed to grow into a thick wad on top of his head, as padding for the burgonet helmet. That let

Batty know this sprig had learned a few matters, while his cheekbones and pale blue eyes let him know he was a Hepburn – they were all called 'The Fairbairn' because of their looks.

He was John Hepburn of Fortune, he announced, a splendid title for a splendid man, all willowy and languidly elegant though his hand rested on the worn hilt of a workmanlike sword. Batty disliked him at once.

Batty and Carruder filled him in and, at last, were let in out of the rain. There were new ostler-boys to look after their horses and the guards watched Ewan unlatch his big two-hander from his back. Carruder laughed.

'That's the weapon of them furrin pay-sojers,' he explained. 'We have had enough of them stravaigin' everywhere, causing havoc.'

They were taken up to the warm of the best room in Hermitage, which had the benefit of better light and a proper fire blazing a welcome in the hearth. There were servants to bring them bread and cheese and a decent pot of ale – good-looking quines, as John Dubh announced when the last of them had swayed her skirts and partlet out of the room. One of them lugged a dirty bucket of black stones and fed one or two to the fire under the approving smile of the Captain.

'Anything come down the waggonway?'

The woman shook her head, left the bucket of stones – coal, Batty realised – and went away, dusting her hands.

Batty went to an unshuttered window and squinted out; the rain had stopped, the trading had started again but even from this height he could see the mean produce – cabbage and dock, a little barley, almost no wheat, some oats. Growing wheat was hard in this country, so oats was a better, hardier affair – but not when folk arrived to strip you of all your hard work.

The Captain looked at them all and grinned.

'I should be obliged if you keep your seats and your temper – what happens next should be interesting, but I don't want it spilling over.'

He had a good brogue, but his speech was dandified by Edinburgh's collegiate and mayhap, Batty thought, some foreign schooling. He wondered if John Hepburn was the Keeper's byblow.

'Riders have arrived and are standing a good bowshot away,' the Captain went on. 'On the other side, so you won't see them from the window. I count two score of them, all Armstrongs.'

Batty and the others looked at one another; the Captain smiled.

'Their leader had demanded a meeting. So I have asked him to be brought here.'

Demanded? That was a word that made the Captain's voice like a badly trained horse – stiff and reined in. Batty felt a cold slide in his belly at who would dare use that to anyone in control of Hermitage. He had a good idea, all the same and was proved sickeningly right when the man himself stepped into the room.

He was tall, but was as broad so it made him look like a new-woken bear. He had a grey-streaked beard, was of ages with Batty and was dressed in half-armour finery, complete with the lobster tails down his thighs, meeting the big riding boots coming up. He had a sword and dagger on him, for the Captain of Hermitage was not about to show any fear of the armed Laird of Mangerton by asking that he leave them at the door.

Archy Armstrong took three steps into the room and stopped, staring at Batty sitting in cushioned comfort with cheese crumbs in his beard.

'So – it is true then. You have the slaughterer of Mickledale. Hand him ower and we'll be gone.'

'I have no such person,' the Captain replied levelly. 'I have Batty Coalhouse, a guest. And the man he is escorting back to the Lothians, Will Elliot.'

'We are just folk of no account at all,' John Dubh offered and the Captain had the grace to look abashed; Ewan sat in grim silence, grasping the two-hander by the *ricasso*.

'I see you all,' Archy Armstrong replied coldly. 'And I will have you hemped by day's close. I will not wait long to find a suitable tree...'

The slap of palm on wood was loud enough to make Batty spill the ale on its way to his mouth. It seemed to astound the Laird of Mangerton.

'Listen to me Archy Armstrong. I have been gracious with you and ignored your demands of the Hepburns of Hermitage to give you audience here. I know you have issues with Batty Coalhouse and mayhap even Will Elliot – though I cannot see why him, since he was ill-used by the Armstrong Laird of Hollows some years back. But they are guests and you have brought a score and more Armstrongs within sight of Hermitage and so fast you probably have not buried the poor folk at Mickledale, the place you claim to be avenging.'

'They are deid and Coalhouse here was fair caught inside...'

'Nebless Clem did this,' the Captain replied sternly, while Batty and the others sat, open-mouthed. 'I had

197

word of him racing back to his lair in the Mutton Pot and you would do better to go there, if you have the courage.'

He took a breath and the Laird of Mangerton spluttered out the word 'courage' as if it had sprung into his mouth like vomit.

'Aye. Pursue the true villains and not your fetid revenge. And mark me, Archy – if you bring numbers of men back within sight of Hermitage again I will track you down, grab you by the lug and haul you back to be dropped into the Pit here.'

He waved a hand in a dismissive flap. 'Get you gone, Laird of Mangerton.'

As if summoned, two big men arrived at the Laird's back to escort him out. For a moment the Laird bristled like an annoyed badger and laid one hand on his swordhilt; the Captain drew himself up and cocked an eyebrow.

'Would ye? Go ahead – and you will meet the Pit early.'

The heat of the men at his back finally let the rancid out of Archy Armstrong, Laid of Mangerton, heidman of all the Armstrongs in the world. He took his hand from his hilt and turned to go – at the doorway, he turned back.

'You will rue the day,' he said. 'Be minded we have a pit at Mangerton too and one day, you long streak of piss, you will be in it so long it will be named efter ye.'

It was only when Batty heard him clatter down the wind of steps, each boot seemingly more angry than the last, that he realised he was holding his breath and let it out noisily. The others did the same, save for John Dubh, who looked admiringly at the Captain.

'What's the Mutton Pot?'

'The worst roost on the moss,' Will answered before anyone could speak and the Captain laughed bitterly and filled the rest of it in. A slash of gully and cut, smothered with gorse and stunted woods, with a grass dip at the centre of it perfect for hiding stolen livestock. You could not use the way in unless you knew it.

'I would love to root Clem and his Broken Men out of there,' the Captain mused, 'but not without double the men I have now.'

Then he managed a smile. 'Not your problem all the same. You have the hospitality of Hermitage for tonight, and tomorrow will be escorted by two of my riders until the Armstrongs give up – they won't attack with witnesses present. You will be back home in a few days, Master Elliot.'

'He will keep coming,' Batty said, half to himself and everyone knew he was not speaking of the Laird of Mangerton.

'Does Clem hate you that much?' the Captain asked. No-one answered and the silence was profound. Everyone – even the Captain – knew how Nebless Clem had been kicked out of his tower and humiliated and the part Batty had in it. He would not stop coming.

Only Will knew Batty well enough to realise that the whipping, bone deep though it had been, had not inflicted a pain as sharp and terrible as the fire Batty had for vengeance. He would not stop coming either.

Chapter Fourteen

The Mutton Pot

Will had watched him leave in the grey light before dawn, a Batty from another time. He had four pistols, all wheel-locks and two of them monstrances that were barely contained by the horse holsters. He had a sword, the basketwork gilding almost all worn off and somewhere in between the apostles on his bandolier lay a brotherhood of knives.

Batty hadn't wanted to do it, but he went to wake Will when he was about to leave only to find him in a dark little hole barely lit by a reeking fish-oil crusie.

'This was mine once,' he said as Batty stepped inside.

'And you carp about losing it,' Batty answered flatly and then let the bag of coin drop to the floor. 'There's the bounty I was given to make your freedom. It is light by my fee and some necessary expense, but since it would all have been lost if Nebless Clem had seen sense I am thinking the Laird of Newark will not be unpleased.'

'You are going after Clem,' Will answered. 'You and I and the others could be sixty miles from here by the end of the sevenday. Leaving all the folk who want to do you harm, leaving starvation and misery and disease – you ken those at Red Cross died of the Sweats?'

Batty had guessed as much, though he wondered how Will had known and said so. Will shifted in his seat on a truckle bed.

'I have seen it before. It took my ma in a night. Day before she was complaining of nothing more than a summer chill or a wee ague. Next day she was dead.'

Batty knew how the Sweats worked though he was glad the disease had not worked on him, even after he had plootered through victims of it out in Piedmont. It began with a strange premonition of oncoming horror, followed by a crippling, violent headache, fever tremors and aching limbs.

He'd always though it was a feature of battlefields and war and when he had seen it along the Borders, he had felt a new fear. He wondered if any of them now carried it and if so when it would show.

'One foot in Paradise, Batty,' Will said sadly.

'Aye well,' Batty said. 'Enjoy the harp music.'

'Why go at all? Because you were whipped?'

Batty took a breath and let it out. 'That,' he answered, 'and the wee girl at Mickledale. He's a fell cruel man and yon Captain here is right — he will not stop. I will not let him stripe another, be it man, woman or even a wee bairn.'

'The Captain is a good man,' Will said softly. 'If you ask, he might help.'

'He might. Or he might prevent me, for the peace of the March. I have shaken loose the Border, it appears and no-one cares for it.'

'It's whit you do, Batty.'

Batty had been aware of Will's eyes on him, for he had gone with him to the gate in order to persuade the guard to let him out. They made his back itch. Will was aware of

Batty's bristle of weapons and steady, grim resolve and the 'good fortune' he offered was genuine and sad; he looked sideways at the guard as they watched the grey figure slide into the last of the grey night. The guard rolled his eyes and shook his head – but he would stay silent on it for a while longer; then go and tell his Captain.

Will stood a long time, staring into the dark until he shivered, a sudden spasm. Then he went to wake Ewan and John Dubh.

–

Batty jerked awake, appalled at himself. The moon was up, the moss rolled away like a sea, studded with a twist of tree leaning away from the sharp hissing wind. Yet night birds were out hunting and calling, soft as snake breath.

He was shamed and afraid of having fallen asleep, if it could be called sleep. He felt feverish and found he had one of the daggs in his hand, plucked from the horse-holster by reflex; he laid the cold barrel against his temple and felt the relief on a pounding head.

The dream-memory was a strange one, back when he had come to join the rest of his family in their war against Saxony. It was because of the family at Micklegate, he thought and all Will had been saying.

–

For a moment Ned's head shook uncontrollably, like a white thistle in the wind; Batty realised his affliction had gotten worse over the years and mentioned it, gently.

'As did Bella's,' Ned answered. 'Until it killed her dead.'

'What was it?'

'Sweating sickness,' Ned answered shortly, which puzzled Batty for though it was deadly, the Sweats took you in hours not years. Ned shook his head and waved his arms when Batty expressed his puzzlement.

'She had no' been right for some time,' he answered. 'The Sweats was just the finality of matters.'

He had looked at Batty then, with the sideways slyness of the drunk.

'You and she were sweet once and she left a word for you, Batty,' he said. 'For a time if we met and she was gone from the world.'

She had left a few words, well remembered by even a sot like Ned.

Look on me kindly — and leave old sins to die of old sins.

Batty had no idea what the second part meant, but was unable to look on her at all, for Ned would not permit it.

'Best leave your sight of her untouched by what plague does,' he declared and Batty, who had looked on the very vomit of Hell and remained unfazed by it, was forced to agree to Ned's wishes; he had never heard of the Sweats being so disfiguring but he knew more than Ned thought he did and honoured the old man's wishes.

The dream ended as he stood by the lichgate, watching her lowered into the ground of a Calais churchyard.

'Buried on English soil,' Ned had declared, still drunk and showing no signs of sobering soon. 'Which I will defend.'

—

He rode up and over the swells of the moss, a rolling sea of tussocks and whin, spattered with the odd lonely rowan and stands of luminous birch. There were thicker copses, too, drenched in the last of the snow, which the wind trailed off like mist. All the way along it he fought to stay awake, fought the hag of dreams.

He found the Mutton Pot easily enough, but finding the way in was never an option unless you knew it, though he saw several that might be. They were half-seen trails that meandered down the side of the bowl-shaped land into thick clutches of leafless trees like claws for the unwary.

All those trails would find a way to the centre, Batty thought, though you'd wander a long time and be tracked by people who stayed there and knew it all by heart. Those same people, he reckoned, would not want folk entering by the porter's gate, all the same, so he slid off Fiskie, left him tied to the weight of the reins and stumped down a way, to where he could crouch unseen.

He was there until the moon died and the first silver of dawn smeared the sky. Then three riders appeared, riding out of the dark shadows, up and over the crest, heading towards him. When they dismounted a good way off, he let out his breath and got it in the cup of his hand lest they see the betrayal of smoke.

After a while, as the cold slithered insidiously into Batty's bones, locking his joints with pain, all three men mounted and rode back. There will be another soon enough, Batty thought. Three at dawn, one or two later in the day, mayhap another at night. Not a task any of them relishes.

Well there you are, he told himself. How do you like it now, Batty, avenging angel without a fiery sword? It will not get any better.

He fumbled out some slices of ham and bread, sipped some decent ale, for he hadn't eaten in a time and, if truth be told, was alarmed about how his stomach had shrunk.

Never a good sign when a man with a belly like a galleon in full sail should suddenly lose it and never notice.

When he was done he licked his fingers and went back to Fiskie, working the stiffness out of his knees and fingers. He fed him a handful of oats and watered him out of his burgonet, then mounted up. He checked the daggs, touched the hilt of his backsword, made a riffle of fingers along the snugged Brothers in the apostle bandolier.

He was ready.

He let Fiskie amble out into the open and then nudged her into a firmer walk heading up to the crest of the little ridge where he had last seen men. He had an idea there was one now who had eyes on him, so he wanted to appear open and slightly stupid.

Now it comes, he said to himself, slouching in the saddle, his shoulders moving with the gait of the horse. A rider relaxed, climbing a trail, in no hurry and off guard. He was about half-way up when the other rider appeared, fifty paces ahead and above him. Batty pretended not to notice until the man called out: 'Stop there.'

Batty stopped and squinted at a brown man on a brown horse with a furriner accent thick as clotted cream.

'I thought it was you,' the man said ambling his horse a little closer. 'I said, no, it cannot be. That man rides too easy for one with stripes all over his back.'

'Oh, I got used to them quick enough. Came back with some friends and blew in the doors of The Scar. You mayhap noticed.'

'Everyone noticed,' the man replied, his voice hardening. Batty shrugged.

'Powerful what you can do with friends. We can be friends if you care for it. I have some decent ale. Would that work for you? What are you called?'

'Vasari is my name. You have too many weapons about you for drinking ale,' the man said. He was at ease now, for he could not see anyone else.

'For protection,' Batty answered lightly, showing teeth. 'No sense in getting off on the wrong foot before I can ask you a boon.'

This was interesting and strange; the man cocked his head but his voice was suspicious.

'It seems we are good friends after all,' he said, 'that you can ask a boon. What is it?'

'You are right,' Batty said. 'As a friend, I want you to go to Clem and tell him Batty Coalhouse is coming. If he plans to run again I will know of it and burn him out of this place.'

'Oho,' Vasari said. 'Perhaps I will stay and enjoy your decent ale and send one of the men hidden behind me.'

Batty shook his head. 'I have been here a while, seen less than a handful come and go and now there is you – what happened to get you this shit, standing out in the cold all night? And alone, too.'

'You are certain of all that?' the man asked, his face a laugh. 'Would you bet your life on it?'

'Life or Primero – you play the hand dealt.'

Vasari spread his hands and widened his smile. 'This no kind of talk between friends. I will go and tell Clem. You wait here, right?'

Batty nodded. 'I will be here.'

The man reined round and rode up to the crest of the ridge, turned, waved and smiled, then vanished over it. Batty drew out the axe-handled dagg and waited for the inevitable.

The inevitable came hurtling back over the crest at a full-sretch gallop, leaning low on the horse so that the mane whipped his face, leaning to one side, away from Batty's pistol hand.

It was in Batty's head that Vasari was riding too fast, aiming to get right round behind him and come up on him that way; then he saw the drawn blade, a curve of wicked smiling sabre and behind it the face, silently screaming.

Now we see how I stand before God, Batty said and levelled the dagg, squeezed hard and waited. Vasari was twenty feet away when the affair went off in a long spear of flaring light and a horrendous blast of sound. Vasari went backwards off the horse's rump, while the mount screeched and threw its head, dancing sideways in fear and confusion.

Fiskie, with the blast and flame coming from between his own ears, did a squeal and a half-hearted buck, but nothing more. Finest horse ever, Batty thought vehemently, though he offered an apologetic prayer to his long-dead predecessor, The Saul.

The smoke shredded, harsh and eye-stinging so that Batty saw Vasari, flat on his back and staring at the sky. He rode Fiskie over and looked down, seeing the dark stain spreading from his side.

'How do you feel?' he asked and Vasari opened one eye and scorned him with it; his arm was tight against his side where the ball had torn through, ripping away his fancy belt, part of his chemise and a chunk of the jack. Plates stuck out like broken bones.

'What did you load that with?' he managed to gasp, while blood pinked on his lips and a bubble formed and burst. Lung shot, Batty thought, levering himself out of the saddle.

'Something for killing vermin,' he replied coldly. 'I will fetch your horse and help you on it. You have someone back in that scrub who can sew you up?'

Vasari licked his bloody lips. 'I will never make it.'

'Of course you will, once you are up. Here…'

He fetched the horse and helped the man on to it; he sat like a half-empty bag of flour, hunched up with glazing eyes.

'Well, here's what you should say when you get there. Tell Nebless Clem that Batty is coming. You hear what I say? Batty is coming to give him stroke for stroke. Not for what he did to me, but for the wee girl-child at Micklegate. He will know.'

'I had no part in that,' Vasari answered, gasping and blowing blood bubbles.

Batty turned the horse to face the right direction. 'Listen friend, I am thinking you had better go there quickly.'

He slapped the rump and watched the horse go up the slope, the man wobbling on its back. He hoped he would make it, but in the end it would not matter for nothing would save him.

If it all went well, Nebless Clem would send out men to pick up my trail, he thought. He will need a dozen and if he has much more than that I am the King of Faerie.

He turned Fiskie, who was still shaking the ringing out of his ears. Batty patted him fondly and nudged him on, singing softly.

'The steed that my true love rides,
Is lighter than the wind,
Wi siller he is shod before,

Wi burning gowd behind.'

--

He lay on his back, staring up at the rough plank roof and then at Clem Selby and Trin, one of his kin. Trin had just told Clem that the man was dying and Clem wanted to know what he had said. Again.

Vasari could hear others moving round about in the dimly lit partitions built under the arching of scrub but he had no strength to turn his head. No desire for it, either. He heard Trin say he was dying and he knew he was dying and the sun was coming up on a new day he would never get to see out.

I should have ridden hard past him, he thought. Turned and hacked at him before he got the monstrance dagg working. Or shot him with my own dagg minute I saw him. Or got off before the crest and used a latchbow from hiding. He wished he had done it differently, wished he could begin again.

He saw Clem looking at him, the leather mask impassive, the mouth beneath it hardly moving as he spoke. He saw Batty Coalhouse and that huge dagg with an axe in the handle, the barrel pointing at him and he thinking then that he might just make it, that it would misfire...

'He says,' Trin said wearily, 'Batty Coalhouse is coming. Vengeance for his striping and for the whipping of a girl.'

The last he said with accusation, for he had been against it at the time, but Clem turned that mask of a face on him and he shut up, as he had done then.

'For a bloody back and a dead girl?' Clem asked and shook his head. 'Who has the grievance here? Man helped steal my wife, my prisoner and my tower.'

Clem thought about it a little longer. 'Send folk to find him.'

Trin rubbed his chin, finding tangles in the beard there. 'There are a dozen ways he could have gone…'

'Send men for all of them.'

'You'd need a dozen.'

'Then send them. We have trackers – send them.'

We have a score of men left, Trin wanted to say. Only that many now and most of those looking to run out if Nebless Clem's luck doesn't change. And that he starts treating them with some respect. There were a dozen who were kin and the rest were like the dying Vasari, defected furrin-fighters looking to get warm, eat well and score some coin.

'We are supposed to be attacking the tower. Taking it back…'

Clem glared. 'We do that when I say.'

'All this for a one-armed old man?'

'Dangerous as canker,' Clem replied, chewing a nail. Then his head lifted like a dog fox scenting love on the wind.

'Did that Will fellow not say something about a woman who held this Batty in thrall? That he did whatever she wished, no matter how foul?'

Trin felt uneasy, but nodded. 'Mintie Henderson of Powrieburn. Who is well connected to the Hepburns and the Grahams.'

If we fail to find Batty, Clem thought, then we will stop charging ower the moss in search of him. Better we find something, a lure he cannot resist. And that will be this Mintie woman.

The man lying on the platform heard it all, thought it foul but could not bring himself to care overly much. He thought about how this had happened to him, how he was laying here when an hour ago the life had been hot in him and now he was staring at the knot whorls in the roof, wishing he could see the stars, feel the night wind. He wanted to be filled with beef and wine, running his hand over the satin skin of a woman, but he had done it all wrong. Should have spotted the guns on the man, but had only seen him strung up, white-naked, being whipped by Clem Selby.

Now here he was, his gut opened up to the light. There was no feeling all down that side, none at all. His ma would have soothed him, but she wasn't here. No-one was. Why are you here alone?

Trin seemed to notice something and peered. Then took a knee and touched a pulse. He knew Vasari was dead, his eyes open and staring at the next world.

Chapter Fifteen

The Mutton Pot, later

Batty withdrew to some high ground overlooking the Mutton Pot, to a place shrouded by ash and downy birch coming into leaf. He fed Fiskie a handful or two of his shrinking oats, gave him water and left him to watch as much of the scrub choked bowl of Mutton Pot as he could.

It was hard toll on Fiskie and himself. You can be rode hard and put away wet for only so long that apologies and excuses no longer cover the agony of aching joints and bad digestion. He looked sideways at the patient horse; we have been to that well too often, he thought.

Will, he realised, was right in just about every way. I am no assistance to anyone here, just a man who shakes up the Border, which will stay shaken by every Name with a grievance that sets out against me, now that they have the time after the end of Henry's war. If I left, few would mourn me and those who did would do it with a tinge of relief.

From his vantage, he watched three men coming up from the Pot, through the dips and over the crests. They rode easy, studying the ground for sign but Batty wasn't worried, since he had not shuffled anything into existence down that way. Instead he thought about what he would do it they started towards him, though there was no reason for that other than the perfidy of God.

He could take the reins in his teeth, unshackle a dagg and urge Fiskie into a gallop, coming down on them like some bold cavalier; the truth of it was an old man wasted too thin by the poisons from his whipped back on a horse staggering under the pain of sore joints.

So he made up his mind, there and then, that he did not care about any of it. He had shot a man not long since and, for the first time in a long while, regretted it. Not that the man could have been spared once he had committed himself – if he had not been shot off his horse, he'd have done Batty harm.

But he had loaded the man on his horse and sent him, weaving, on his way with no more thought on it than he needed the dying man to deliver his message before he died. Now he hoped Vasari had died before he did; Will Elliot was right and always had been – Batty Coalhouse needed to be gone from the Borders; sooner or later Clem Selby would die, killed in a raid or destroyed by the snotters and shivering of winter.

Batty had ridden a little way west, with half a mind to reach Berwick and consider what he did next – mayhap find the nuns, snug in their new home, beg a night or two and ride on to the coast, into France or Germany. Visit Michaelangelo if the old sot was still alive – he laughed at the notion, felt fey and shivered.

It came as a surprise to him, then, to find three mounted men ahead of him and coming on steadily; he had not thought the ones he saw that determined or clever. Then he thought they would must be three other trackers for Nebless Clem. Then he saw the lead figure raise a hand and wave and knew, with certainty beyond his aged blurred vision, that it was Will Elliot and that, riding on either side, would be Ewan and John Dubh.

He waited for them to come up and was met by the harsh, violet-ringed eyes and face of Will, was surprised when he spoke.

'Is he dead then? Nebless Clem?'

Batty shook his head and Will sighed. 'I had hoped for it, seeing you still alive.'

'Hoped for it,' Batty repeated, bewildered. 'Is this the man who keeps telling me to leave the matter alone?'

'Not possible now, I am thinking,' Ewan offered quietly.

'A man came to Netherby,' John Dubh added and, while Batty looked confused, Will hauled on the reins of his horse.

'We spotted a sheltered place where we can have a fire,' he said. 'Let's go there and I will tell you why Nebless Clem is now deadlier than any canker.'

It wasn't far, Will's hidden place, but all the way there Batty fretted with impatience to find out why Nebless Clem was more dangerous than before. While Ewan made up the fire, Will sat opposite and finally told him.

A man had arrived at Netherby, staggering and crawling and it was a wonder to everyone who saw that he had made it at all. His back was lashed to ruin and the bone, he was already feverish with the afterclap of shock and the cold.

He was Thomas Ower The Moss, which was the only name he had since he was Broken from the Hendersons by some heinous misdeed. He had been a Broken man since, running with others of his kind until swept up by Nebless Clem.

'He had refused, or so he claimed,' Will said, 'to be part of Clem's latest plot.'

He stopped and Batty sat for a while, then sighed.

'Am I to pay for the rest?'

Will shook his head. 'Clem is set on capturing Mintie Henderson, in order that you be flushed out to try and free her. He was told you are in thrall to the Mistress of Powrieburn.'

Batty was rocked for a moment, the others saw his mouth work in astonishment, like a new-landed salmon. Finally he managed to say 'God's blood' and then: 'We must go there.'

'Not me,' Will said vehemently. 'I will never set foot in that garth again.'

Batty stared at him. 'Because she has never seen you hirple like a cripple? This, I think, outweighs any vanity.'

'Not vanity,' Will said miserably. 'I just could not bear to see her again.'

'We have Netherby on our side,' Ewan added hastily before matters boiled up more.

'They have sent out trackers,' John Dubh added. Batty sat while John Dubh put something in a pot and wreathed the area in tasty smells; Batty's mouth watered. It was a good place, a sheltered dell with running water so the horses could drink when they chose and need only be hobbled. Fiskie did not need even that, Batty thought; he needs the rest. And so do I while I work out what happens now – he was still bemused by the fact of Mintie being dragged into this.

'He will want to catch the place in daylight,' Batty said, working it out in his head. 'He will come down on them just after dawn.'

'Why not at night?' Ewan demanded. 'Covered by the dark, he could get close...'

Because Powrieburn is a bastel house, Batty told him, thick-walled with a thick door and an iron yett behind that. You couldn't burst it in, or smoke them out from the slate roof. Besides, there are roosting ravens which will fly up if disturbed by riders in the dark. And a good dog even if it appeared to be built of several different ones.

'Mintie's bastel is like the one at Micklegate,' he explained, 'which Nebless Clem broke into only because a bairn fretted over her dog and opened the doors.'

He stopped, seeing the tattered, bloody body. When he looked up, Will was staring back at him; he nodded once.

'That will be the fate of Powrieburn if he gets in.'

'All the more reason for going there,' John Dubh answered; Will lowered his head.

'I will come close to it. I will fight with you Batty. For the last time.'

'Netherby cannot send men to it – not their lands, not their Name – but they will tell the Hendersons, who will send men to help,' Batty answered. 'Clem will never break in.'

He looked from one to the other. 'Our job is to stop him ever returning for a second attempt. If he wants to lure Batty Coalhouse out to a fight, I will give him that.'

'It may be a trap,' Ewan said thoughtfully. 'It will have the same effect, after all, as having this woman held prisoner. Rather than go to the trouble and blood it would take to break into this Powrieburn and seize the woman and all the feud that would come after.'

'I am aware,' Batty said sardonically.

'You have a plan?' John Dubh demanded, ladling something into a bowl.

'Fight. All save for you, who will take Will back to Fife.'

'They will not,' Will said firmly and smiled sadly. 'You are not the only one with one foot in Paradise.'

—

They rode hard and without stopping more than a breath or two. They crossed the Thief Sike and swung north, then swung south to come up on Tinnis Hill from the sheltered side.

The dark loom of it washed Batty with old memories. He had been ambushed on that innocent looking dome, blasted off his horse and spilled down a drop. Mintie and Will had turned out to find and rescue him and when he looked at Will, he saw he was remembering the same thing. They grinned at each other, rueful, and shivered.

Ewan and John Dubh knew nothing of the Faerie that hagged Tinnis, so they were unconcerned as the dawn spilled up, all rosy and fired. They tethered the horses and fed and watered them, then stumped to a vantage point and looked down.

Powrieburn, an ache of old familiar, lay a good gallop away, marked by a spill of smoke that showed the occupants were up, making fires. There were a lot of men slouching about the place, at doors and in the garth. Batty thought he saw Bet's Annie at one point, but could not be sure.

'The garth and yett are both open,' Ewan declared and Batty cursed the young eyes that saw what he could not. It was not a surprise; there would be wood to carry in, mulch from the stalls to be got out – you could not constantly be opening and locking two doors.

But there were two big men on either side, watching and ready; the Hendersons had clearly sent Mintie men to help.

They sat for a while longer while the morning spread to a dance of loveliness. Oystercatchers swooped, reminding everyone how close they were to the firth at Solway. Larks soared and wood-pigeons called one to the other or argued with the ravens. Those black birds of Powrieburn, Batty thought. Every cry they give reminds me of the first night I arrived, to where the frightened, determined and brave Mintie had come out of Powrieburn to take a message from me. He glanced at Will, sitting with his back to it all; he will recall it too.

'Will ye not keep watch?'

Will shook his head. He would not look at as much as a stained plank of Powrieburn's outhouse. Batty shook his head with exasperation.

'Then move to the ither side and watch for riders. Come tell me at once if you see same.'

He did not say why but neither Ewan nor John Dubh needed an explanation; if this was a good watch-point for Batty, it would also be good for Nebless Clem and his men.

Batty wanted to see a flurry of riders come down on Powrieburn and veer off when they saw how defended it was. He wanted to see them wheel like birds and scatter. He wanted to know where Nebless Clem was…

'I havna seen a single Faerie,' John Dubh offered up, sounding offended. Ewan chuckled.

'Well, at least you can tell folk you spent the night on a Faerie hill and had no bad for it.'

We're not off it yet, Batty wanted to tell them. He remembered when he had been here before, the storm, the Hen Harrow's cunning plot to box him in on this very hill. He felt the comforting weight of the axe-handled dagg, which had belonged to the Hen Harrow and which he had not needed once Batty was done with him.

Now he sat on the hill waiting for another and had no fear of Faerie, or even considered them much. If I hear the tinkle of silvered bells mind, I will soil myself he thought.

There were no delicate chimes, just the opposite; Will came crushing through the bracken, breathless and afraid.

'A dozen riders,' he managed. 'They have dismounted and left horse-holders – the main of them are coming up on us.'

'Riders from the Hendersons?' Ewan offered. Batty looked at him, pouch-eyed and sour.

'Ye think? Having circled half-way round the Hill to come up on it? Well, you stay and find out for sure, last of the Lovats. When you do, gallop like a tail-fired stirk and see if you can catch me up with the news.'

'I thought we were here to face them off,' John Dubh growled. 'To seek out Nebless Clem and finish him.'

On our own ground, Batty told them. When their numbers don't outweigh our gallant bravery. They laughed, soft and bitter.

'We head west,' he added. 'See if you can keep up with me. If we get divided, make north and then east to Edinburgh and on to Newark's castle. God willing, we will all meet there.'

The sun was up and at their back, casting long twisting shadows of them over the tawny land ahead.

'If you see Nebless Clem,' he added, urging Fiskie onward, 'go at him. With him dead, all will be ended. If not – keep riding and follow me.'

They all nodded, pale-faced Will with his sword already in hand, John Dubh grim as old stones and Ewan, his hauberk hitched up to his waist, big sword on his back and his long legs white and patched with cold.

They rode on down the west side of the hill, picking through the tangled bracken and stunted bushes. Then Ewan pointed out the riders.

There were six, mayhap eight, Batty thought but he could not see any of them looking like Nebless Clem. Neither did anyone else.

'Well,' Batty said. 'Draw your weapons and ride at them. Don't spare shot or steel, get through and keep riding.'

He said it more easily than he felt it; there were eight at least, he thought, two of them unshipping lances, one with a latchbow. No firelocks of any kind – unless he was mistaken about the latchbow. He wanted to call out to Ewan with his better eyes, but thought better of it and drew one of the big daggs out of its saddle holster.

Then he blew out his cheeks, tried to ignore the roiling of his bowels and kicked Fiskie. The beast leaped forward gamely, caught a foot in the bracken and stumbled; Batty felt a rush from heel to crown, a shock that left him trembling. Bigod, beast, dinna do anything so foolish as fall here…

To his right, he saw Will, sword out, leaning low and he almost cried out with delight at him – gaun yerself wee Will. Show them how much of a cripple you are not.

Then he aimed himself at a rider, a man amorphous behind a beard and hair, a metal breastplate rusted to the colour of dung and a six-foot length of lance couched like a noble knight. He was determined and confident, looking to skewer his opponent without even getting close enough to worry; he never had time to realise the horror of his mistake.

Batty triggered the dagg, it spat a plume of fire and the man's head vanished like a squeezed blood blister; Batty rode through the mist of it, holstering the empty dagg and hauling out a new one. He heard Ewan and John Dubh making warcries and hurling foulness in their own tongue, half-turned but could not see them. He saw Will lumbering after him and waved him on.

He rode on for a while, then risked stopping and turning Fiskie to face back the way he had come. He saw Will come up and felt a stab of shock at the way he was riding. Behind him were cries and shouts and the clash of steel; get away, he wanted to shout. Get away from them. Run.

He knew they would not run. Not ever now.

He moved to Will and saw the sallow, shocked face, the way he held himself. Then he saw the latchbow shaft waggling slightly and at an odd angle low down in Will's side. Batty holstered his pistol and got close enough to grasp it; Will gasped.

'Caught a clankie,' he said. Batty felt the play in the shaft and took a chance, gripped hard and hauled it out; Will gave a sharp cry and started to fall off the horse until Batty held him up. When Will was steady, Batty looked at the point of the bolt, saw the blood and flesh on it. Not lung, was the best he could come up with from his long experience, but there was fat on it that showed it had gone deep and driven in fabric and filth.

'Can you ride?'

Will nodded. 'The others...'

'When they are done looting their dead, they will be along.'

Will wanted to say they were leaving two against six at least, but the words didn't form on his tongue and he had to concentrate hard on not falling off.

'Stay with me,' he heard Batty say. 'We will make for the Saltburn Bridge.'

'We are supposed to fight Nebless Clem,' Will managed – or thought he did. He did not hear if Batty replied.

Batty had said nothing and kept it that way, having to lead Will's mount with his one good hand all the way down to the Saltburn brig. The Saltburn wasn't a big stream – you could step over it further up – but the road led down to where it cut through the moss, a wheen of years having made it a long drop to where it gurgled over boulders.

The brig was a wooden affair, built so that packhorses full of Solway salt could cut a long way round to Edinburgh. It was timber, too narrow for carts and with a railing so rickety and low that folk didn't dare ride across it, but led horses quietly.

'Dinna take a tumble here,' Batty warned but the lolling figure said nothing; Batty let out his breath when they were on the far side. He left Will in the saddle, praying to God the man would not fall, praying to the Devil that he could manage to get him back up again; Will moaned and his breath wheezed in and out – but at least it was still going in and out.

Batty wanted to attend to him, but there was something more pressing and he dug it out from under the jack – two cloistered rolls of powder and the last of his slow match.

He moved back out a third of the way on to the brig and set his charges, hoping they would not just fizzle out, having no containment to shout against. Even fizzing would be good, he thought. Might set fire to the old timbers if they were not too damp. Below him, the river seemed to gurgle distant agreement.

He set one charge there, then moved back and set the other on the timbers at the end. These he managed to pack under stones. Then he went to look at Will as the sun blazed up.

'It will be a nice day,' Will observed.

'Any day is where you live to see the close,' Batty declared and then cursed, wishing he had not trotted out the old saw so glibly. He led Will a little way to where a choke of hawthorn and rowan held a sunken glade which provided some cover, then heaved Will off on to the soft bracken; Will's legs buckled as soon as they touched earth, but Batty stretched him out on his back, then covered him with their blankets. He looked back, squinting into the sun in the hope of seeing Ewan and John Dubh riding up, but there was nothing.

He wanted to stay, light a small fire, make some broth, examine Will's wound more thoroughly – but it was too close and if Ewan and John Dubh had gone down to the mulch, then their enemies would be moving west.

He did what he could for Will, all the same; a trick of God had laid him out where the sun blazoned like a torch and he could see what was what. It wasn't good. Will's jack had padding but no plates, neither horn nor metal. It was fastened by toggles of bone and when he laboriously unfastened it, something large fell out which made his own belly flip back and forth.

It wasn't Will's innards, it was the bag of coin, slashed where the latchbow bolt had hit it and gone off at an angle. Now that the wound was exposed, Batty could see it had gone deep. He was no chirugeon, but Batty knew the wounds of battle, knew that this was a belly wound which was invariably fatal no matter what it had hit. Knew it had probably nicked the liver.

'Bad is it?' Will asked and Batty managed a laugh.

'Thought your innards were falling out – facered me a bit. That bliddy bag of coins.'

'Saved my life, though, eh?'

Batty fumbled out his flask and drank, then offered it to Will, who drank and coughed; Batty knew it would do him no good in the long term, but the short one made Will sigh with satisfaction.

'Good medicating Batty. Whit is it, or dare I ask?'

'Ma's tonic,' Batty lied. 'Should have a daud of beef in it but there's no time to making broth.'

'Does it work?'

Now there was plaint in Will's question and Batty tried to ignore it. 'Everytime someone got dinged – usually my da – Ma would make this. Send me out for all sorts of herbs from mugwort and cockspur grass to lamb's cress. There isnae a wee bit of greenery I am not familiar with. Mixed it with powder-proofed brandy and called it 'musket ball tonic'. My da swore by it.'

'Ball tonic,' Will repeated dreamily while Batty worked around the hole in his side, badly fretted where he had torn out the bolt.

'My da was sick as a rabid dog once, for eight or so long days,' he went on, to keep Will's mind off the pain. 'Ma fed him her tonic every day, sometimes twice and on the ninth, his fever broke, he coughed and spat up a caliver shot, which was all his bad cess rolled into iron. Sat up saying he was friskier than a March hare.'

'Away…' Will said, softly disbelieving and then his head lolled. For a second, Batty panicked but then he heard the breathing, ragged but audible and sat back, heaving a relieved sigh. He used his neckscarf to bind up the wound and levered himself to his feet, squinting into the sun. He thought he saw a shape, but heard a brief wet cough behind him and turned back to Will.

He slept, breathing uneasily. When Batty touched his lips he came away with blood on his fingers. When he turned back, he saw two horses and wished he had managed to reload all his pistols; the axe-handled dagg was ready, so he hefted it in his worn fist.

He didn't need it. The lead rider was Ewan, the handle of his big sword harsh as a cross against the diffusing dawn and he trailed another horse which Batty thought was riderless until they got closer.

There was a shape across the saddle and it made Batty's heart lurch. Ewan did not dismount on the rickety bridge, but rode quietly on to it, pulling the reluctant horse behind him. He turned once to make sure the body on it didn't foul on the ragged handrail and, when he walked off the far end, he stopped and looked at Batty and the lolling Will.

'Is he bad hurt?' he asked hoarsely and Batty could not reply for fear Will might hear it, so he squinted at the load on the second horse and asked if that was John Dubh and if he was hurt bad.

Ewan climbed down stiffly, went to the second horse and began hauling the body off; when Batty went to help he saw John Dubh, eyes staring at morning clouds he could not see and a latchbow bolt almost through his neck. His good hand shook then.

'Wee spalpeen got away,' Ewan explained wearily. 'We had killed everyone else, but that yin reined round to running when John Dubh chased him, springing like a deer. Would have got him, too, if the bastard had not turned and shot. *Bratach salach* got clean away and no doubt has raised the others.'

Batty looked at the bloody pale face of Black John and thought how the man with the latchbow had killed two of them and ridden to safety. Stands well in the sight of the Devil, he thought dully, then drew Ewan aside and told him how Will fared, quietly, close enough for the fog of their breath to mingle.

'Well, there it is,' Ewan said. 'Mayhap we all should have gone back to Will's wee fortalice when you telt us.'

'He insisted otherwise,' Batty answered, watching as Ewan explored the body of Black John, ransacking it for anything of use or value. Then he heaved the dead man by his shoulders to the edge of the drop.

'Canna give him proper burial, but I have said what words are needed and taken what he will no longer miss. I dinna want that whip-man to get anywhere near him.'

Batty nodded and helped him roll John Dubh off the edge. There was a slither, a pause and a thump. Batty made the cross, then looked up across the bridge. There were riders, small still but growing shadows with the light at their back.

'I have a plan to ruin this bridge,' he told Ewan, who nodded, hefted the great sword off his back and then nodded to Batty and held out his hand.

'It has been an honour and pleasure, Master Coalhouse,' he said, 'but they will be on you afore you can load Will back on a horse. Fire up your match when you will; I will hold them.'

Last of the Lovats of Beauly, Batty thought with a sudden pang in his chest, fierce and hot, that almost sprang tears to him. He watched the man lope back across the bridge and then hurried to get Will.

'Thwarted them again, eh Batty,' Will whispered as he tried to help his way on to the horse.

Grit, Batty thought. Will always had a deal of that. Now the bolt had broken something in him and he was starting to choke on his own blood. The nearest help was Graitna, heart of Armstrong country and no safe place for any of them. In his head, he drew a map of the country he knew well enough and realised how much of it hated him. He heard Ewan's voice from somewhere in the past saying 'If a man is judged by the number of his enemies, ye are mighty indeed, Batty Coalhouse.'

Batty went out along the bridge and knelt where he knew his first slow match began. He called out to Ewan, seeing the riders coming closer; one or two dismounted and he was sure he could see the masked figure of Nebless Clem urging them all on.

Ewan turned briefly, big sword in both hands. 'Fire up yer bridge-blower, Batty. Do not wait for me. *An rud a theid mun cuairt, thig e mun cuairt.*'

What goes around comes around.

Batty wanted to rage at him, but he knew what Ewan was doing and why. He watched the sparks fly from the dagg when he pressed the trigger, watched the slow match flare and blew more life into it. It hissed like a snake and set off on its way.

Ewan did not wait, especially for the boy with the cunning latchbow – he went forward, big sword held above his head like a banner and roaring out 'claymore' in his own tongue. A latchbolt hissed past him, a rider came at him and he swung while running; the horse shrieked and went down, front legs smashed. The rider went out through the ears and Ewan ignored him, plunging on.

Seeking for the head of the snake, Batty saw, running to Nebless Clem; cut him down and all is done with – another rider tried to skewer Ewan, but he danced sideways and cut the man in the middle as he went. A bolt struck him, staggered him, but he did not fall...

Batty became aware of the slow match and recoiled from it, back along the bridge to the far end, where he lit the other. The first one went off in a shower of sparks and pops, the smoke obscuring any sight of the battle beyond. Batty hauled himself up into the saddle.

'Can ye ride?' he demanded and Will nodded and managed a bloody smile.

'Steeplechase on a Truce Day, dinna worry about me.'

'Aye, you will take the silver bell for it, for sure.'

Batty reined around and they went off, leaving the clash and shouts until a roar and a fetid heat on Batty's back told where the second charge had gone off. He risked turning to look back and saw timber flying in the air.

That was it for the bridge, he thought. And for the last of the Lovat Frasers.

Will was half in and half out of the world, knowing they were running and trying to feel the urgency of it. All he felt was a great sense of loss, but that would be because of Batty's singing.

'They buried him at the mirk midnight,
when dew fell cold and still,
when the aspen grey forgot to play
and the mist clung to the hill.'

Chapter Sixteen

At the bridge

Clem sat on the bay while peewits called and swirled and Parcy took the lists and gave the bad news – six dead, two so badly hurt they'd need taken back to shelter by two others. Ten men lost, though Skelf was constant and nagging in saying how he killed two of the northern caterans with his latchbow. Parcy grudgingly confirmed one a certainty – 'shot through the neck, by God. Nae man lives with that.' The other he thought likely to die, shot in the belly by Skelf, who preened and strutted with it all.

The bridge was the worst of it. It had been the easy passage for little pack ponies of salt from the Solway to make it up on to the moors and then to Edinburgh or Berwick. No-one much cared to go after salt, since disposing of it afterwards was complicated and likely to attract attention.

Now it was broken at the far end and the remainder of it lurched and hung like a drunk fallen on a fence. It would collapse, everyone agreed, at the first foot on it and they said it firmly, because they knew Clem was likely to ask and it saved tension all round if he realised no-one was about to risk it. Not even him.

The only way over the burn, as was pointed out to him, was a detour of eight miles across the bracken and then eight miles back to the other end of the bridge to try and pick up tracks. It looked like rain, as Sleekeye pointed out, so haste was advised.

Clem could feel their heat and their eyes. Sleekeye, no doubt, had been telling them how this would gain them nothing and they were forcing it at the expense of raiding for the winter and finding somewhere warmer than the Mutton Pot scrub. He knew Sleekeye was only the voice saying what they all thought, knew that they hadn't liked what had been done to the girl at Micklegate – even the Broken Names, who were bloodsoaked at the best of times.

He hadn't liked it himself. Afterwards. Tried to excuse it as necessary, a way of forcing the da out of Micklegate but that was a lie; the bastel houseplace had fallen like a fat apple and he had been tempted to stay and make it his new home. But the others had glowered and scowled until Sleekeye had dared to whisper in Clem's ear about how this was Armstrong land.

He glanced at the wreck of the bridge, at the clouding sky, then at Sleekeye.

'We go after Batty Coalhouse,' he said.

–

Batty halted after a while, making the excuse that he was checking his direction, though it was really to give Will a chance to straighten up in the saddle before he tipped off.

'Where are we headed?' he asked and Batty told him, light and smiling.

'Langholm – we will just skirt the north of the Debate-able so we don't bump into Armstrongs. There will be warmth and shelter there. Then we head back to Edinburgh and Fife.'

'The tower is burned,' Will whispered and Batty acknowledged it. Langholm's tower had belonged to the Maxwells but the Earl of Hereford had washed war over it three years ago, burning it to a blackened husk.

There was the Smith Tavern, all the same and the risk of being too close to Hollows and Canobie would be worth it to give horses and Will a rest.

'Won't they follow?' Will asked and Batty reassured him that they might try, but it would rain soon and, with luck, they'd be in front of warming fire eating stew with meat in it while Nebless Clem plootered through the mud of the moor.

'Thwarted them again, eh Batty?'

They rode on, hunched into a soft, persistent drizzle until Batty saw a light, a corpse-candle affair so wan he had to squint to convince himself it was real. It was, filtering from under the badly fitting shutters of a bastel house.

It was a dumb shadow in the night, surrounded by two or three smaller shadows of outbuildings, but Batty rode them up close enough to be heard and then called. He had to do it twice before he heard wood clack and a voice sailed out of the unshuttered slit.

'Who are ye and what do you want?'

'Travellers, needing warmth and shelter. One is an injured Will Elliot…'

'And the other is Batty Coalhouse,' the voice finished. 'Aye, I have heard. You ken we are Armstrongs here?'

'I had hoped for Christian Armstrongs.'

'Get ye gone,' the voice answered coldly. 'Else we will come out and vengeance ourselves on the slaughterer of Hollows.'

'If you could,' Batty spat back, 'you would have already. Instead you will huddle there until the moudiewarts chasing us come up. Nebless Clem will ignore you and take over your outbuildings and anything in them he needs.'

'Would we be better off if you were here when he arrived? I dinna think so. Begone.'

Begone. Nae Christians here – try up the dale. Batty remembered Minty telling the story an eon ago, laughing when she had laughter in her. That was gone; he turned Fiskie's head and rode on, dragging Will behind him.

They rode on while the rain filtered away, but gathering clouds veiled the sun. Batty raised his head and bathed in birdsong. He knew he was heading in the right direction but had no clue what lay ahead, save that the Armstrongs would be somewhere in it if he stood poorly in the sight of God. He knew Nebless Clem feared them, too and so would be riding cautious, throwing riders out as scouts.

In the end, horses decided it; they stumbled more often and almost pitched Will off, so Batty steered them in the direction of a stream, little more than a rill and followed it to where he found a ruin half-hidden by birch.

This was no recent victim of the English purge on the borders but an older affair, where Names had looted and pillaged until no-one wanted the place. It was solid walled, the remains of a slate roof at one end, but the stones and slates had been plundered over the years by neighbours who valued the treasure of them.

It had lain uninhabited but for rats and birds, long enough for birch to grow through some of it, trunks thick as a man's forearm. It was also shaded and hidden by them and Batty took a chance.

He helped Will off the horse and laid him under the shelter of the slate-roofed end, covering him with Fiskie's horse blanket. Then he dared a fire, little and made with wood that smoked only a little blue haze. He unsaddled the horses, brushed them as best as he was able, until Fiskie started in to grunting with the pleasure of it. Then he fed them what fodder he had left and finally made a decent gruel of grain and wind-dried cod, listening to the cushie-doos murmur back and forth.

Will barely ate a mouthful, his breath a heavy, broken stutter. There was blood on the horn spoon when Batty took it and that made him frown. He stared at the man, his face waxy and the colour of old cream. He had grit, for sure, but he would die unless he got better care and the thought drove a blade of sorrow and panic into Batty, so that he almost sprang up to saddle the horses again.

He watched the beasts cropping grass, thought of all the times he had seen blood in the drinking bowl or on the lips of men wheezing desperately to live. He could pick up a stalk of grass, sign the cross over it to consecrate it as a Host and give absolution to Will, but he would not do it just yet. Instead, he watched him in the poor light of day, surrounded by birdsong.

Will was aware of it, could not open his eyes to look back at Batty but still could see him. He knew he was dying but no longer felt the fear of it. If you are stuck under a great rock you can't move, with no hope of rescue, what do you do?

Count the blessings of your life? Not many. Consider the blessing that it won't be troubling you much longer.

Batty thought that in a different world they would just have looked into each other's eyes, and Batty would have said: 'You're dying' while Will confessed that he knew, but was afraid. That's all they would have said if they'd been talking straight from the heart and Batty had stared into the eyes of dying men too often to know how impossible it was to live like that.

And Will thought of the world moving forward without him, not noticing he was gone. Am I wicked for thinking of a world that ends when I do? Not ending with respect to me – but every set of eyes closing with mine.

'How do you feel?' Batty managed to ask and Will smiled.

Dying is nothing, he wanted to say and he had no fear of it in his mind. But living? Living was becoming a field of sheep hefting to a hill, wandering where they pleased. Living was a gliding owl in the dark. Living was a good horse between your legs and a caliver under one leg and the rolling moor with a stream fringed with trees along it and the bulk of grey shape that might be Hermitage or Heaven.

He wanted to say all that, but all he managed was 'fine'.

Batty felt a chill on his neck and went to pull the blanket up round Will when the pigeons burst away with frantic flaps; he turned, reaching for the axe-handled dagg in his belt, then looked up into two faces, bearded and tense.

'Dinna jerk that fast,' one said. 'Pull it slow and let it drop.'

Batty looked at them steadily, then let the axe-handled dagg drop to the ground with a thump. They weren't runaways from one of the paid-sojer companies, they were Broken Men in dirty trews and scuffed boots and ragged jacks, splintered and cut from hard use. Border men and the worst of them. The one who had spoken had a latchbow, raised almost to his shoulder. This will be the one who boasts about killing three of us.

'Well,' said the other one, 'wid ye look at that. Batty Coalhouse, what Clem has been chasing and trembling over for all this time. Meaner than a stepped-on adder, bloody-handed and terrible, they said. Whit is all the fuss about, eh, Patey?'

'Ah kilt three of them,' Patey replied, lowering the latchbow and grinning.

'Two,' the other corrected and Patey hawked and spat.

'Three in a while – look at him, Tam. Belly-shot and dying.'

'Well,' said Tam again. 'Here ye are, having been sounded out as a tusky boar and found squatting like a fopdoodle.'

'Nebless Clem will be happy for you,' Batty growled, wondering if he could reach the tribe of knives across his chest, or the one in his boot, or even his backsword.

'On yer feet,' Tam ordered, sneering. 'Put yon one good hand on your heid and stand up. Face me.'

'Watch him, Tam,' Patey warned.

'Shut yer breadhole, Patey,' Tam growled and then eased a little, his smile all lopsided and brown. 'I'd as soon have Patey put yin of his bolts in your face, but that would mean us dragging you on to a pony and carting the pair of you away back to Clem.'

'We could try the Armstrongs at Hollows,' Patey put in. 'Pound for pound they will pay the best price for him.'

Tam half-turned, considering it. 'Clem's nose will be out of joint ower that.'

They both laughed, then Tam signalled Patey to hand over the latchbow. 'Go fetch up the ponies.'

Patey scowled at him. 'I am the one for this weapon. You couldna hit a bull's arse at touching range. You get the ponies.'

Tam scowled, then turned to Batty. 'Get yourself free o' that blade at your side.'

Batty got the baldric over his head and the backsword slithered to the ground. Tam's feral grin got wider.

'See, Patey? When you pull his fangs he's a wee tamed hound. I'll get the mounts – watch him close, mind.'

He stumped off, clashing through the undergrowth. How did I not hear them come up, Batty wondered? They are bulls, not foxes.

He felt himself come over loose, felt his mouth fill with spit and start to zing. He measured the distance to Patey and his latchbow. Then he started to reach inside his half-opened jack; Patey made a warning gesture, but Batty made a whimpering sound.

'Here,' he said. 'I have money here. Take it and let me go.'

He hauled out a handful of silver and let it spill, catching the light; Patey's mouth dropped a little and he stared.

'How much more is in there? Bring it all out.'

Batty half-rolled his body, feeling a knee shriek. At the same time he plucked out Brother Throw from the tribe of knives banded in the apostles across his chest and flicked it.

Something hissed past his shoulder, then Patey cried out, a gurgling sound, and staggered sideways. Batty dipped to the backsword, drew it and lunged, but Patey was on his back, kicking like a beetle and Batty had nothing much to do other than to look into the shocked eyes while blood from Brother Throw's neck slice sluiced down like a scarlet scarf.

Batty said nothing, simply leaned the sword into the new hole and pushed until Patey shut up all sounds.

Then he rescued Brother Throw and wiped the blade clean on Patey, sheathed it and went back for the dropped dagg. He heard the crashing as Tam lurched back with the ponies, saw him as he came into the clearing.

'Ye are right, Patey,' he was saying, 'we will go to the Armstrongs…'

He had time to be briefly shrill when the bang went off and the flare soared out of the barrel. Then he was slung away like some discarded bag, hit the last wall of the ruined house and slid down it leaving a snail trail of gore.

'Thwarted them again, Batty,' said a voice and turned to where Will was weaving on his feet, sword in hand.

'If you have burst open yon wound to leaking, I will beat you with a bridle.'

'I am pert as a rutting buck,' Will said and then his legs failed him so that he sat down, a bewildered expression on his face.

'Up,' Batty said, shoving the pistol into his belt and extending his hand. 'Nebless Clem might be close enough to hear that so we should not wait around for it.'

'I thought you came to kill him,' Will said, his voice a whisper. Batty scowled.

'I will. I would just prefer not to have to break a wall of his men to do it.'

Will managed to climb into the saddle with some help from Batty and for a time he looked upright and alert, but Batty saw him droop and slump. He did not want to stop, all the same, so he led Will's beast and took the easiest way he could find, always heading west, towards

Langholm. Though there was no certainty of decent help for Will there, no proper barber-surgeon, only beldames with skill and potions that would get them burned if a decent witch-finder took it into his head to go hunting.

The only such medical I met inspired no-one, Batty remembered but then I was out of it for most of the affair and only my ma told me how his hands were clean and his nails trimmed, which was a good sign for her.

The wee barber-surgeon, whose name Batty did not know and wished he did in order to offer daily prayers, had cut and tied the stump of his arm and even offered help swaddling the body of Batty's da. His ma, ruined by grief, barely functioned and Batty came out of his fogged condition only once, enough to hear the chirugeon offering his ma some 'small beauties'.

That had been maggots, which his ma had used to root out the rot when Batty's stump started in to healing. That unknown wee tooth-pulling hair cutter with his Paracelsus skills saved my life, Batty thought. Though there are some as would think that a waste...

What do they think has happened to make old fools like this?

Batty jerked round at the sound of Will's voice, which seemed strong and yet came from a lolling husk. He'd though to find intelligence in the face, but it was wobbling like a bladder on a stick and the mouth moved wetly and when silent, hung open and drooled.

Is it more grown-up when you keep pissing yourself, and can't remember who called on you this morning?

Aye, well done Will Elliot, Batty thought. Who is younger than me by a score of years and yet has beat me to the tape. If he lives, I will tell him of this moment...

The thought made him guilty and ashamed because he had come to believe Will when he said everything bad that had happened to him came from Batty. Mercifully, Will had given up on sense and though he spoke, said nothing Batty could understand.

If either of us could choose, he thought, we would pact with the very De'il to alter things back to when we could dance all night, or lace our own shoes.

Better having faith in that than knowing God will make no change and they will always now behave as if crippled or foolish, sitting through days that seemed too thin and where dreaming had more substance.

Age whittles away at beauty, saws away at strength, blunts sharpness of skill and wit. Few are born with a treasury of those traits. Fewer still manage to beat off the relentless attacks of Time. I have done so for too long and thought I held my own, Batty thought, then chuckled. Maybe I should have drunk more often from the Holy Grail when I had it in my hand. If you believe it…

The biggest mystery of all is – why am I not screaming?

–

They came up through a soft day and the haar rolling up from the Solway, cold enough to make lawyers keep their hands in their own pouches. The milk-mist had no rain but it soaked everything, leaving clear diamonds trembling on stalks and petals and clothing and beards.

It made the cross that loomed up a sudden, frightening beast that caused Batty to jerk and set Fiskie snorting; he looked guiltily back at Will, but his horse was plodding weary and had noticed nothing.

It was a tall cross with a nimbus, slouching on a three-step base. Defiantly Catholic these days, Batty thought, but a defiant Scotland embraced it – but he knew where he was now and felt better for it. In another few steps the dark shadow of the old chapel slid out of the mist.

It was a squat, unhandsome affair with a slate roof still intact and, though wee kirks only a few miles away on the English side of the Border had been Reformed years before, the ones on the Scots side went relentlessly on.

This one, however, had seen the ravages of raid and counter-raid so that the wee men of God had fled for the safety of Glasgow, because the kirk was dedicated to Saint Teneu, mother of Saint Kentigern, apostle to Strathclyde and founder of the city of Glasgow. Whenever fire and steel threatens, Batty thought, you run for that sacred place that can never be violated – your ain home and bed. There God will show you your folly of belief.

Good old Saint Thenew, Batty thought. He had ridden this way before, but had never stopped; the value of the place then lay in the narrowest, easiest crossing of the Esk with a step of stones that took you dryshod from one side to the other in less than a minute. It came up to the hubs of two-wheeled carts, which could also be taken across it and you might risk a four-wheeler if the river was not flooding.

Now the building was all of it. Batty was sure it had been maligned with hauntings and worse, which is why its stones and slates were still intact; the double doors were open wide and had been badly battered before this, but the locking beam was inside, propped up against one wall in case folk arrived here desperate and pursued. The inside was a scatter of timbers from broken pews, the shattered glass of magnificent, decadent coloured windows and the litter of smashed idolatry – but it had been mostly left alone.

Batty brought the horses in and unloaded Will, who tried to help but had no strength. Batty put him under a part of the roof with more slates than holes, wrapping him warm while he attended to the beasts. There was little left for them to eat, so once he had unsaddled them, he led them out one by one, then pegged and hobbled them so they could chew grass.

After that, he fetched the wood of the splintered pews and started a fire. He reckoned there would be little light and less smoke from the dry wood inside the church and fairly certain that Clem and his trackers would not come this way — at least at first.

He made pottage with the last of their stocks — cabbage soup with some oats and a sniff of bacon. It was liberally dosed with ransom, wild garlic, a deliberate ploy by Batty. Will made murmurs of appreciation and managed to get some down him before he gave up and sank back, exhausted.

Not that it will do him much good with a belly wound like he has, Batty thought as he watched him and supped. In a while Batty would expose the wound and sniff around it; he fully expected to smell the wild garlic and confirm that Will's liver and lights were pierced. From there it was a step or two from the end.

But the taste and warm will keep him this side of Heaven for a while and maybe if we reach Langholm…

He slept, couldn't say for how long, but when he woke it was the dying of the day and he started up thinking he had heard something moving. He scrambled up, found the axe-handled dagg and went out to where he had hobbled the horses; they looked up at his approach, calm and rested.

The night was cool and clear, the haar shredded away by a wind that staggered clouds over the bloody sunset; somewhere a hunting owl screeched. Batty went back to where Will lay, fetched out a brand from the fire and stuck it where it gave extra light for what he wanted to do.

He took the old wrappings off to expose the wound, a coin-sized hole blotched with blue flesh, turning black, speckled with puffy sick white around the edges. He cleaned the wound with a clean rag and then started to rebind it, having to shift Will to do it. When he had finished, he turned into the stare of Will, a dark affair from a face the colour of spoiled cream.

'Bad,' Will said. 'Want you to know I am sorry for griping at you. You keep saving me but I am thinking this time you cannot.'

'Away,' Batty said dismissively and then felt the touch of Will's hand. He knew it was meant as a warm gesture, but the skin was dry and felt like a lizard claw.

'When I am gone,' he said and Batty snorted.

'Ye have a dance invite then?'

'When I am gone,' Will repeated, 'leave me here. Wrap me up, tie me tight and prop me at the altar – I like the idea of scaring the Jesus out of anyone who creeps in looking for slates.'

'Just because you have lost God,' Batty answered roughly. Will's chuckle was feather light.

'I have. Is it not the worst irony? Here am I without God and there is you, who could never be persuaded to him, now wanting to believe.'

'I drank from the Grail,' Batty answered and wondered if it was true. The Lord was still a vicious bastard in his everyday life was what he thought – and yet he would pray to him to spare Will.

'I want ye to know I'm as proud as a new rooster to have ridden with ye,' Will added, his voice fading. He lay back and closed his eyes, so that the shadows made by the lancing sunbeams softened his hollowing cheeks. Sleep made him look like he did when he was a wee boy.

'Ye are a wee rooster, right enough,' Batty said softly, then fell to the painstaking annoyance of reloading the axe-handled dagg.

It is a dread matter, watching the approach of death. To know that hope is gone, and recovery impossible and to sit and count the grey hours until life leaves. In a while there would be the secrets of the heart, buried and hidden for years, poured out by a being no longer able to keep the doors closed. The strength and sleekit of a whole life will fail when fever and delirium tear free.

Batty had heard them many times before, strange tales told in the wanderings of dying men, full of guilt and crime that those who stood by the sick person's last bed have shifted away in horror and affright, no matter that they were hard men, fell cruel in the ways of war. But they had the same secrets and were afraid to see that, at the last, they would spill them forth like vomit.

They left that poor wretch to die alone, raving of foul deeds that had mattered to him.

–

He started awake into the dying echoes of a dog fox screaming and the rattle of wings fleeing the trees. He knew what it was at once and cursed his luck; he had thought to give Will and the horses more rest – and himself, if he was forced to admit it – but the dawn was spearing light over the horizon and all was undone.

He heard them prowling, talking in low voices and then someone pressed the doors and felt the barrier of the beam.

'Some yin is inside,' a rough voice declared and the answer to it was a growl of spit and scathe.

'Aye, wake them up why don't ye?'

'Might be haunts,' another voice offered, rich with fear, but the scathe had plenty left for him, too.

'No' much of a haunt if it needs to bar the door, is it?'

Batty fumbled for his pistols. He had started to reload them but the poor light, his poor eyes and the treachery of pain in his knuckles had allowed him only two before he gave it up, vowing to himself to load the last 'in a minutey', once he had rested his eyes.

He found the axe-handled dagg and brought it up, found his baldric and backsword and dragged it close, then levered himself up, listening to his knees crack and complain with sharp stabs of pain. Will never moved, which was a blessing at least.

Then a voice he knew said: 'Lever up the beam and get in. It's him, I know it.'

Batty watched the blade slide through the splintered door seams and under the bar, then it went up, there was a tremble and a grunt as the man wielding it raised the bar off the trunnions and let it fall. It clattered loudly to the remains of the flagged floor. The doors swung inwards.

'Coalhouse. Step out. You have annoyed us long enough and caused folk out here to be resentful of their lost kin. If I turn them loose, there will be no parlay.'

It was Nebless Clem, that familiar drawl Batty had recognised.

'Come ahead, you skull-faced child beater.'

Clem growled and muttered, exhorting men through the door and no-one was willing because they knew what would happen; Batty suspected Clem promised silver he didn't have and one was gullible enough to become the Forlorn Hope and crash through the castle breach.

He lived long enough to realise where greed had got him; the ornate Saxon dagg spat deafening noise and a blinding flare of flame which ate his face and sent him backwards into his crowding mates, who recoiled in horror.

Batty dropped the dagg and took up his backsword, in time to face the fear-masked howl of a second man, his own sword up and coming down like the wrath of the Devil. Batty had time to throw up a block but the shock nearly drove the sword from his grasp and his opponent felt it, grinned manically and started to bore in for the kill.

Save that Batty kicked him in the shin, hard enough to crack bone; the man fell away sideways yelping, but there was no time even for a brief moment of triumph – yet another took his place and stamped forward swinging right and left.

Then he came on, all fire and flashing steel, forcing Batty to back, away from the poor firelight and until his back slammed a pew. The man who followed, relentless as avalanche, was grinning and twirling.

Once, Batty had thought to learn the proper way of the sword and he knew the ways of it, saw it in this man's supple wrist and easy moves. He fought desperately, knowing he was outmatched from the start, hearing the wee Bologna *maistre's* pawky voice, a grate on all those sweaty hours in the *salle*, with its stink of liniment and fear; *the glide to the outside high line should be executed in one movement from one's own engagement in sixte, Monsieur. It should end in the adversary's outside high line.*

The blades spanged and shot sparks – *the answer to it is a parry – la! – with third and riposte to the low line, which is detached, or outside high line, which is contact.*

This was no *salle* elegance, no Lippo Dardi expertise; Batty dropped low, feeling his knees screech. He scythed, caught his opponent by surprise and booted him in the cods as he rose up again – save that he missed and hit the upper thigh. It was enough for the man to yelp and fall backwards, clattering into the man behind – Christ's blood, they are lining up to hack lumps aff me – but he was up and away like a cat before Batty's savage backsword cut chipped up stone where he had been. The man took advantage of Batty's off-balance to lunge, pinked him in a rake up the wrist.

Cursing, Batty spun away, shaking his hand in agony, spraying blood in fat drops, but determinedly hanging on to the sword; he turned to face the man, who saluted with an insouciant swish-swish – and came on again.

Or he can parry counter of fourth and riposte to the inside high line – detached or contact – or a flanconade in fourth.

They locked hilts and faces – and Batty spat on him, which made the man reel back with a cry of outrage. He recovered well enough to glissade Batty's mad whirl of cuts and thrusts until the strength bled out of them. Batty backed away until the altar racked his back; now the men fanning out on either side of his opponent could not circle round and backstab him.

Instead of parrying and riposting, he can also counterattack with the time thrust or passata sotto...

The backsword wasn't the weapon for it, but Batty was sobbing for breath now and backed hard up against the altar; from somewhere came more shouts and the squeal of too-excited horses.

He lunged, felt the almost contemptuous glissading parry, took the brunt of the enemy's hilt on the side of his head and went sprawling; he lost his grip, heard the backsword clatter. Someone screamed and a pistol went off with a roar and blast of flame that silhouetted all the heads facing Batty. Too many, he thought, struggling for sense.

'Not so much after all, Batty Coalhouse,' his opponent sneered, though he was breathing hard and limping from the kick. He saw Batty start to move toward the distant sword and gave two small steps and kicked it further away.

'I had heard you were a wolf with fangs of steel. I had heard you defeated the Armstrong lord of Hollows, for all he had a two-hander. I am Tam of the Shaws and I have you Batty Coalhouse,' he gloated.

So ye have, Batty thought, feeling sick and drained and dizzy. Too auld, too slow, too everything that was bad...

Tam of the Shaws had put the point of the sword to his neck and the steel was cold as an icicle, though it broke out more sweat on him and kept him from speaking. Yet his mind ticked – why was there shouting and fighting? Why had a gun gone off when Nebless Clem's men had none?

'Away, ye moudiewart wee pox sore,' said a new growl of voice and Batty watched, bemused as Tam o' the Shaws reared up like a goosed mare and let the sword fall from his hand. He was looking round until he thought to look down a little.

The Ape grinned up at him, a dagger driven into the cloth of his cods, hard enough for him to feel the point. The Ape turned the grin on Batty.

'The King sends his regards.'

Batty got to his feet, swaying; there were men crowding everywhere and a deal of them with grey faces in the sudden torchlight, knowing their fate but unable to fight to the end, in case God or the Devil stepped in and saved them. Tam of the Shaws had a luminous face and a mouth twisted with fear; the Ape pushed his point harder and Tam whimpered.

Will was lying where he had been before, though the blanket was off him where folk had kicked and trampled over him. Batty felt a lurch then and confirmed it when he knelt, almost falling as he felt his neck.

Will was dead.

The truth of it drove a gasp from Batty so that he could not stand and had all his efforts straining to keep from falling over prone.

They had almost made it. They had almost thwarted them all. Batty cursed God until he started to choke on his own incoherent spit; someone's arms went round him and raised him on to wavering legs – he threw them off.

'This man,' he managed eventually, 'was raised in a time of blood and dying, of war and burning water. He never turned his back on folks in trouble and when he rode with me I had no complaints.'

'We'll gie him a decent kisting,' said a voice and the granite cliff face of the Randi King loomed into Batty's view. 'We owe you for that.'

249

Chapter Seventeen

With the Egyptiani

Mair sleekit than a buttered otter. That was Merrilee Meg's take on Nebless Clem, who had contrived to make his escape yet again. Batty found that out after a score of hours thinking he was back in the Swan, the Dutch fluyt that transported Maramaldo up and down the Baltic.

The Swan was the worst ship in Christendom, whose rats knew more about sailing than the half-dozen apes they had as a crew. He was relieved to find that what he rode in, swaying under flapping canvas, was one of the Egyptiani covered carts.

When it stopped, the King heaved himself up the side and dropped to the bed of it, a great flat clunk of sound that rocked the cart to and fro. The King grinned.

'Awake then is it?'

'How long have I been out?'

'Long enough,' Meg answered and put the delicious balm of a cold compress on his forehead. 'Yon whip scars ye have are a right sight, no mistake. Some of them have been stretched broken so that your back will look like auld Egypt writing from now on. Your lovers will go mad trying to work out the message.'

'Well, we are making camp for the night, having avoided Graitna and trying to avoid Carlisle,' the Randi

King said. 'Headed south to St Cuthbert's Fair once we have set you back on your feet.'

'My thanks for that,' Batty managed. 'How did ye ken where I was?'

The King waved dismissively. 'We have oor ways and I owed you for the rescue of the Ape.'

'Bliddy wee hoormonger,' Meg threw in bitterly. The King laughed.

'Ye wonder where he gets the grit for it, considering how he is handled most nights by yerself, mighty Meg.'

She rose in a waft of stale sweat and perfume, tossed her head and declared her intent to fetch Batty some broth. Outside, Batty heard the low murmur of talk, the tinkling clash of anklets and bracelets, the sound of wood being cut.

'Aye, aye – be assured your horses are revelling in comfort.'

'Will?'

The King sighed. 'A bad end for a good man. We left him by the altar as you raved over it so hard. Tied him a decent carpet all the way from the Mongol lands and sat him with his face uncovered. He will scare the horses, so he will.'

Merrilee Meg snorted, whether at the joke or the way they had left him, and he exchanged winks and she swayed off dropping over the side of the wagon. The King watched her go and chuckled.

'Aye, sometimes I envy the Ape...'

He seemed to say that every time and Batty often wondered if he had been there. Probably not – for all his grim strength, King Billy did not like magic and knew what Meg could do with a sample of seed.

'Not if you had seen him with his hair full of straw in the garth at Carlisle,' Batty growled back and the King admitted it with a shrug.

'I thought he was lost, for sure. You are welcome to travel as far south with us as you care.'

Batty said nothing and the King eased himself a little, turned sideways to seek something hidden and turned back, grinning.

'The wummin are cleaning and loading your fine pistols, we have recovered all your wee knives – but your sword is a ruin. The blade is broken at the tip and bent in the middle. I have it, but unless there is sentiment in it for you, I would advise you leave it here. Egyptiani smiths are noted for bringing the dead back to life.'

Surprisingly, Batty found the sentiment in the old blade – but a useless edge was just that and he said so. The King nodded sagely, then thrust a burlap wrapped package forward.

'A wee bit too fine for the likes of yourself,' he offered, 'and a duellist's weapon. I can see it hanging in pride on the wall of your wee tower, all the same.'

Batty unwrapped the burlap to find his own sheath and a new sword in it. It was a backsword of sorts, but for all it had a basket hilt in the Scottish style, Batty thought it had been fashioned elsewhere, particularly because backsword by tradition were sharp on one side only and this one had an inscription cut into the blade: *Si Deus pro nobis quis contra nos*, the King told him.

If God is for us, who will stand against us – it made Batty think of Templars and that made him uneasy. It made him think of Sister Faith and her insistence that he was Michaelangelo, that he had drunk from the Holy

Grail instead of the rough-carved wooden bowl she had handed him to keep safe.

He hoped she was safe still, as he studied the sword, the way the blade was a double edge from the midpoint to the tip, how the hilt was composed of two solid side guards surmounted with a woven design in the Scottish fashion. It was a matter of lethal beauty and he thanked the King for it.

He saw the genuine delight in Batty's face and cracked his own with a big smile. 'I am sure you will leave as soon as you can. Seek Clem and use that fine blade to cut off his eyelids to complete his beauty.'

He leaned forward so his wrecking reef of a face was inches away. 'I have admired yer derring-do for the longest time. There's the rub of it. Time. The only enemy ye will never beat – but you have had good innings. Time you left the Border lands, Batty Coalhouse, or you will end at the ither end of that chapel with Will, staring each other out until the Second Coming. Or dance in the air like all Clem's men are doing, waiting for the crows of dawn.'

He leaned back a little. 'Ye have the siller for it – ye have replaced your belly with a bag of coin, I see. Enough to live comfortable. Dinna worry – it is safe enough until you want it.'

'Will's ransom,' Batty said, suddenly remembering it. 'Belongs to a wee lord out in Fife and I will needs take it back to him.'

'That's the ither direction,' the King pointed out. 'I can give you some men to make sure you get there – but it is my fondest wish you never return to these parts. Now that the war is no barrier to them, your enemies are stirring forth and will eat you.'

Later, Batty found the strength to leave the wagon and sit by the fire in the camp, surrounded by people talking in what seemed half-a-dozen tongues at once. Women swayed among them, cooking and serving while others, men included, worked willow into baskets, or horn into spoons.

He sat beside Megs, who brought him mutton stew and they ate and talked. Batty learned that they were heading down to Applecross and the horse fair.

'Though it is not only for the horses,' Megs added and smiled gently. 'Also to meet others and get them wedded. The King calls it improving the bloodline.'

Batty knew it well enough – this was one of the larger Egyptiani groups, but there were others and they needed to find mates so that, as the King had memorably said to Batty once before 'we don't end up with droolers who have an extra limb.'

'Are you with us?' Megs asked and Batty shook his head and explained what he must do. She nodded as if she had known.

'You need a good woman,' she added. 'There's Philo over there, a field in need of ploughing since her man died of the Sweats. She's the one who cared for you and knows the ways of herb and chant.'

'A dangerous profession,' Batty responded, though he had to admit the Philo in question was dark, tinkled with brass and had a shelf of chest that moved well. He felt Megs' scowl and was urged to tell her of the five women abused and hanged by Nebless Clem.

'Everyone was told by the Mistress of Blackscargil that they were Egyptiani women, but that was a lie. For a' that, Clem sought revenge on you, which is why the Ape was seized.'

'Who were the poor quine?' she wanted to know and Batty told her. She shook her red head and looked into the flames; for a moment, Batty thought she was working some heinous spell on Clem and did not like being near it.

She felt him shift and turned. 'You and I have been together often enough for me to know that commingling is no' a problem with you. Is it maritals that puts you off?'

Commingling. Where did she get it from, he wondered? At the same time the memories of it welled up and he felt himself urging in the groin, enough to make him grunt. She knew well enough what was happening and her smile grew salacious.

'I have no desire to saddle a wummin wi' an auld wreck like me,' he hastened to add. 'Everyone tells me I am too auld, too slow and the rest.'

He levered himself up and made for the cart, hoping he could heave himself up by the wheel and clatter back into it.

'I wid have ye, Batty Coalhouse,' he heard her say.

Christ wummin, I plough you once a six-month, if that and you never ask payment, though you always take something I never miss and am never aware of. All very fine for a witch with red hair, but you are twenty years younger and there is a big change between a rare swiving and being married on to me.

He wanted to say it, but his mouth was dry and he crawled into the bed, feeling flushed and cold at the same time. He fell asleep and when he woke, she was at his back and his hand had been dragged between her thighs, high up against the heat of her.

He tried to pull free and felt the thighs close.

'Best liniment for what ails your fingers, Batty,' she breathed. 'It will ease your stiffness.'

Her own hand was where stiffness was being encouraged and he wanted to tell her to leave off, but failed. Spectacularly.

She lay with him all of that night, which was unusual from the other times. He woke briefly, feeling her fingers tracing the still-raw scars on his back, as if reading runes. She knew he was awake and he felt her wine-breath on his ear.

'Ye are too thin by far. I liked my Batty with more belly.'

And a clean shirt. And washed armpits. Once a wummin gets ye…

He fell asleep to her breathing, wondering if she was touched by some curse that made her want auld fat men. In the morning, she was gone from the bed and he was still wondering.

Chapter Eighteen

Eastwards, up the Liddesdale

He moved through the mist, hoping it would last well into morning, aware of the heat of the Armstrongs and Elliots and Nixons to the north, the Milburns, Dodds, Charltons and everyone else he had antagonised to the south, over the river in England. If he could just stay mouse-quiet and unseen until Hermitage...

He rode in silence, thinking on her and what she had said. 'You are a lonely man,' she had offered, her voice soft in the dark.

'No more than you,' he had replied. 'But I am an older man who can live with my loneliness, quietly. You are young, and it must be difficult to accept your loneliness, right in the middle of a' yer ain folk. You must sometimes want to fight it – which is why you make the offer you do.'

She had struck his arm, hard enough to make him wince with her little nut fist.

'Fool,' she said. 'There is eighteen years between us, that's all. A good man is a good man, no matter the silver in his hair. Youth is not the only lonely time – you keep coming to my house but you cannot rid yourself of your loneliness. I have it in me to help you forget it, but you never stay long enough, as if the feeling of cleaving to another kicks you to your feet.'

Her voice tailed to a firm sadness. 'I have decided this will be otherwise.'

'The King may think different,' Batty offered, a little afraid and knowing it was exactly as she said. She laughed.

'He has never lain with me. He fears the magic. Part of why he wishes me wed to you.'

Batty gawped and she laughed. 'He kens you will not stay with the Egyptiani and that we will leave once wed. He kens also that I am the best sense you will get for achieving your goals – your ain tower in a place of peace.'

I've enjoyed every age I've been, even the one where I lost my arm, he thought now, shuffling along the Eskdale. Every scar is a badge I wear to show I've been present, the hat-plumes displayed proudly for all to see. Nowadays, I don't want the face and body of the likes of Hepburn at Hermitage, the Fairbairn. I want to wear the life I've lived and do so for the longest time.

He thought about Will and how the world had not ceased because he was dead, how everything flew on despite his lack of presence in it. Death is not an evil. It takes away good things and the desire for them. Old age is the Devil, Batty thought, because it deprives us of all pleasures, leaving us only the appetite for them. Pawky folk that we are, we fear death, and we desire old age.

He met only the wool men, Forsters from Caddy-shaws near Hermitage. They were coming up the Eskdale looking to sell good fleeces in Graitna, to men who would ship them out of the Solway to the Dutchies. Good, clean wool would bring premium prices in a world ravaged by sheep-scab and Caddyshaws nestled in the armpit of

Hermitage, which had allowed them to raise the sheep in safety.

They knew who Batty was – who did not ken of the one-armed, heavily armed rider who scorned the rest of the Border and all his enemies in it? Tam Forster opined this, grinning brownly in the lights of lantern and fire. Since he offered decent ale and a plate with fish in the gruel, Batty worked out that he considered it only his due to speak freely.

'Them Armstrongs out of Mangerton will pact with the De'il to feel your collar,' Tam offered, passing good bread.

'The ones of Whithaugh might even brawl with their Mangerton Laird if it meant grabbing you for themselves,' said Johnnie Forster, Tam's younger brother. 'You made them look daft and they didnae care for that.'

'I had no hand in making them look daft,' Batty growled, spitting out fish bones. 'They managed that themselves.'

'Weil,' Tam answered, beaming from under the waterproof round his head, 'it is a fine, saft night and if it rains harder there is room underneath the cairt for all o' us. The Armstrongs are no' oot and aboot in this wet moonlight – and Nebless Clem is half-way to Berwick.'

This last was news to Batty, which he realised Tam had known all along, for he had a sleekit look.

'For a wee shilling or two,' he said, 'I can mayhap tell ye why.'

Batty knew why. He would be going to Malatesta before the man packed up and moved south. He would be looking for men and Malatesta, who hated Batty as much as the next man, would be likely to offer them.

Tam saw his chances smoke away and scowled, burying his bad cess in a mug.

He woke into another saft day of mizzle, where the rain never fell but hung in the air, drenching cobwebs with diamonds.

The high ground wore a shroud of silver, the path up to the little wood was a glittering net and the soaking earth smelled rich and sweet while the drips pitted and patted as he rode Fiskie away from the wool-sellers.

Batty did not wait to say goodbye, or take a hot posset; he wanted away from Tam and Johnnie and struck out along his original path until he could not see them, then turned more north than east. He did not trust them.

Not long after, when the sun was more than a milk wash in the east, he looked back towards the Esk and a sharp flick of light caught his eye. He knew it was the point of a slung lance, knew it well and waited until he saw two or three more. Men were riding up the Eask and in a little while would come on the wool seller brothers.

Armstrongs, he was sure of it. A small patrol, six or eight seeking news which they would get from Tam and Johnnie Forster. A one-armed man who was certainly Batty Coalhouse, heading east along the Esk, no more than an hour ahead.

Will they hunt down their quarry or go back to the warm of Mangerton? Or maybe even Whithaugh. He knew the truth – they would hunt down their own grannies if commanded and Batty would have sold his soul there and then to the Earl of Hell for two things – a glass with *eau de vie* and his youthful eyes returned.

'What shall we do?' he breathed to Fiskie, who whuffed back at him. Batty nodded – what we always do.

'Run,' he answered.

And then he was off, forging swiftly and feeling the heat of them on his ravaged back.

They rode too hard and for too long, down dips and up slopes until Fiskie's breathing made Batty stop. He looked back; a dark figure tottered over the far rise behind him, a cloak flung off his shoulder and trailing like a wedding train. He raised a wavering caliver, there was a plume of smoke and, an eyeblink later, the faint pop. Batty waved to him in savage exultation – missed, you bugger…

Then he cursed as a horseman breasted the crest, the big, powerful beast blowing hard, but urged into a new run. In the moment before Batty turned his head and started to urge Fiskie on, he saw the face. Knew it. Maurie Armstrong of Whithaugh, the one he had humiliated at Mickledale.

Out with some kinsman, hunting any whisper of a one-armed man. Batty had fumbled out a dagg and turned Fiskie to face Maurie, thinking he'd have to be quick or the others would swamp him like fever.

Maurie had flogged his fine horse into a final canter, but it was failing and finally stopped entirely, blowing. Maurie raised himself up in the stirrups.

'Hold hard, Batty Coalhouse, or I will blow out what brains you have.'

He kicked and cursed the horse into a stumbling trot, half-falling through the clinging bracken; it must have been a long, hard ride to get this far from those treacherous wool-selling brothers, Batty thought – for once, a chasing horse is worse than mine for wind.

Maurie had a pistol, which Batty realised must have been a deliberate action – there was the one with caliver, too and he imagined others would be so armed; the many daggs of Batty Coalhouse would be legendary now.

Maurie shot, which made the horse shy sideways at the blast and put his aim so far off he probably did not even hit the ground. Shrieking with fury, he savaged the bit, kicked with his spurred boots and the animal squealed and lumbered on.

At the last moment, Batty raised his pistol and fired, with Fiskie standing sideways; now we find how well we stand with God or the Devil. At that moment Maurie's horse had enough and stopped, flinging up its head in time to take the ball in the upper lip – the explosion of blood and brains, the high screaming of the horse, the smoke… all of it pinned Batty to the spot.

Riders materialised into two firm shapes and Batty reined Fiskie away from that, sticking the dagg back in the horse-holster and hauling out another. He fired, just as the nearest rider, wet-mouthed with fatigue was suddenly aware of who he was riding at. Wishing he had unshipped his lance, astonished as if he had stepped through a portal into fairyland, the last thing that went through his mind was a half-ounce of soldered lead shot.

He went backwards in a cloud of pink mist, as if hauled by the Devil's scaly hand – Batty shoved that dagg in the empty holster and hauled out the new backsword, kicking Fiskie straight at the remaining man.

This one managed a desperate parry and backed off, trying for room to slash and stab, but Batty pressed home. The man's face was red and sheened, he had a look of utter terror and his eyes rolled up into his head when the backsword hissed round and down; blood flew up and he yelped, collapsed moaning and whimpering off the horse.

There was a sudden, eerie stillness, broken only by the grunting of Maurie, who was pinned by his dead horse and struggling to escape; he went quiet when he saw Batty loom out of the clearing pistol smoke.

'You will hang for this,' he said and Batty looked down at him and smiled like a fox in a hen coop.

'I will hang you myself...'

'Och, Maurie, you will not,' Batty answered mildly. 'You will dine out on the tale of how you came quim-hair close to catching the terrible Batty Coalhouse – again – but was foiled by a poor mount and too many enemies. Again.'

Batty winked at the fallen man. 'There will be twenty at least who stood with him and you fought them all to no avail,' he added, 'and, with some luck, your limp will only add to the attraction all the weemin will have for you on the dancefloor.'

Even pinned and in pain, Maurie found a twist of smile, hearing what he would have said if the circumstance had been reversed.

'Get you gone, Batty. One day I will have the price of these dead from you, with interest.'

Batty did not hesitate; more men would be coming up and he wondered, already, why he had no seen them. Clutching his new backsword and exultant with the fact that he had survived and won through, he could not care less. He felt better than he had since he'd originally left Edinburgh and wondered if Meg had spelled him.

'*Si Deus pro nobis quis contra nos*,' he said and knew it was too enigmatic for Maurie to comprehend. He rode off, leaving Maurie yelling for his men and trailing a discordant verse or two after him, laughing in between.

> *'If God had let her work her utmost spite,*
> *Nae doot she'd have killed the man outright,*
> *But he is saved and for all her Malice,*
> *She looks to hang upon the Gallows.'*

Chapter Nineteen

Hermitage

Hermitage boiled like a fish cauldron and Batty found himself almost ignored as he shambled Fiskie up to the gloom of the castle. In the end, Toddie Graham saw him and trotted through the shriek and litter of carts and people.

'Batty,' he said, bemused. 'I thocht you were away out in that Fife. What brings you here?'

'I was that way inclined,' Batty answered, 'and still am. I need only the rest of today and the night and then I will continue. What's occurring here, then?'

Toddie was a big-chinned youth who had contrived to hide what he considered defect under a beard, but that had backfired and simply made his lower face massive as well as hairy. Batty, who had known Toddie as a wee lad, was facered to see the streaks of grey in it.

'Right slorach, is it no'?' Toddie responded, then looked right and left to find who was in earshot. 'Wicked Wat has only gone and declared his intent for a Truce Day at the Reidswire. We wait for the reply of Hume.'

'Christ save us,' Batty offered. 'Bad enough all the work and hazard of a Truce Day without the new Wicked Wat in it, he who has seldom been seen stirring to any work.'

265

Toddie chuckled. 'Aye well, he still isnae – the Captain has been packed to the Reidswire with wood and canvas to erect the shelters and booths. We can only hope that Hume says naw.'

Batty doubted it. Wicked Wat Scott, of Branxholme and Buccleuch, was newly appointed Warden of the Middle March in Scotland and determined to stamp his mark on it. Alexander Home was similarly smelling of new wood and paint for the English Middle March; they would both posture in their finery and make a clear declaration that the war between nations was done with, but the war against rapine, theft and slaughter had now to be fought.

Batty was surprised to see Harry Rae in the solar, twice surprised by how he felt glad about it. Rae cocked an eyebrow at the sight of him.

'Ye look better than last we met.'

'In Netherby,' Batty added, showing he remembered. 'Hot work after that, but Blackscargil is returned to the Grahams and Nebless Clem sent whirling intae the moss.'

'I hear Will Elliot died,' Rae said blankly. 'I am sorry for that – were you there for it?'

Batty admitted it and then sat, divested of his jack and boots, squinting at his daggs in the fire glow and fretting that Philo had drenched them with too much oil.

'What brings you here yerself?' he asked and Harry shrugged.

'I bring the news of all the world to Edinburgh.'

'As filtered by Sadler,' Batty added grimly and Henry laughed.

'Losh, no. There is a fifth outbreak of Sweating in England, down Shrewsbury way if you wisely wish to avoid it. John Caius is writing the first full contemporary account of the symptoms of the disease.'

He took a swallow from the cup of wine; Batty realised he was not about to be offered, so he crossed over and poured for himself.

'There is a debate in Valladolid concerning whether the indigenous folk of the Americas have human rights or not.'

'You say?' Batty queried, tasting the wine – a decent hock, he realised. 'Well, the Spaniards are a bit late coming to it.'

'I do say,' Henry went on. 'No doubt it will be the main thought on the mind of new Pope Julius III, recently elevated to the triple crown.'

'Which of all these marvellous events will concern the Upper Ten most in Edinburgh, d'ye think?' Batty asked. Henry shook his head.

'Dinna ken, dinna care. I bring the facts and await exodus or revelation.'

Batty acknowledged the jest with a raise of his cup, then went back to studying his guns at the fire.

> *'Out o' the lady's grave grew a bonny red rose and*
> *out o' the knight's a brier. And they twa met, and*
> *they twa plat and fain they wad be near; but in*
> *the end all angels rise and men are wise to fear.'*

'That's a nice song,' said Rae and it was only then Batty realised he'd been singing it. It took him a moment or two to recall that he'd heard it over and over out beyond the Balkans.

'A wee tune for fighting men,' he added and Harry smacked his lips round the wine.

'With angels in it? I didnae ken such folk cared for angels much – and many of them will care less for such Catholics in the years to come, I surmise.'

'Indeed,' Batty declared. 'You are right.'

Rae was silent for a moment or two and then huffed. 'As I have said, ye looked like a burned boot that had been kicked round a muddy garth as a fitba' last time we met. Yet here ye are, fresh as new dawn and singing songs about angels.'

'I drank from the Grail,' Batty answered and found a patch of linen which he used to try and lighten the oiling on his daggs. 'Besides, a wise man told me the secret of good health.'

'Which is?'

'Never to argue with a man of opposing view.'

'Away,' Harry Rae declared, scathing and slack-mouthed. Batty grinned.

'You are right,' he answered.

He remembered the song being sung after hard fighting and men crying over it, cheerful though it seemed. But that was because they were listening out for the voices not singing, the ones who would never sing again. Harry Rae had never experienced it and probably never would unless he stood poorly in the eyes of God or Satan, for the business of war was not in his nature. Only causing it.

Batty did not say anything and, after a long and pleasurable silence, Harry broke it, gruff as goats.

'I hope you are gone afore the Captain gets back. That cloth ye hold is a Dutch lace doillie to stop creishie heids rubbing on the good fabric of his chair. Cost a wee fortune, but lets the great and good know he has taste.'

Batty looked guilty for a moment, then went back to cleaning the pistol pan. Somewhere outside a hound howled.

'I have a favour,' Harry Rae declared and Batty's heart foundered. He turned a heavy head and saw Rae holding something between the thumb and forefinger of one hand, a slim, silvered affair, domed at either end and no longer than half a ring-finger.

'This is the stock of our trade,' Rae continued. 'There are secrets here.'

He twisted the affair so that it unscrewed; inside was a tightly rolled piece of paper, which he withdrew.

'Secrets,' he said, 'for the eyes of the great and mighty.'

Batty had seen wee pieces of paper like this before, spilled from Needle Tam's geegaw cases and said so. Harry Rae huffed dismissively.

'Many are used,' he answered dryly, 'but only the most loyal and trusted get the silver. You know why it is this shape?'

He did not wait. 'If you are taken by surprise, you swallow it.'

Batty was unsurprised, but equally unsure it was safe to do such a thing – he had seen long-time silversmiths turning blue with the exposure to silver and he did not trust the process of ingesting it.

'If you ever rediscover Will Elliot,' Rae added, reining round, 'you might try his dead insides for one like this – perhaps a little longer. Not swallowed.'

Inserted. Batty recoiled at the idea, but knew one sure thing about it.

'Valuable to you, is it?'

Rae chuckled. 'Mair valuable to you, I am thinking. Make the effort and then quit the Borders forever. That will make it worthwhile to me.'

Batty rode on, musing on what he had heard. He did not like spywork and vowed never to go near the dead Will in his church tomb. The endless nag of it, all the same, almost took away the delight of Falkland stables, where the royal horses were kept.

There were 200 in stall and room for more, so Fiskie had a royal night in the dry, massaged by a brush in the hands of two servitors while Batty ate lavishly of stew and bread and greens. He brought Fiskie an apple later and, though he had a proper bed, stayed with his horse and slept warm and dry.

In the morning, he rode on to Newark Castle.

There was scaffolding everywhere and what seemed to be too many people, milling like maggots and unnerving Batty. He found the Lord, was invited to the solar, half new wood and the rest old char.

He presented the scuffed worn bag of coin and told how this was less his fee and how Will had died. The old Lord's seamed, pouched face seemed to droop even more at the news, but he shook Batty's hand.

'Ye did well, in the fight here and efter; I have heard tales of it. Good luck to ye Master Coalhouse. I would advise you take your fee and travel far from Scotland, all the same – folk have been here looking for you and Will.'

The way he said it was meant kindly but had the word 'monster' unspoken in it. Batty ate frugally and lay in a cot for a long time, thinking on how hard he and Will had struggled to get here and how it now seemed like mist on glass.

They were all right, the ones who breathed 'monster' to themselves. Batty had hundreds of monsters inside him wearing his face as a mask. Screaming and trying to tear him apart and all for sound reasons, while he fought furiously to hold them back in the mind-twisting chaos it made inside him.

I am losing, he thought. I am being dragged into the abyss, crying and begging to get out from there again and to be myself.

So Meg had told him, a soft voice and a sweet breath in the dark. If you have to fight longer, the real Batty is lost forever.

Chapter Twenty

Moss and moor

He had no idea why he did it, other than the hagging of Harry Rae's words. He did not like the idea of that church at the beginning and even less now with the swirling fetch of those killed in it.

But he went because of Harry Rae's words and the warning from Newark; it didn't sit well with him that Will had carried secrets for one lord or another, or even one country to another. That he had been paid for it and by the English spymaster Sadler, through Harry Rae. Somehow, he had considered Will above that sort of war.

Yet he plootered Fiskie through the dark and wet, hunched in a waterproofed leather cloak and a grim realisation that he had known nothing at all about Will.

About anything.

He left Fiskie in the dark and struggled almost blindly down to the Esk, followed it a little way and came up the worn steps to the church. He saw the light inside and felt his heart loop at the sight. For a long moment he hovered on the razor edge of quitting. Just leaving the place and all the revelations it might still hold. Will would have advised it, for sure – but he quelled that, almost savagely; Will had been no less of a liar than everyone else, about God, about right, about sense...

He crept in and saw the horn lantern beside the body; the place reeked of mould and death, but the rug the Egyptiani had used to wrap Will was gorgeous, the gold and silver wire in it bouncing the light like the halos of angels.

Batty breathed soft, unshipped Brother Throw from his family of knives and moved to the light; Will looked back at him from dark sockets and Batty, no stranger to the ways of death, had to take a breath in through his nose – he would gag if he tasted it, he knew – and moved the lantern closer to Will's belly.

It was slit open and Batty rolled saliva round his mouth and spat it out sideways; they had been here. They had taken what Will had hidden; Batty was almost grateful for it.

'Is this what you seek?'

It was proof, when he later thought of it, of how strong his heart was that Batty didn't fall down and die on the spot. His head thundered, all the same and he turned as fast as his joints would allow, knife up – but the voice was strangely familiar and he wasn't surprised to see a face he knew.

Elfin, framed in red – even artificed, that hair was beautiful – and smiling, soft and sad. Meg held up one hand and in it, long as both her ring fingers, a slim wand bounced light of the silver.

'Jesu, wummin,' Batty managed. 'You risk killing me with tricks like this.'

'I hoped you would nivver come,' she answered, 'but I knew that moudiewart in the pretty cote would persuade you. Told you of its value, did he? Paying you for its return to him?'

'Told me it was more valuable to me. Offered no payment, nor was I inclined to wanting it.'

Meg's smile broadened. 'Then you are blessed. Did he say you should take it and run far away?'

That was true and the length it took Batty to think about replying confirmed it for Megs, who leaned forward and untwisted the silver length.

'Stuck up his arse,' she said crudely. 'Did you ever hear of such a thing? Did you ever consider the likes of Will Elliot, Land Sergeant as was, would even contemplate such a thing, never mind do it?'

'I did not,' Batty managed hoarsely.

'God knows when he did it, but he will not have visited a privy in all the time it was in...'

'Aye, aye,' Batty interrupted. 'You have acquainted me with the regard he held for the contents and all of how much I did not ken of the man.'

She slid out the thin rolls and opened them. 'I ken you dinna read, but I do.'

Batty tried not to be surprised by this and failed; she chuckled.

'My King insisted on it and so I sat moodily through all the lessons he provided from some wee priest running for his life from the forks and flames.'

She held the unrolled paper up, so that it stirred in the heat of the lantern. Batty saw it had ornate writing on it, the sort that was printed and looked Germanic, though it might be any tongue.

'Nae secrets of plot or counterplot here,' she said. 'This is a writ from the Goldsmith's Company in London which says "pay to the bearer the sum of one hundred silver shillings". You know what that means?'

'Who ever presents it there will get the coin,' Batty answered and turned briefly into the black stare of Will.

'There are eight of these wrapped up one inside the other. And you don't have to go to Lunnon – any goldsmith moneylender will do. There are several at Appleby, for example.'

'This is Will's rewards for services,' Batty intoned dully, seeing it now. She nodded.

'Tha earliest date on one is six years since. Clearly Harry Ree knew it and thought it like a benefice in a will from a close friend or relative. I am sure he considered coming back here with enough men to keep banditry at bay, but he is weel kent and constantly watched. The great and good would want to know what he was doing.'

Batty looked at her and grinned. 'But you have it now, so no-one would question that you are not entitled.'

'Just so,' she said, almost triumphantly – then pushed the notes at him. 'I would like to keep the wee silver container, all the same.'

Batty did not want to know why – or where she planned to push it if things came to that. He had realised that anyone finding the notes would be rich, even if the *testoons* were devalued of more silver, as Fat Henry had done before he died.

He took the notes, squinted at them and knew, for the first time, how important the skill of reading and writing was. And how absolutely anyone could claim the reward for these wee bits of scribbled paper.

'We had best go,' she said suddenly. 'I have waited here, trembling, for someone to arrive, hoping it was you and praying you were first. I dare not rely on the Lord's Grace much longer.'

Batty blew out the lantern at once. He did not want to ride – it would get darker and he could smell rain. 'Who else do you see coming here?'

'No friends,' she answered laconically and Batty slithered after her, down to the Esk and along the bank. Her mount was closer than Fiskie and she wanted him to get up behind, but he thought that was unkind to the beast.

They rode in silence for a while until, finally, he had to ask why she came to hunker down and wait in the remains of a ghostly old church. She laughed, a trill that sent a course of warm feeling through him.

'I wanted to warn you, to give you what Will concealed and we Eyptiani made sure he kept while we wrapped him in the rug. Harry Rae knew something of it, but that big pipe Will hid up his nethers was Will's own business and no wee secret message.'

'The war here is done with,' Batty answered, not wanting to admit that the revelation of Will carrying secret messages back and forth was so strange, given what he had known – or thought he had known – about the moral man who hated the Borders and wanted only peace.

'It is not,' Meg answered shortly. 'Wee Mary will grow into a crowned Catholic and there are those here who will want mair Lutheran than that. The English boy-king is assuredly against Catholics. The rides will go on, too, until there is no border at all.'

The thought struck him. 'Is that why the Armstrongs took him to Hollows all those years since?'

Red Meg shook raindrops off her hood. 'Naw, they knew nothing of it, though Will had to swallow one of his secret silver cylinders. Puked it up afterwards, right into the hands of Wicked Wat Scott. Naebody else found out what was in it and it did not harm Will.'

He was harmed enough, Batty thought glowering so hard he eventually woke from it and wondered why he did not steam. And also where they were going.

'North,' she said. 'Up to Mosstop. They dinna care for Armstrongs nor Nebless Clem, even though he is one of them.'

She smiled sweetly. 'Nor Grahams. Clem was born in Mosstop and his faither was rough handled by the young Dickon. To death. Clem has never forgotten it, though he will flat-out lie if asked whether he was raised in such a place as Mosstop.'

The coal mine, Batty thought. Dirt smeared churls digging up black stones – Nebless Clem would want to put that stain well behind him.

Just as the first of the dawn sparked out over the Solway, Batty felt them on his back. When he turned, he saw it was the same for Megs.

'Eight or ten,' she confirmed, head up as if sniffing, with her red tendrils snaking round her face.

'Run,' Batty answered.

They managed a decent trod for an hour, heading for the faint eldritch lights of Mosstop but having to go sideways to take the sting out of the clim, looping round through the bracken and the morning birds.

The sun came up like a flash of gold and soft rain lisped down to diffuse it into a molten morning; their shadows stretched out like faerie.

Batty stopped to ease Fiskie's wheezing and when he looked back, he could see the dark figures following on, closer every step.

'Do we run or fight – I am sure that's Nebless Clem.'

'Run,' Batty declared and saw her pout.

'I thocht you wanted Clem at the end of your sword-point,' she said and he glowered at her until she laughed.

'Him, aye. Not seven mair like him in villainy and bastardy.'

They stumbled on and Fiskie came to a stop, head down and blowing hard. Megs turned her younger beast to face the men and hauled out a matchlock pistol; she began to blow on it, trying to bring the match back to life.

Batty wanted to tell her to not be so daft, but something whirred between them like a fat fuggy toddler. Meg pointed her pistol, there was a pause and then a long flare of yellow light and a thunderous noise making the horses stir.

Batty kicked Fiskie into life and they rode on. 'Did ye hit any?'

She turned with a look of feverish delight and an empty pistol. 'I did not, but they will take time finding that out.'

There was one – there is always one, Batty thought sourly – who rode harder on a better horse. The De'il looks after his own and neither he nor God was averse to watching a wee stushie and making bets on it, with souls as the prize.

This one got close enough to stop and risk a shot from his own pistol, a brief pop and burning shine that coned out from his weapon. Batty heard it hit Fiskie in the arse, a slap of sound and a jolt; Fiskie staggered and whuffed and kept running. Good man ye are, Batty thought and headed him towards the glowing lights of Mosstop.

Help me to remember, Lord, that nothing will happen this day that you and I the gither cannae work out…

He had barely finished when he felt Fiskie stumble, then come to a stop. It gave him time to get his feet out of the stirrups and the big axe-handled dagg out of the saddle holster – then the beast fell sideways and Batty rolled free of it.

He lay, confused and blinded by dirt and dawn sun. Someone gripped his wrist and pulled hard on it; her voice said: 'nae time for a doze, Batty.'

He rolled over and got to his knees in time to see Fiskie wheezing hard and lying down. Behind him rode a figure, holding his pistol muzzle up to the sky and wearing a triumphant smile.

'You are Batty Kohlhase from the Germanies and I claim my prize.'

A bliddy Deutcher, Batty thought, getting to his feet. A reiter, too, yin o' those wee clever riders who wear black and trot aboot in a *caracole*, a circle round the enemy where they discharge pistols. Naw swords or lances here. Gunfire. The modern way of it…

At Pinkie Cleugh, the mounted Spanish company under Dom Pedro de Gamboa successfully harassed Scottish pike columns with this and Batty would have bet his last bawbee on this being one of the arrogant moudiewarts who had done it.

'Up and run, my man…'

Meg's voice was urgent and Batty felt a leap of sheer terror when he saw the reiter start to level his pistol, grinning. He wasn't even going to trot a half-circle.

Batty found the axe-head a hand length away and rolled to it, leaving the big German cursing and trying to aim. Aiming is no what you Deutcher jackals do, though is it? What you do is fire into a mass of men where ye cannae miss…

He levelled the dagg and fired. It sparked, fumed out smoke and blasted his eyes with a light as bright as the sun. The reiter jerked as if someone had kicked him; for a moment there was a look of utter bewilderment on his face and he took long enough to look down at the hole in his fancy breastplate. Then he fell off the horse with a noise like a tumble of tin kettles.

More men were behind him, one with a latchbow. He saw a strange face and heard the familiar voice; 'I want Batty alive. Alive d'ye hear?'

He got up as the latchbow wavered in his direction and for want of anything better he hurled the empty dagg. Once before that had served him well, but it was not meant for throwing and Batty did not even know if he hit the man. But the pistol was gone…

He shoved Megs ahead of him and staggered up the street behind her, into shadowy figures who were yelling outrage. Batty dragged out his sword feeling the hot stabs in his knees and the drag of the money bag inside his jack – and the beginnings of despair.

They met people as they staggered in a hard run, but they all scattered before the onslaught of a snarling man and a wild woman with hands full of blades; those who foolishly closed in behind were all but run down by the plunging horsemen – a beast skidded out on the rutted mud and slithered half-way down the street, spilling the rider to roll over and over.

There were shouts and screams – Batty ploughed desperately on towards some strange conical knolls; if they could get in among them, it would break up the charge and slow the horses.

Men now stared at them, eyes wide with astonishment in black faces. There was a tall structure with a wagon under it, but four horses were attached to the wrong end, facing the wrong way. It was a big affair of timber and metal, the sides all slanting outwards. It dangled with chains and men paused in heaving rain-sodden coal from straw creels into it to stare.

A voice called for Jackie to get up and let loose the brake. 'Awa' wi' ye,' it added and then scattered away from Batty and Megs.

He recalled it, heard the handsome Fairbairn mention it as they stood in the solar of Hermitage, warmed by a coal fire.

The waggonway.

'There,' he bawled to Megs, her wet skirts wrapping her; she stumbled and almost fell – the drum of hooves grew deafening and Batty whirled.

The horseman was yelling out that he got them, waving his sword with a mad grin from a face framed with straggled hair under a burgonet. Batty slashed back and forth, advancing on him – or rather the horse. He did not want a plunging horse near enough to cause him damage – but he had to get close enough to make the beast rear up and veer sideways with a sharp squeal.

The rider went off, hit the ground with a sickening thud and rolled almost to Batty's feet, where he stared up, his eyes swivelling. Batty booted him hard in the cods and turned to Megs stood at the waggon, undecided and almost dancing with panic.

'Up,' he declared. 'On to the thing. Get on it.'

'The horses are on the wrong side…'

Batty hefted her up then shoved her up on to the high thick wooden sides of the waggon, the iron wheels flanged on to the wooden rails. She growled curses at him for putting his good hand on her arse, but it was more because he still had the sword in it.

'Here…' a voice declared indignantly and Batty grabbed the owner by his filthy collar and hauled him off his seat to thump on to the ground below. Then he kicked the brake loose, just as the rest of the riders came galloping up.

It was loaded and slid away with agonising slowness, while Batty thumped it as if it was a recalcitrant horse and demanded it speed up. Megs perched on the coal and hurled curses at the riders. One latchbow bolt, Batty thought in a sudden panic… he moved to drag her down over the coal and behind the sides.

Clem saw the huge wagon rolling away, saw the figures and knew his prey was on it. He cursed them from Hell and back again – but he spurred after, even as he saw it was desperate. His own horse was a good one and all but blown; the ones behind were worse.

Batty watched the rider closing, saw the strange face – he had a new mask, just the nose itself and not anything round it. Did nothing for him. Batty wished he had a pistol left; all he could do was bounce in an agony as the man closed and the waggon rolled faster and faster.

'The horses…' Megs called out and Batty saw the tethered beasts, four of them being dragged reluctantly along. Used to pull the empty waggon back up to Mosstop, he realised and it was going too fast for them. They stumbled and squealed and if one went down, the drag would slow the waggon.

He leaned down and slashed it free – just as Nebless Clem closed and, with a desperate growl, hurled himself from the saddle.

He missed the edge of the waggon, caught the trailing end of the slashed tether and hung there, twisting side to side and with the toes of his big boots scuffing the sleepers as the waggon picked up speed.

Too slowly; Batty cut free the rest of the horses before he realised the weight of Clem dragging behind it was almost as bad and he cursed, started to lean over with the sword poised to stab…

The blast sent him careering backwards, dazed and blinded by smoke, that part of his mind not shrieking and gibbering registering the sole word – pistol.

The monstrance itself sailed over his head into the dark and then, as if in some fevered horror dream, he saw Clem haul himself over the edge of the waggon, his backsword clenched between his teeth like a pirate boarding a galleon.

Meg's scream shattered Batty from his fog; Clem, in the act of lurching across the heaped coal to skewer Batty, suddenly recoiled with a sharp cry, flinging up his hand to ward off the black lump. Megs gave a 'la!' as if she had scored a point in some debate – and heaved another lump.

The waggon lurched and rattled and Batty realised it was going too fast, laden with coal and three body-weights it should not have and no horses to keep it within the bounds. We will melt, he thought remembering the smart academicals who had predicted it. The uterus of a woman. that weaker sex, will fly out…

'Get to the brake,' he roared at Megs as Clem crawled over the coal, gave a savage growl and sprang like a tiger, just as Batty managed to get to his knees, which was enough to bring up his sword in time to block the vicious cut; the blades rang like bells.

Batty realised that the waggon was now rocking hard, had hit a long, flowing stretch and had picked up speed. Clem's coat was slathered with black, his face plastered with a paste of rain and coaldust – yet he came on, slipping and sliding on the shifting surface as Batty did. They fought in a farce of wild strikes and cuts, off-balance and without finesse. I am betting sure you had a better idea of how this would be, Batty thought savagely. A wee finesse of salle and then a triumphant foot on my corpse for all to see.

But not on this teetering horror filled with coal.

Clem slashed, fell sideways just as the cart rocked the same way; he spilled on to coal, his sword went spinning away into the dawn and Batty, with an exultant shout, brought his own up.

He would have finished him and knew it. Finished him there and then and not caring if the man was unarmed or not – but the waggon lurched sickeningly and Megs screamed. She didn't have the strength to work the brake and Batty dropped his sword to the coals and sprang to the brake instead leaning on it, feeling her heat and panting breath. They both worked it, there was the smell of charring wood, but the waggon did not seem to slow much – then something dragged Batty away from it and Clem swiped at him with a lump of coal.

'Bastard...' Clem yelled. 'I will finish you this day...'

Batty took a wild blow designed for his face, but which grazed his forehead instead. It was sickening enough, drove sense from him and pain in. There was a second slash which blew the breath out of him; he realised Clem had a knife out and had cut the top buckle fastening of his jack.

There was a sudden flurry of movement and the pressure on Batty was released; he rolled over and sat dazedly up, in time to see Megs and Clem locked like stags, heaving and straining. He was raining foulness on her, about being a gyppo trull and what he would do when Batty was no longer a danger…

She screamed and it looked as if she was going into faint and could manage little else. Batty struggled up, searched frantically for his sword and scrambled to fetch it; there was a sudden sharp cry and a distinct crack which made him turn, half-afraid of what he would see.

To his surprise, he saw Clem locked in a wrestling hold any Cumberland man would be proud of, his face twisted with anguish and his arm clearly broken. Megs glanced at Batty's open-mouthed surprise.

'A bothersome man or twa',' she said bitter with stored resentment and did not need to say more.

She let Clem drop to the coals and he slithered down, where he struggled weakly with a useless arm and a blinding pain. Batty was not about to let him lurk in some dark coal hole, waiting to do bad – but she took him by the arm and pointed.

'Journey's end,' she said and Batty whirled; the waggon was rocking and rolling, far too fast, down to a cleared area of cobbles and coal-heaps – the coal store near Hermitage. At the end of the relentless trackway stood a bulwark of earth and sleepers and iron, surrounded by waiting packhorses and more straw creels.

Clem had recovered and was not for giving up; Batty dragged the half-conscious Megs to her feet.

'Jump,' he said.

She hesitated; then Clem sealed it by growling through his pain and grabbed for her sodden black hem. She was already hurling herself over the edge.

Batty went the other way, in a blur of sky and grass. The landing slammed him into mud and coaldust and he tasted it, tasted blood, too, where he had nicked his tongue. He rolled over a few times and bounced almost to his knees; he had lost Megs and looked for her.

There was a crash, a great rending sound of tearing metal and splintering wood. Shouts. Batty saw Megs lying a few yards away and moved to her, cradled her head, was blasted with panic – until she moaned and fluttered her eyes.

Someone moved behind him and he started – but it wasn't Nebless Clem and he continued attending to her until she came round enough to be got upright. They staggered on down to the cobbles; there was a milling crowd and a great scatter of coal and timbers. No-one seemed concerned, but they were all excited – some were fighting with each other and Batty looked at it, bemused.

'Your jack,' Megs said wearily and he saw it had burst open where Clem had sliced it – and shot a bag of silver out like a gift; Batty's heart lurched into his throat. His fee, in a bag the size of a new baby's head, spilled like frost among a sliding heap of two tonnes of coal, shattered timbers, burst sleepers, broken waggon wheels...

And a sword. No-one cared much for it, save that it was in the way, to be shoved casually aside by folk hunting the glitter of silver among the black gold of Mosstop. Batty lurched to it and picked it up. His sword, still fine through the coal smears.

'That won't serve you,' said a too-familiar voice. Batty turned to see Clem easing his broken arm into his belt,

286

snugging it up. His coat was ripped and more black than the green it had been before; his false nose was torn off, leaving a parody of a skull, stained with black mud. He reached his good arm to his waist and Batty wondered if he had got his sword back – but what he saw was the swift, vicious uncoiling of the whip from round Clem's waist.

'I should've never listened to that Graham wummin,' Clem growled, his voice a thick mucous of hate and coal dust. 'I should have kept on with this until you were flayed.'

'Good advice for the Egyptiani, too,' Batty managed, hefting the sword. 'You'd have found the seven wummin you handled cruelly were Grahams and Forsters. Maybe even a Selby.'

Clem had heard that since and it was not inclined to improve his mood. Batty waved the sword, trying to stop Clem spotting Megs hobbling away to safety.

'Come ahead, ye skull-faced shit-eater. This sword has your name on it.'

There was a moment of peace, where the sun lisped down on the scrabbling coal heavers backing away from Clem and his whip. He lashed it out once, a sharp crack that ruined air; people yelped and scattered.

Batty saw at once that Clem wanted a knife in his other fist, the one that would not work for him. It was a standard – knife and six feet of coarse leather, tempered to a thin, fine leather end studded with barbs. Even when lashing bound slaves, a good whipmaster would have a knife ready.

Clem drew back his arm and leaned into the strike. He needed distance but even a solid hit from the middle of the whip would ruin Batty's day; as it was, the sharp snap of it near his face made him rear back in alarm.

'I will blind you, you one-armed dog. Then I will string you up and finish what I started. I will lay your backbone open to the world...'

Batty closed on him with a lumbering rush, knowing that the key to the whip was distance; the hiss of it was loud, he flung up his hand in panic and felt the cracking sear of it along his forearm.

He yelped, lost the sword and ploughed on to where Clem sidestepped like a *toreador*, leaving Batty to stumble on until his foot caught and he fell, rolling over and over. The whip cracked again and again – his head reeled from a blow and his burgonet slid off and dropped to his feet.

He fumbled out Brother Throw and flicked it, more hope than expectation – but he heard Clem yelp and took the chance to rush him again – with the same result.

Crack – he fell sideways, the breath driven out of him with a strike to the jack; when he risked a look he saw a vicious slice in it, exposing cracked horn plates. He would not last long like this – he rolled over frantically as the whip sliced up spirals of coal splinters. It was here he found his sword and swept it up, feeling the black dust on his palm sweat like flour on oil.

Clem laughed. Batty rushed him – and this time Clem seemed unable to wield the leather coil. He tugged and tugged and then panicked as Batty closed in; beyond him, Batty saw Megs, both booted feet planted firmly on the outstretched tail of barbs.

At the last, Clem dropped the whip and hauled out his knife, but Batty was not waiting for any salle honour – he slashed the broken arm, which made Clem reel away, shrieking at the new pain. Then he slashed from the other quarter, hit Clem's wildly flailing wrist and cut it almost off; the knife went spinning off like a bar of gold in the sunrise.

'I will slay you…'

The howl was heartfelt, seared with pain and frustration and fear. Batty did not care about it.

'Away,' he growled back. 'You couldna pick your nose, even if you had one.'

Clem went to his knees, babbling. Batty sheathed his backsword, bent and took up the handle of the whip.

'I have only ever used yin on bullocks,' he said in a growl, 'but I ken the way of it…'

He drew back his arm and was stopped by an imperious command. He turned into the lean, handsome face of the Captain of Hermitage, who smiled.

'Ach, Batty – dinna spoil it. This is a legend waiting to happen – and if you sully it with vicious, you stain the brave act o' yer light of love.'

Men closed in and hauled Clem to his feet; he yelped once with pain and struggled a bit until a gauntleted hand smacked the back of his head.

'I will get ye,' he panted at Batty, who waved his wearied hand.

'Come ahead if ye can unkninch yer neck from the tree the Captain of Hermitage will find for ye.'

'Well done,' the Captain declared, beaming.

Aye, you would think that, Batty muttered to himself, given that you are young, fetching as a cavalier and full of that nonsense. Yet he saw Megs smiling, too and gave up the whip. When she crossed to him, drew him into her embrace, he felt the full sun of the day strike him like a furnace of gold.

They stayed at Hermitage, in a decent bolster bed and having had to wash all over for the privilege, a snell task that bothered Batty more than her. They ate well and paid for it by telling the Captain what had been done – or most of it.

Batty watched Megs flirt with the Captain and marvelled at himself for bridling up like a spoiled dog. In the end, when they went to the room through the knowing looks and little jeers, neither of them had the strength for anything but sleep.

'Tomorrow, Appleby,' she said with finality and Batty was too weary to argue. Mayhap he would purchase a new horse, though the memory of a dying Fiskie lay on him like cold haar. That and the vanishment of his axe-handled dagg and Brother Throw – as if all the old accoutrements of a vicious life had been stripped from him.

It was all part of the whole and he had learned that a long time ago. He had also learned that if you must leave a place, leave it the fastest way you can. Never turn back and never believe that an hour you remember is a better hour because it is dead.

He said as much and got a tired grunt back. 'Women too, I am betting,' she said.

Batty was clever enough to say nothing. He realised there might be a bit more of that in his future.

Author's Note

Most of this is fiction, set against a true tale – the Rough Wooing (a later term) was the period where an ailing Henry VIII tried to assert his power to ensure the union of England and Scotland with a marriage between his young son Edward and Mary Queen of Scots. The more violence he used, the more violence he met from Scots who would not be forced.

In the end, he died without having resolved what he had wanted. For a time the Lord Protector of the young Edward VI tried to carry matters on, but it was clear the English had reached their limits – and there were other armed bands causing trouble in the south.

The Battle of St Monans was the last throw and it failed. I recommend you look up the work on this vanished epic written by Leonard Low (no relation). You can find it on Amazon and elsewhere.

In the end, the war stopped, mainly because the French wanted it. They got Boulogne back and the Scots got all the English-seized fortresses and castles in Scotland.

It might have seemed to many that, at last, there was peace along the Border lands – but there wasn't. The raids continued for decades, right on until the death of Elizabeth I and the accession of James, already King of Scotland and now of England, too. There was no more

Border and the reivers realised it, though the last to do so were the Grahams, who had to be sent out of the country.

The Grahams were as wicked a crew as any in the Borderland, but none of their crimes justified the viciousness with which they were murdered, dispossessed, and banished in the name of law and order, and with the full approval of the King, whose hatred seems to have been acute. For too long a time at the turn of the 17th century, Jeddart Justice prevailed – which is to hang first and try later.

As late as 1614 a proclamation was issued forbidding any Grahams to return from banishment in Ireland or the Low Countries, yet there were still those who were willing to run the risk of coming home.

Batty, I feel, would have approved.

Glossary

APOSTLES – A collection of wooden, stoppered flasks filled with an exact amount of powder and ball for a single pistol or caliver shot, which made for quicker and more reliable loading. They were suspended by a cord from a leather bandolier worn by arquebusiers, seven flasks in front and five in back, for a total of twelve, hence the name.

BARMKIN – A defensive wall built round a castle or keep, usually with a walkway for sentries.

BATTLE OF ST MONANS – The Battle of St Monans doesn't exist in any military credits of Scottish history and you can blame Oliver Cromwell for it. In 1650 Cromwell transported all the Scottish records to the safekeeping of the Tower of London where they remained for ten years until he was replaced by King Charles II. The records were returned to Scottish shores, but disaster struck when a ship sank near Newcastle, taking 85 barrels of papers down to the salty deeps. It took the records of 1548, 1550 and 1551 and among the losses were details of the Battle of St Monans.

Some 900 died. The combatants were the High Admiral of England and James Stewart (Mary Queen of Scots' half brother) who are not minor figures in the history of events. Bonnie Prince Charlie's two victories 200 years later at Prestonpans and Falkirk did not have such a loss of life and both these conflicts have memorials and innumerable books on the subjects.

BILL – An official warrant, issued by a March Warden or the like, demanding that a suspected miscreant present himself for judgement. If ignored – fouled – then someone appointed by the Wardens would go and bring him to justice. This was Batty's job until the war stopped all Warden activity.

BILL – Derived originally from the agricultural billhook, the bill consisted of a hooked chopping blade with several pointed projections mounted on a staff. The end of the cutting blade curves forward to form a hook, which is the bill's distinguishing characteristic. English bills tended to be relatively short, putting them at a disadvantage against the commonly used pikes of other countries.

BIRL – To spin round.

BLACK MEAL – A payment made, in coin or bartered goods (grain or meal), to the more powerful family who could do you harm. In essence, the 16th century Borders were run like Mafia bosses and paying to keep them away was sometimes the only recourse. Origin of the word 'blackmail'.

CALIVER – An improved version of the arquebus, in that it had standard bore, making loading faster and firing more accurate.

CRUCK HOUSE – A building made of a frame of curved timbers set in pairs. Used to build small huts up to large barns, it was the simplest cheapest building method of the medieval age.

CRUSIE – A simple container with a wick that provided light.

DAGG – A pistol as opposed to a long-barrel musket.

DEBATABLE LAND – An area ten miles long and four wide created by edicts from both countries about settling it or raising any permanent structures. The area's people ignored this and powerful clans moved in, notably the Armstrongs. For three hundred years they effectively controlled the land, daring Scotland or England to interfere. It became a haven for outlaws of all sides.

FUGGY (or FOGGY) TODDLER – Affectionate name for the wild or moss bee because of its slow, droning, bumbling flight. They still make nests on the surface of the moors.

HEMP – Hanging, from the material used to make the rope.

HIRPLE – Limp.

HOT TROD – The formalities of pursuing reivers, usually by the forces of the Wardens. Up to six days after the seizure of any cattle by thieves taking them across the other side of the Border, the forces attempting to recover them and apprehend the guilty were permitted to also cross the Border freely in pursuit. They had to do it with 'hue and cry, with horn and hound' and were also obliged to carry a smouldering peat on the point of a lance to signify the task they were on.

HOW BULLS RUN AND CHUCKIES ROW – Scottish interpretation of what academics in university do all day. How bulls run is self-explanatory. Chuckies are small, smooth stones and row is simply a dialectic for 'roll'. In other words – an explanation of how the world works.

JACK – The ubiquitous garment of the Border warrior – the jack of plates. Most ordinary Border fighters had a jack, a sleeveless jerkin with either iron or the cheaper horn plates sewn between two layers of felt or canvas.

JALOUSE – To surmise or suspect.

KERTCH – A kerchief, usually used by married women to cover their hair.

KISTING – Funeral. A kist is a chest or a box.

LATCHBOW – A cheap crossbow, light enough to be used from horseback, with a firing mechanism as simple as a door latch. The power was light but at close range it would wound or kill an unprotected man and knock the wind out of one wearing a jack.

PERJINK – Proper, neat.

PRIMERO – 16th century poker where you attempt to bluff your competitors out of betting against you. Players *vie* or *vye* by stating how high a hand they are claiming to have and can flat-out lie to overstate it. It was played using a 40-card deck, but there are no surviving written rules, only descriptions.

RIDE/RIDING – The raids mounted by one reiver family, or Name, against another, either for robbery or revenge. Depending on how many family members and affiliated Names you could get to join you, these were brief affairs of one night or ones involving several thousand men who could lay waste to entire villages and towns on either side of the Border. The usual Riding times lasted from Lammas (Aug 1) to Candlemas (Feb 2).

SLORACH – Any bog or morass or filthy mess you might step in.

SLOW MATCH – Early firearms were called 'matchlocks' because they were ignited by a smouldering fuse called a slow match, brought down into the pan. Keeping a slow match lit required constant vigilance, a good manufacturer – and no rain. By the middle of the 16th century, pistols with a wheel-lock mechanism were being made, which utilised an iron pyrite to create sparks and a cover for the pan, which was more reliable.

SNELL – Cold, icy.

TESTOON – Coin minted during the last days of Henry VIII, with more copper than silver in it, so that the portrait of Henry on one side wore down to the copper on his embossed nose becoming known as 'coppernoses' as a result. They transmuted, eventually into the English shilling.